Paving Paradise

J. Harris Anderson

Paving Paradise

J. Harris Anderson

Blue Cardinal Press • Rixeyville, Virginia

Published by
Blue Cardinal Press
18601 Bluejay Way
Rixeyville, VA 22737
www.BlueCardinalPress.com

Library of Congress Control Number: 2020924783

Trade Paperback
ISBN: 978-0-9911645-7-8

Copyright © 2020 by J. Harris Anderson

All Rights Reserved

First Edition

Cover image by Leland Neff
www.LelandNeff.com

Cover design by Carol Gana

Back cover author photo by Anne Whiting
www.AnneWhitingPhotography.com

Also by J. Harris Anderson

The Prophet of Paradise
A Paradise Gap Novel

The Foxhunter's Guide to Life & Love
An Inspirational Novel

For more information: www.BlueCardinalPress.com

*"They paved paradise
And put up a parking lot
With a pink hotel, a boutique
And a swinging hot spot
Don't it always seem to go
That you don't know what you've got till it's gone."*

*Joni Mitchell
"Big Yellow Taxi"*

Chapter 1

It began as a trickle of ebony tar creeping across the crest of the mountain. The thin vein broadened into a rivulet and cascaded over the apex like coal-black blood gushing from a head wound. Expanding, gaining force, it uprooted trees, lifted boulders, and carried them along as if they were twigs and pebbles roiling in a bubbling ooze.

The torrent widened, then split into three writhing tentacles.

One slithered toward the kennels, blanketing the huntsman's house and outbuildings.

Another swept across an open hayfield, entombing the summer grass under a thick layer of gelatinous pitch. Ancient monuments in the private graveyard tumbled over and disappeared.

The third came for the main house at Montfair.

Thumper Billington stared out a second floor window, speechless and unable to move, watching the tide surge toward his home. The caretaker's cottage melted away like a child's sandcastle hit by a crushing wave. The stone foundation of the barn offered no resistance and the structure collapsed with a creaking moan. The swirling mire engulfed the first floor of the house. Thumper felt the heat through his bare feet as the asphalt forced its way between the floorboards. The sulfuric stench of creosote enflamed his nostrils. Tears swelled from his eyes.

Just before he succumbed to the swarming darkness, Thumper saw, coming over the mountain, a horde of steamrollers, hundreds of them, churning onward, tanks leading a conquering army. At the front of this relentless force, in a machine bigger and more powerful than all the others, was a man in a rumpled brown suit. He stood in the open cockpit, as if driving a chariot. His bald head glistened and his striped tie flapped over his shoulder. He grinned with a cartoonish leer, his lips curled in a mix of disdain and exultation, his eyes ablaze with triumph.

Thumper heard himself croaking out the words, "No! Stop! Stop! Don't!"

His feet were kicking wildly against the searing heat throbbing up through the floor.

Blackness enveloped him. Breath came hard. The final suffocation drew near.

He felt a gentle touch on his arm, a tiny spot of relief from the steaming flood. A soft voice sounded beside him.

"Thumper, it's happening again."

Waking with a jerk and a grunt, he turned to see Janey Musgrove, her distress evident even in the heavy darkness.

He was dripping with sweat, a sheet tangled around his feet.

A few moments passed as he sat on the edge of the bed, waiting for his heart to stop racing, his lungs to soothe back to normal respiration, his eyes to adjust to the shadowy dimness of the room.

"I'm all right," he said. "You go back to sleep."

"You need to get some sleep too," she replied. "We've got to be at kennels by dawn."

He arose and went to the bedroom window. The landscape was black with tinges of gauzy gray, but it was the reassuring darkness of deep night in the unlit countryside. The irregular contours of Virginia's Piedmont, formed by the forces of nature and not the leveling blades of machinery, could be discerned in the faint moonlight. The horizon stood punctuated by arching rows of treetops.

"Still there," Thumper Billington whispered. "For now anyway."

****

Thumper and Janey moved off from the Montfair barn just as the late August sky blossomed into a blushing pink. He rode his most seasoned hunt horse, retired steeplechaser Lenny. She rode Bee, whose racing career lasted less than a furlong but ever since had served as a reliable mount no matter the skill level of the rider.

It was a short hack to the hunt club's kennels, housed on Montfair property. Four others awaited their arrival on the final morning of summer hound exercise: Crispian "Crispie" O'Rourke, huntsman; Patrice "Patti" Vestor, first whipper-in and Crispie's significant other; Ryman McKendrick, Thumper's joint-master of the Montfair Hunt and whipper-in; Nardell Raithby, honorary whipper-in and Ryman's SO.

As the final two joined the group, Nardell leaned in toward Janey and said quietly, "Thumper looks like crap. Still not sleeping well?"

"This thing about Frank Worsham's farm, that he might be selling, has him really worried."

"We're all concerned about that. If Frank sells out, what next?"

"Exactly. What next?"

Patti Vestor opened the gate to the kennel yard and thirty-seven foxhounds—mostly tri-color, well-muscled, and eager for the chase—swarmed out, bounced and pranced around their huntsman's horse.

Crispie blew a short note on his horn and the pack obediently fell in behind him.

"All right, me fine lads and lassies," he cooed to them. "Come along then. Come along."

He picked up a trot, Patti to his right; Ryman on the left; Thumper, Nardell, and Janey spread out behind. In good order they moved off from the kennel complex just as the first full rays of sunlight beamed over the Blue Ridge Mountains.

Five of the six riders were seasoned equestrians. Thumper, Ryman, Nardell, and Crispie had been riding since childhood, Patti for more than two decades. The past year had brought monumental changes to Janey's life. She had discovered foxhunting by chance and was now fully immersed in this little-known world of horses and hounds.

Naturally athletic, she took to riding easily but was far from ready to handle the young Thoroughbreds favored by the hunt staff and lifelong horsemen like Thumper. Her assigned mount, Bee (short for Buffoon's Ballet), was more the babysitter type.

Dr. Janey Musgrove, PhD, was a recognized expert on the subject of fringe religions. Her research work had taken her around the world and honed her skills at observation and description. Her analytical mind churned as the group moved along on this summer morning through the verdant countryside of Virginia's Crutchfield County (an area named for one of Thumper's maternal ancestors).

Covering ground on horseback, she noted, reinforces the connection to the natural world. The rider senses each step, every subtle feature of the terrain. The horse's muscles respond as the animal moves across the varied surfaces— long smooth strides over open fields, short choppy steps along a rock-strewn trail, shoulders hunched cantering up a steep hill, haunches tucked sliding down the other side. The rider feels the flow of signals through legs, hands, and back. Muscle reacts to muscle, spine connects to spine, blending the two sentient creatures into a perfectly melded partnership.

Gone is the buffer of thickly treaded tires, the mechanized force from an unfeeling motor, the cradling comfort of finely calibrated shock absorbers, climate-controlled interior, ergonomically engineered eight-way seat—all those automotive marvels designed to separate humans from the sensation of raw propulsion. Only flesh and bone remain, moving over a landscape unaltered by the artificial influence of asphalt.

She inhaled the aromas of field and forest, marinated in three months of humid swelter, as the scents rose in waves and swirled unseen in the stew of August air. The morning mist floated away to reveal a vibrant azure sky. Bright red cardinals, shrill blue jays, and darting brown sparrows reveled in the warmth and abundance. In the distance a woodpecker tapped its jackhammer beat.

Much of Janey's life had been a vagabond existence, rootless, always at the ready to go wherever the next story took her. This, though, was starting to feel like home, a life with stability, revered traditions, permanence, where the land was used for productive purposes and cherished for more than its monetary value.

Why, she thought, would anyone want to tear this up and pave it over?

Chapter 2

Myrna Billington hurried along West Olive Avenue in Burbank, California. The noontime sun mandated light clothing and large sunglasses. Myrna hoped the shades would conceal the deep circles under her eyes. She was sleeping no better than her brother, three thousand miles away, although for different reasons.

As she neared the corner where South Orchard Drive intersects to the right, a large man stepped out of the cell phone repair shop and blocked her path.

"Going somewhere?" the man asked.

A few more steps and she'd have reached her destination. *Why here? Why now?*

She took a breath and replied, "Yes, I'm meeting someone for lunch."

"You have money for lunch?"

"She's paying."

"How nice. And how is this helping you meet your obligation?"

"It might just be the answer." She tried to step around the man. "I have to go. I'm already late."

He did not let her pass. "Being late seems to be a habit for you."

"Look, this is for real. But I have to get there to meet my friend. She's the only one who can help me."

"This friend will lend you money?"

"Maybe a little. Enough to get where I need to go."

"Go? You're not going anywhere. Not till you've met your obligation to our mutual friend."

"I have to. It's my only hope. It's complicated, but I own a piece of property, in Virginia. I need to get back and make arrangements to sell it. I can pay off what I owe and everything will be okay."

Towering over her, the man reached down and removed her sunglasses. "This had better be on the level. Our friend has become very impatient." He locked his eyes on hers. His work had honed his ability to tell when someone was lying. He nodded. "You can go to Virginia. You can go wherever you like. But there's no place you can go where I can't find you." He studied her face and then added, "You look like crap. You should try to get some sleep." He slipped her sunglasses back on and stepped aside. "Go. Enjoy your lunch. I'll be watching."

****

Gloriana Devereaux was waiting at a table in the Tallyrand restaurant when Myrna arrived.

The two women made forced small talk, an effort on Myrna's part to maintain the pretense that they were friends—in fact former sisters-in-law—just meeting for a casual lunch at a low budget eatery. She asked about Augie, Glo's son and Myrna's nephew, how his studies at the UCLA film school were going. Fine. And Glo's husband David? Also fine. How about Glo's job at Pymsdale Development? Yes, all good there, too.

Myrna's response to Glo's inquiry about Claudette, Myrna's older sister, began with a dismissive shrug. Oh, you know, living the charmed life in the Big Apple with her husband and kids. Any new acting opportunities on the horizon? No. How about the vintage clothing shop? Business doing okay? Not great.

Myrna's answers were short, tense. She had not yet removed her sunglasses.

"You said you needed to talk to me about something," Glo remarked. "Is everything okay?"

"No, everything is definitely not okay." She took off her shades and dropped them on the table.

"Geez, you look terrible."

Myrna tried to force a smile. "Won't get any acting gigs with a mug like this, will I? Unless Wes Craven puts out a cattle call for scary extras."

"So what's wrong? Tell me the truth."

Myrna sagged into a slouch of surrender. "I thought I'd finally hit on something that was going to work out for me. I've come to grips with the fact that I'm never going to make it as an actor. Oh, sure, maybe the occasional bit part or crowd extra, but nothing more. I've been scraping by, living above the shop. But I've had another dream for many years and decided it was time to make it happen."

"What was that?"

"If I wasn't going to be a success in front of the camera, I decided to try my hand behind it. I've always been fascinated by the pioneering women in the film industry. Not so much the actresses but those who made their own films. I guess that spark came from my mother's interest in movies. I mean, heck, she even named me after one of her favorite actresses…back when they were still called 'actresses.'

"I wanted to do a documentary, maybe a series, about some of the other women, the writers and directors. I've done tons of research and have the whole plan worked out. But I needed funding to make it happen. I shopped it all around town and no one would bite. The idea sounded interesting, but who did I think I was to do something like that? I had no credentials as a filmmaker. Everyone I approached essentially patted my little head said, 'That's nice. Now go back to your shop and sell old clothes.'

"I figured it was over, that I'd failed again. But I picked up a job as a crowd scene extra and during a break I was telling another would-be actor about my idea. She said she knew a guy who might be able to front me the money. Said he wasn't part of the mainstream system, did his own thing his own way, what he called 'alternative financing.' "

"Sounds kind of shady to me."

"Shady? Yeah, it was shady all right. What I didn't realize, or blindly chose to ignore, is that 'alternative financing' is a euphemism for 'loan shark.' But I knew this project couldn't fail, so I took the bait. He fronted me a sufficient bankroll to get things started."

"So where's the project stand now?"

Myrna stared out the window of the restaurant. West Olive Avenue was bustling with people at lunchtime. Without her sunglasses on, the glare hurt her eyes. "It doesn't stand at all. It's dead. A flop. A disaster. Turns out I was no better at making documentary films than I was at becoming a famous actor. And now this fellow wants his money, which I have no way of paying back. And if I can't come up with it, well, I'm facing some pretty scary consequences."

"Oh, my God! So, you mean like broken legs, smashed kneecaps?"

"C'mon, Glo," Myrna sniggered, "That's what they do to men who can't pay up. Women? No, there's a different kind of payback plan for us."

"Jesus, Myrna! Look, David and I aren't wealthy, but if you need a loan…"

"I can't ask you to do that. And the amount I owe this guy is way more than you and David, or anyone else I know, could ever cover. There's only one way I can see out of this."

"What's that?"

"I have to sell my share of Montfair."

"You're kidding. Thumper would never agree to that. You might be able to convince Claudette, but never Thumper. And they'd both have to agree to let you do it."

"I know how it works." Myrna's voice was sharp with frustration and bitterness. "My dear parents made sure their two golden children would keep their irresponsible youngest child from breaking up that beloved property."

"Maybe Thumper would agree to buy out your share."

"I already tried that. It's been a few years, but I doubt anything's changed. He and Claudette have both done a pretty good job of managing the assets that went to them when our parents died. Me? Not so much. I was sure my acting career would take off and I'd be rolling in fame and success. But, well, you know how that's turned out."

Glo reached over and squeezed Myrna's hand. "You just never got the right breaks. You have more talent than most of those famous people can ever hope to have."

"Yeah, sure. And a lot of good that's done me. Anyway, when the inheritance money was gone, I asked Thumper if he'd be willing to buy me out. Or maybe he and Claudette could do it jointly. They both said they couldn't afford to. But, between you and me, I think they thought I'd just blow through that money too and didn't want to see it go to waste."

"And would it have gone to waste?"

Gazing again into the blurry distance, she said, "Yes, I guess it would have. Back then anyway." She turned to Glo. "But I think I've got a better grip on reality now. The star-struck kid has become the practical realist. Although a dead broke practical realist who owes a hunk of change to a scary guy who has an even scarier guy working for him and who keeps popping up out of nowhere to remind me. And with hints of what might happen if I don't come up with the money soon."

"So what can I do to help?"

"I just need enough to get back to Virginia and try to figure out how to sell my share of Montfair. My old car wouldn't make it across the country and I don't even have enough for airfare. If Thumper and Claudette won't buy me out, maybe I can find some other way to make a deal happen. I know it's a wild idea, Glo, but it's the only hope I have left."

Glo pulled her checkbook from her purse and started writing. "I can float you enough for airfare and whatever incidentals you need. Will that help?"

"Oh, my God, yes! That will help immensely. I can't thank you enough!" She reached out and took the offered check. "Oh, Glo, that's way too much. I only need enough…"

"Look, just spend what you need. If you don't spend it all, fine. You can return whatever's left. But if you need more, let me know. I may not be independently wealthy, but I've got good job security and a steady income."

"You should have soaked my brother for more than you did. You let him off too easy."

"No, the divorce wasn't his fault any more than it was mine. We both just finally realized we weren't right for each other. He'll never leave Virginia or give up foxhunting. I wanted to return to California and horses aren't my thing. Thumper's a good man. Not perfect certainly. He's got his faults. But compared to some others I know…well, let's just say old-fashioned Virginia gentlemen are a rarity these days."

"I suppose you're right. I can't say I've encountered very many, maybe not even one, in all the years I've been out here trying to make it. And look where it's gotten me."

"You'll be okay. And if there's anything else I can do to help make this happen for you, I'll give it my all."

"There is one thing. Don't say anything about this to Thumper. I know you two keep in touch about the kids. I need to feel things out first, come up with some other reason for being there and develop a plan to make this happen. If he just gets hit with the idea cold, even given my desperate situation, he's likely to dig his heels in and say no just out of principle."

"I see your point. Yes, he can be pretty stubborn when it comes to his 'principles.' I won't tip him off. Anyway, I have a feeling this will all work for you. It's about time life finally cut you some breaks."

"Gloriana the Optimist."

"That's me."

****

Glo's cell phone rang as she walked the short distance back to the Pymsdale Development headquarters. She wasn't happy when she saw the caller ID.

"Did you enjoy your lunch?" the man asked.

"That's not why you called."

"Of course it's not. How do you know the woman you had lunch with?"

"She's my former sister-in-law, but still a good friend. I was married to her brother. Actually, she was the one who introduced us."

"It seems your friend has a track record of arranging things that don't work out. So why did you write her a check? She's not on the official list of recipients. You wouldn't be taking on some freelancing, would you?"

"She needs to take care of some family business, but she's short on cash so I loaned her some traveling money."

"And what is this family business she needs to take care of?"

"How is that of any interest to you?"

"I'm asking the questions. You don't need to know why."

Glo had a strong suspicion why Myrna's situation was also this man's concern. But she knew better than to press the point. "Okay, fine. The reason is she's having financial problems and needs to get back to Virginia where she owns a piece of property, so she can make arrangements to sell it."

"Is this property deal on the level?"

"There are some complications, sort of a convoluted will with some restrictions. But, yes, the fact that she owns it and it's worth a lot is on the level. I can't see how that has anything to do with our arrangement about…"

"I suggest you stick to the business matters that concern you and not pry into other dealings. That's all for now. I'll be in touch when the need arises."

Chapter 3

Glo was back at her desk when she heard Smith Bondurant, her boss, coming down the hallway. He was talking with Maurice Pymsdale, whose father had started a small land speculation business that grew into a development behemoth of international proportions. Maurice ran the resorts division, a chain of luxury facilities that included hotels, conference centers, golf courses, and other sporting activities suited to the local geography.

"Yes, sir," Smith said, "I'll get right on it."

He strode through the outer reception area of his office suite and into Glo's domain where she held sway as his trusted personal assistant.

Tall, broad shouldered, with perfect grooming and a gleaming smile, Smith projected the essence of corporate elegance. His tie alone cost more than most people's car payment. His suit's price tag came close to a typical teacher's annual income. He was well compensated for his work as Pymsdale's vice president in charge of site selection.

"I need you to make some travel arrangements for me," he said. "Mr. Pymsdale is eager to get things rolling on the Mid-Atlantic project. He's thinking something in Maryland, Virginia, or North Carolina. I need to establish a base in that area and start checking out sites, get a feel for the terrain and the local sensibilities."

"When do you need to leave?"

"As soon as possible. You know Mister P., he doesn't like to wait around, wants results and wants them fast.

There's a resort he's familiar with in Virginia, some town called Middleburg. Small by our standards, but he knows the woman who owns it, a former media exec he's had some dealings with. He said I should establish a base there, a handy central location. And they'll take good care of me."

"I know the place," Glo said. "Salamander Resort and Spa. Very nice, you'll like it."

"Oh, right, you used to live in Virginia."

"I've been away for several years, but I get back from time to time. My daughter's in school at…"

"Okay, great." Glo's personal life had never been of much interest to Smith Bondurant. "Get me booked at this Salamander place and on a plane ASAP."

"If it would help, I can give you a tip about the local area, someone who could be an asset once you're on the ground. Sort of your Sherpa for the wilds of Virginia."

"I'm listening."

"Cuyler Corley, he's a developer in Northern Virginia. He'd be a goldmine of inside information. He'll also know where some possible site options might be."

"And how do you know this guy?"

"He's my ex-husband's cousin."

"All those people are inter-related, aren't they?"

Glo took offense at that remark, but she couldn't voice her true feelings.

"It's an old Virginia family, a lot of history. A contact like this could save you a huge amount of time and effort compared to starting cold. And, trust me, most Virginians—the old-fashioned ones anyway—are still wary of newcomers. Especially a smooth-talking type from California."

"Fine, make the contact."

As Smith closed the door to his office, Glo grabbed her phone and hit Myrna's number. "When you get to Virginia, get in touch with your cousin Cuyler. He just might be able to help you."

Chapter 4

Thumper poured Janey a glass of cabernet sauvignon from Gray Ghost Vineyards and a healthy splash of Wasmund's Copper Fox single malt Virginia whiskey for himself. They settled into their evening postprandial routine, nestled in the leather club chairs in Thumper's study, surrounded by stacks of books and research materials. Janey looked forward to cooler autumn weather when the massive stone hearth would again be ablaze with a cozy fire. But on any night, warm or cold, it was now her favorite place to be.

The decision to resign from her teaching position at George Mason University was a risky choice. Devoting herself to a full time writing career was an uncertain path. She'd finished her latest work, an account of the founding and fledgling days of The Ancient and Venerable Church of Ars Venatica (aka The Church of Foxhunting), earlier that summer. The initial responses from potential publishers were encouraging. The company that published her first two books—studies of fringe religions around the world—was interested in her new one. But her agent, Danella Kernan, felt this one was worth shopping around before closing a deal.

The implication did not escape her that she was able to give up her adjunct professorship to spend her time writing, and also riding, in part due to Thumper's largesse. She knew she was seen by some as his "kept woman," an image further tainted by her recent arrival to the local community and her rapid adoption of the foxhunting lifestyle.

Others, though, saw how she and Thumper made a suitable match. His better friends were thankful that this newest relationship was with a woman more his intellectual equal. Her modest Mid-West demeanor stood in happy contrast to the fiery temperament of his second wife. That short-lived marriage was now officially dissolved and Shelagh McGrath was back in her native Ireland.

Janey picked up a newly arrived copy of Thumper's most recent work, *The Foxhunter's Guide to Life and Love*. He had authored half a dozen well-received books on such topics as the Constitution, the Presidency, and the Supreme Court. His most widely read work was a biography of his late father, who served eighteen terms in the House of Representatives. This new one, though, was a radical departure from that world, admittedly a vanity project done in part for his personal amusement. Inspirational, in a lighthearted, tongue-and-cheek voice, it allowed him the chance to be his true smart-ass self rather than the scrupulously detailed academic.

"I love the cover," Janey said. It showed two foxhunters, a man and woman, holding hands. Little else was visible, directing the focus to the hands, the lady's adorned with an engagement ring, leaving the rest unidentifiable but universal.

"And your thoughts on what's between the covers?"

"I'd have preferred a pseudonym for me. But other than that, I think it's great."

"I dropped off copies for Crispie and Ryman to read. I'll be interested to see what they think. Nardell and Patti too. And I'll pass a few more copies around Saturday morning after we're done hunting."

"I can't believe summer is almost over and hunting is about to start up again."

"Your first autumn opening meet." He reached over and refilled her wine glass. "A cause for celebration."

"I hope you're able to sleep better tomorrow night. It's going to be a pretty early Saturday morning for us."

"It's amazing to me that Frank would even consider selling his place. And to Cuyler Corley of all people."

"But if he does sell, wouldn't it be better to have someone in the family buy his farm?"

"Cousin Cuyler?" Thumper grunted in disdain. "The Corleys, first the father and now the son, have been playing both sides for decades."

"Both sides of what?"

"The line between preservation and development. Cuyler's father, Leeland, came from a hardscrabble background in the southwest part of the state, down around Pulaski. As a young man he swung a few fortunate land deals down there, parlayed his profits into the development craze outside the DC suburbs, and made an even bigger killing. He started cozying up to the landed gentry farther out, saw that as a good way to find more opportunities to pick up land on the cheap, sit on it for a few years, and then make more millions when the growth reached that area."

"I'm no business expert," Janey admitted, "but that sounds like a pretty good strategy to me. As long as you've got the money to invest and can sit on it for awhile."

"No argument there. It's just that his strategy involved a hefty dose of duplicity, pretending to care about history and preserving the country lifestyle when his true motivation was to find the next bargain land deal."

"So how did he become your uncle?"

"He met my mother's younger sister through his newfound connections. He was certainly charming, enough to charm her into marrying him. That gave him even greater access to potential deals before anyone else. And he jumped into the whole country gentleman foxhunting thing. He owned racehorses, gave lavish parties. But it was all pretty much a front."

"Is he still alive?"

"Yes, but not well. He had a stroke about a year ago. His son, my dear cousin Cuyler, has succeeded him, sticking to the same business plan. He even adopted the old man's style."

"How so?"

"The trick is to not look too slick. You can usually tell who's nouveau and who's authentic 'Old Virginia' around here. The real locals, no matter how wealthy they might be, don't put on airs. Their clothes may be well-made but they're understated, not exactly shabby but they might show a little wear."

"I still have a lot to learn about this world, don't I?"

"We seem to be pretty good subject matter for your anthropologist's eye."

"That's me. Margaret Mead transplanted from Samoa to the wilds of Crutchfield County, Virginia."

"Kinda lost your neutrality though. I don't think Doctor Mead ever took up cohabitating with the chieftain of the village."

She chuckled, and blushed slightly.

"Anyway," Thumper continued, "Cuyler's style is just like his old man's—wear a rumpled brown suit, speak with a laconic drawl, appear to be disarming, and you'll soon discover your wallet is empty before you know what's happening. And if Cuyler gets his hands on Worsham's property, it will only be a matter of time before my nightmare comes true."

He took a swig of whiskey. "Enough of that. On a happier note, any news from our favorite agent?"

"Nothing lately, she's still shopping the book around. And she's also pressing me about what's coming next."

"And what will that be?"

"I wish I knew. Ryman's been at a loss about where to go with his Church of Foxhunting idea. Says he's waiting for inspiration from Saint Hubert. But no telling when, or if, that might hit. Otherwise, I haven't come up with anything else."

"I know that feeling well. You finish a book, and then you think, 'Damn, can I do this again? Or was that my last hurrah?' But then something else strikes you, and you're off on the next one."

"So true. It's just that uneasy time when you're waiting to find out what's next."

****

"Hallelujah! Saint Hubert be praised! His message has arrived!"

Ryman McKendrick's exclamation rattled the walls of the small cottage he shared with Nardell Raithby.

She leapt up from the sofa in the front room and ran down the hall to see what the commotion was about. Ryman stood in his cramped office, waving a book and continuing his shouts of exultation.

"What's going on?" she asked.

"I've found it! Saint Hubert has delivered his blessed instructions. And he's used Thumper as his anointed messenger." He held the book out for Nardell to see. "Look! *The Foxhunter's Guide to Life and Love*. It's all right here. The Seven Principles of the Foxhunter Model. For months now I've been struggling with what Saint Hubert wanted me to do next. And all the time Thumper was right next door mapping it out."

He thrust the book into her hands. "Go. Read this and you'll see. The ten commandments of the Foxhunter's Faith have served as the foundation. And these seven principles will now carry the message forward, and to a much wider audience. The masses await! This is what comes next!"

Chapter 5

Thumper and Janey, riding Lenny and Bee, arrived at the Montfair kennels a little before 7:00 Saturday morning where a dozen dedicated practitioners of mounted foxchasing were assembled.

Among the hardcore hunters were Mildred Preston, joint-master of the hunt; her husband Dr. Joshua Preston; Marva Henderson, honorary secretary; Bing Sensabaugh, club president, retired banker, and, at 81, Montfair's oldest active hunting member; Marie Hardesty, Bing's lady friend; Cecelia Broadhurst, local real estate maven and patron of the juniors riding program. A few other faithful members filled out what would be a small but eager field of riders for the opening day of autumn hunting.

All but two wore polo shirts rather than the tweed jackets and ties typically associated with this portion of the hunting season. (The scarlet and black coats are not worn until "formal" season begins in late October.) The two exceptions on this steamy morning were Bing and Marie, neither of whom had ever hunted in anything less formal than jacket and tie and never would.

Twenty-seven foxhounds milled about, most of them not venturing far from their huntsman's horse. A few of the young ones, those just starting their hunting careers, cavorted around the fringes of the group. An occasional stern command from Patti and a gentle call from Crispie kept them from drifting too far away.

Thumper noticed that Ryman and Nardell had not yet arrived. They would be hacking over from Fair Enough

Farm, the neighboring property owned by several generations of the McKendrick family.

The official start time was approaching, hounds and riders were eager to be off. Thumper was about to call the group to order and make opening announcements when he heard hoof beats approaching through the morning mist.

"Brother Thumper!" Ryman called out as he and Nardell rode in at a brisk trot. He was riding Clyde, a Thoroughbred-Clydesdale cross that had been his father's favorite hunting mount. Fergus McKendrick, Ryman's father, had dropped dead from a massive heart attack exactly one year earlier, a fact no one took note of this morning.

Nardell rode Gabby, her gray Arab/Quarter Horse mare, a compact package of energy best suited to someone like Nardell who could ride anything with four legs and hair.

Ryman's exuberance at this early hour took Thumper by surprise. He'd slept somewhat better the night before, but the threat of changes brewing around the Paradise Gap community still troubled him.

"You're unusually spunky this morning," Thumper said as Ryman pulled up next to him. "Another outburst like that and you're likely to scare off the game before we even cast the hounds."

"Ah, fear not! The game will be obligingly waiting for us. Saint Hubert has given peace to my soul. A good day is assured."

"So you're back to where you left off last season, huh? Think you know where the foxes will be and how they'll run before we even move off?"

"Did Saint Hubert disappoint you even once last season?" Ryman challenged.

"It was an excellent season. But many factors could account for that. Whether or not the influence of a little known saint who's been dead for thirteen hundred years was one of those factors is impossible to say."

"Still the doubter, are you? Well, guess what. Our beloved patron saint has chosen you as his newest vessel to spread the word."

"Has he now? And what if I don't feel like being a word spreader?"

"Hah! You already have been. Who do you think guided your hand to create the next building block for the Ancient and Venerable Church of Ars Venatica?"

"What the hell are you talking about?"

"*The Foxhunter's Guide to Life and Love*, of course. The Seven Principles of the Foxhunter Model. With Saint Hubert's guidance, you have perfectly crafted the follow up to the Foxhunter's Faith. Those ten commandments the unknown Hunting Parson created served as an excellent start. But the message needs to be broader, to show how Saint Hubert's guidance applies to a much wider audience than those of us who actually ride to hounds. You've provided the key that will unlock the message to the world. Saint Hubert be praised!"

"Damn! Now I'm sorry I gave you a copy. I thought the whole Saint Hubert thing was fading. I'm not sure I want you using my book as part of your wacky Church of Foxhunting thing. I own the copyright, and if I say you can't…"

"Thumper," Janey said gently, "maybe now isn't the best time to discuss this. Everyone's ready to go. You and Ryman can hash this out later."

Thumper was still steamed. "There's nothing to hash out. I won't have him…"

She placed a hand on his arm and said, "For me. Can you let it rest for now?"

The pleading look in her eyes took his anger down several notches. This was about more than just getting the hunt started. He could tell she had something else to say.

"Yes, you're right." He turned to face the group of waiting riders. "Well, it's the start of another season already.

Wonderful to see everyone here. Mildred will be leading second field, I'll be leading first. It looks like a fine morning, but scent will vanish quickly with the rising heat, so we don't want to delay. Mr. O'Rourke, let's go hunting."

Crispie was riding Kashmir, his number one mount, a tall, well-formed, dark bay Thoroughbred now starting his sixth season as a huntsman's horse. A short note on the horn brought the pack to attention and the hounds fell behind Crispie as he trotted away from the kennel yard toward Gretchen's Bottom, a low-lying area along the northwest edge of the Montfair property. The lingering dampness there made it most likely that scent would hold if a fox had recently passed that way.

Patti took her position as first whipper-in to Crispie's right. She rode Pennywise, a strawberry roan mare of indeterminate breeding. They made a good match as each conveyed a hint of mysterious past and whose reddish-blond hair and pink, freckled complexion suggested they were different species from the same mother.

Nardell moved up to Crispie's left and Ryman took the drag position at the back.

As the field of riders fell in behind Thumper, Janey moved Bee alongside Lenny. "Maybe Ryman's idea isn't all that wacky," she half-whispered. "Okay, so the whole Saint Hubert thing is kind of out there. But, to be honest, I can see where he might be on to something. You did lay out an inspirational plan, foxhunting as a metaphor for life, that it should always be about chasing something, some goal to work towards."

"And," he replied, "you've been wondering what you'll do next, how to follow up your book about Ryman and his church of foxhunting. Would it die out or somehow keep going? And now you see a way for it to keep going, which means you can keep writing."

"Is that such a bad thing? You said you did your new book mostly just to amuse yourself. So it's not like you had other big plans for it."

"Look, you and I are the only ones who know the truth behind Ryman's visions, those strange sightings that led him to think Saint Hubert was sending him a message. Maybe I should just show him the evidence and see if that shakes him back to reality."

"I'd rather you didn't. Not just yet anyway."

A hound opened with an eager "Awooo!"

"That's Warwick," Thumper said. "If he's on to something, it's sure to be a good line. Looks like some action might be about to start."

The hound sounded his alert again and the rest of the pack went to him, confident he'd found a fresh line of scent.

Thumper grinned and shook his head. "Well, Saint Hubert be praised!" he said mockingly. "The game is afoot. I guess we'll have to finish this discussion later. Time to kick on."

He squeezed Lenny into a smooth canter and a dozen riders moved off across the dew-dampened fields following twenty-seven happily hunting foxhounds.

****

Post-hunt horse care and tack cleaning completed, Janey led Bee from the barn out to the large paddock next to the training ring. She stood at the gate and watched as he began to graze leisurely on the lush grass. A movement to her right caught her eye. She turned to see two young foxes cavorting just inside the paddock fence line. Healthy and energetic siblings from the spring birthing season, they were behaving like adolescent boys play-fighting—pouncing, running away, stopping, crouching, then springing and repeating the same moves. They were practicing the skills they would need to survive—stealthily tracking, killing, and eating mice, rabbits, and other small mammals as well as birds, including domestic fowl when the opportunity arose.

Unaware of the human's presence and unthreatened by the horse, they leapt, rolled, and ran steadily closer to Janey. She watched them with a mix of observation and amusement, careful not to move and cause a distraction. Their path brought them closer to her and, when just a few feet away, one of them looked up and saw the biped. They froze, stared at her like kids caught misbehaving, then pivoted and dashed away.

Janey returned to the barn where Thumper was hanging up his cleaned and oiled tack. "I just had a fox encounter of a different sort," she said. "Two foxes, actually."

"A brace," he replied, using the term for a pair of foxes.

"Young ones, siblings I assume. They were having a great time playing in the pasture, completely oblivious to my presence. We think of them as such elusive creatures, at least that's been my impression anyway. But these two were just letting it all hang out in broad daylight."

"We have to remember," Thumper said, "that it's really their turf we're on, not them on ours. They were here long before we were. And it's our responsibility to help them stay strong and healthy. Life in raw nature can be pretty rough, sort of like Hobbes said about human existence; 'Nasty, brutish, and short.' For foxes that can mean things like the scourge of mange, food shortages, invasion by other animals such as coyotes who kill foxes and drive them out of their territory. So we do what we can to help the fox population."

Janey recalled her conversation with the huntsman when she was gathering material for her recent book. "Crispie told me how he puts out chicken necks with an anti-mange medication to help prevent that. And the chasing season is timed to stop when the vixens are giving birth in the spring."

"You know," Thumper mused, "we're so habituated to the term 'fox *hunting*' when these days it's really just about chasing. Although I suppose the 'hunting' part suggests that we have to hunt around first so hounds can find a scent to chase, more like we're hunting *for* the fox. But no one wants to see a fox killed or even hurt. I guess it's sort of a trade-off. We help them stay healthy and well-populated and in turn they provide us with some challenging but ultimately harmless recreation."

"Well," Janey noted, "harmless for them anyway."

Thumper chuckled. "You're right. If anyone's not going to finish the day standing upright, it's far more likely to be someone among the chasers than it is the chased."

"When I was traveling around with Ryman and Nardell on their Church of Foxhunting missionary tour last year," Janey said, "a couple of the clubs we visited were called 'drag hunts.' We never stayed very long in one place so I wasn't able to get much in the way of details, but it was my understanding that they didn't chase real foxes, something about using an artificial scent."

"That practice has been around for a long time," Thumper replied, "and it's expanded over the years. It's mostly used where territory is limited and the fox population is slim to none. Someone lays a line of scent in advance, with twists and turns the way a fox would run, hounds then follow that and the riders follow the hounds. Their reward is a pile of kibble instead of putting a live fox safely to ground the way we do it.

"One of the first clubs to use this method in America was interested more in controlling the time spent hunting, which is hard to do when you're chasing live game. Myopia Hunt in Massachusetts is based just outside Boston and has been using the drag method since its founding in 1882. The original members were mostly professionals such as lawyers, bankers, and such who wanted to get out for a morning chase and then conduct their business the rest of the day. So by following a drag line they could keep to a fixed amount of time, maybe a couple of hours, then wrap things up and get to their offices."

"Myopia?" Janey asked. "Seems like an odd name for a

hunt club."

"Oh, yeah, that. Well, given their professions, most of the founding members wore glasses. So some wag came up with the name 'Myopia,' and it stuck."

Thumper started toward the tack room door but stopped for a moment of reflection. "You know, when I think about it, it's possible the overall fox population is better off than it might otherwise be if it wasn't for foxhunting. And there's also the element of land preservation. After all, we can't chase them if there's not enough open country to ride through, which means their natural habitat is protected. So another harmonious aspect to the arrangement."

"I've heard, though," Janey said, "that foxes are pretty adaptable, that they can live in cities as well as in the country."

"True, but it's hardly a happy arrangement. City folk tend to think foxes are cute little critters as long as they're just a cartoonish figure out in the countryside somewhere. But not so much when they start raiding their trash cans or attacking their pet cats or small dogs. And more development means more roads and more traffic, which is a far greater danger to foxes than foxhunting will ever be."

Having studied cultures in diverse parts of the world, Janey's frame of reference extended far beyond the limited environs of Crutchfield County. "There's danger for people, too, when humans and animals start sharing the same territory. Foxes might be a nuisance in the city or suburbs, but when you think about the potential for cross species transmission, the risks become much greater."

Thumper shook his head. "Ah, Doctor Musgrove, your scientific knowledge far exceeds that of a humble old country boy like me."

"It's not all that unusual," she countered. "Animals like bats and rodents carry pathogens that can infect humans. Mosquitoes and viruses like West Nile and Zika, fleas and bubonic plague, ticks and Lyme disease—the natural world is rife with all kinds of dangers. We may not think much about that in the developed world, but I've seen the results of that on a much larger scale in places like Africa and parts of South America. Foxes may be just a small part of the overall ecosystem here. But when people take over animal habitat, they expose themselves to dangers that are harmless among the wildlife population. The ripple effects can be disastrous, for both people and animals."

"Well, let's hope our efforts to support the local fox community will assure a safe and healthy future for those youngsters you saw."

Janey thought about mentioning the possible impact on the fox population that might result if Frank Worsham sold his farm to Cuyler Corley. How would the presence of an assisted living facility affect the local fauna? And would this one project start the domino effect, opening the door to more development? Fearing such speculations would only fuel Thumper's steamroller nightmares, she chose to keep those thoughts to herself.

Chapter 6

Frank Worsham pulled up at the shop he'd always known as McKendrick and Sons Farm Implements. Now, though, there was a bright new sign on the building that read "McKendrick Farm & Home Equipment" and beneath that "Sales and Service."

Frank opened the front door and allowed his constant companion, a Golden Retriever named Merle, to enter first. Stepping in behind the dog, he found Barstow Reinhardt in the showroom, explaining the latest improvements in string trimmer technology to a potential customer. A few other shoppers milled around on this Saturday morning, examining the riding mowers, chainsaws, generators, and other products. A row of larger John Deere tractors sat parked outside.

"Morning, Frank," Bar said. "Be with you in a minute."

"No rush," Worsham replied. He looked around and studied how the place had changed in the year since Fergus McKendrick died. Bar Reinhardt had taken on part time sales duties in addition to his role as head mechanic. Fergus's granddaughter Shelton, known locally as Sheltie Lou, quit her job as a veterinary pharmaceuticals rep on the West Coast and returned to Paradise Gap to help save the family business. A hefty dose of capital investment from Bar's personal savings provided the funds to keep the shop going. Shelton's business experience and MBA training ushered in a new spirit of modernity and a well-crafted approach to marketing.

Farming was the primary focus of life in Crutchfield County when Shelton's great-great-grandfather started the shop in 1885. A succession of sons, down to her father Ryman, had maintained that focus over the ensuing generations.

But changes had come, and more were coming. The local population was transitioning away from large farming operations to smaller "country properties" that required different equipment. As Shelton's demographic studies showed, the future would see the lot sizes become even smaller, requiring little more than a mid-sized riding mower and an assortment of gardening tools rather than agricultural tractors and attachments.

In addition to those trends, there would be no more "and Sons" carrying on the McKendrick name. Ryman's brother, Teedy, had died young without heirs and Shelton was Ryman's only child.

Another change Worsham noticed was Bar's attire. For decades he was never seen in anything other than grease-stained white overalls without a shirt underneath unless the temperature dropped below freezing. Now that he was spending time in the sales area as well as the service bay, he conceded to wearing mostly clean overalls with only a few stains to confirm he still got his hands dirty handling the trickier repair jobs. Under the straps of the overalls he wore a dark blue polo shirt emblazoned with the McKendrick logo. A further concession was the presence of a black patch covering his missing left eye and part of the surrounding scarring. The absence of his left ear, however, remained clearly evident.

At six four and two hundred eighty pounds, Barstow Reinhardt cut an imposing figure just on his size alone. With his sartorial choices and battle scars, he was easily the most recognizable figure in Crutchfield County. He also knew tractors and related equipment better than anyone in the area, possibly in all of Virginia.

That knowledge had convinced a new customer to go with the higher priced string trimmer. Bar directed the man to the checkout counter where Muriel Hudkins waited to ring up the sale.

He then turned to Frank Worsham. "Thanks for waiting, Frank. How you and Merle doing today?" He reached down and stroked Merle's soft fur. The dog smiled up at the large man with a happy, welcoming Golden Retriever grin.

"We're both doing fine," Frank replied.

"Merle looks great. All healed up from that surgery?"

"Jumping around like a young pup. I can never thank Ryman enough for making me take him to the vet. I'll never know how he was able to tell Merle had a tumor, but he saved my dog's life."

"Ryman's been doing some strange things since his daddy died. I've pretty much given up trying to figure it out."

"Is he here today?"

"Nah, they're all out foxhunting this morning."

"Oh, right, it's that time again. Guess I forgot. Maybe I'll catch him next time."

"He ain't here much these days. We see him from time to time but he's mostly leaving everything to me and Sheltie Lou. Fine with us 'cause when he is here he's more interested in spouting off about his stupid-ass Church of Foxhunting ideas than he is about the shop's business."

"There's another reason why I stopped by, something I wanted to talk to you about. What do you think the resale value might be on that John Deere 7830?"

"What! You just bought that last fall. I figured that was gonna serve you the rest of your working days. And then continue on once your kids took over the farm."

"That's just it. None of the kids want to stay in farming. Can't say I blame them. It's a difficult way to make a living. Even harder now for smaller operations like mine. Hell, we got people saying all the cows have to go because their farts are causing global warming. And half my income comes from beef cattle, farts and all. Oh, and we gotta get rid of vehicles that run of fossil fuels. You ever heard of a tractor that runs on electricity?"

"Shit, Frank, that's all just a lot of politicians blathering about things to get attention. Ain't none of that gonna happen, probably not in our lifetimes anyway."

"Maybe not. But it's got me thinking. It might be time to get out while I'm still able to enjoy some retirement years. Betty and me can get an RV and do some traveling, enjoy ourselves for a change."

"And there's Cuyler Corley waving a hunk of cash in your face."

Bar's comment took Frank by surprise. "You know about that?"

"Hell, Frank, anyone who stops by the Paradise Gap General Store knows about that."

"Oh, right. Luella."

"You know she runs the store mostly just to be the hub of gossip. Like they say around here, if you want to spread something, don't telephone, tell Luella."

"Nothing's for certain," Frank declared. "But I admit it's got me thinking."

"You know he'll be looking to pick up your land at a bargain price. That's how he works. Like his daddy before him. Whatever he's offering you, that land will be worth easily twice that much, maybe a lot more, in the next five or ten years. He'll just sit on it till the time's right."

"I know all about that history with him and his father. But he told me this deal is different. He wants to give something back, a legacy for his father and others like him."

"Others like him? You mean multi-millionaires who don't give a shit about anyone but themselves?"

"No, he means people who need nursing care and want to live out their last years in a peaceful country setting."

"And you believe that?"

"He showed me the plans. Already has the concept sketched out. Not a housing development or anything like that. An assisted living facility, with a low profile, limited occupancy."

"Hey, Frank, it's your property. Do whatever you want. As for your 7830, I'll have to look into resale options. But I can tell you straight up you won't be able to recover anything close to the original price. Especially with all the extra features you had us add."

"I'd appreciate having a number to play with. If I do decide to make a deal with Corley, the tractor won't be any use to me."

"Yeah, not something you and Betty are going to tow around behind your new RV."

Both men turned at the sound of the front door opening. A small, wiry man entered. He wore a billowy white blouse, light blue wool trousers held up with leather suspenders, and tall black riding boots.

"You're late," Bar snapped.

"Yeah, I know. I was helping Ansel with a difficult horse. Took longer then we thought."

"The correct answer is, 'Sorry, Mister Reinhardt. It won't happen again.' And that outfit ain't appropriate."

"Yeah, whatever. Didn't have time to change, or I'd have been even later."

Miles Flanagan breezed past Bar and headed to the stock room behind the sales counter.

"Arrogant little asshole," Bar muttered.

"Strange outfit he's wearing," Frank noted.

"Always something odd about Miles. This is just the latest. He's gotten into reenacting thanks to Ansel Hart."

"The farrier?"

Bar looked at Frank with his one eyebrow raised. "You know another Ansel Hart around here?"

Worsham chuckled at the remark. "No, I guess not."

"Miles got kicked out of the last place he was living. A fairly routine occurrence for him. Ansel took him in, lets him work off part of the rent by helping some with his shoeing work. And now he's got him into this Civil War reenacting crap. Just what we need, Miles Flanagan riding around with firearms and a sword. Only a matter of time before he shoots or stabs someone for real."

Chapter 7

Thumper was in his study Monday afternoon when his phone rang. He was surprised to see Myrna's name on the caller ID. So much time had passed, he'd forgotten she was still in his contacts list. For a moment he hesitated, not sure if he should take the call. But he steeled himself and hit "Accept."

Five minutes later he went to the kitchen where Janey was helping Natasha Nutchenko, Thumper's housekeeper, prepare dinner.

Both women noticed the troubled look on Thumper's face.

"We have a houseguest coming," he said. "My sister Myrna will be arriving Thursday evening. Not sure how long she'll be here. Probably not very long. Just wanted to let you know."

"Miss Myrna?" Natasha asked. "She has not been here for many years. Not since…"

Thumper cut her off. "Well, she's coming now."

He turned and went back to his study.

"Woof!" Natasha's English was still flavored with her Polish accent. W's sounded like v's and her syntax retained some awkward constructions. "Miss Myrna? I have not heard her even mentioned since…well, it was not good after Mister and Missus Billington died."

The knife Janey was using to dice an onion remained halted in mid-slice. "A falling out over the inheritance?"

"I am not knowing the details. But there was much anger from Miss Myrna. She did not like how things were done. She went back to California and has not returned since. Mister Thumper does not tell me much about these things. I am not knowing if they have talked before, but I am thinking they have not. Miss Claudette, his other sister, comes to visit sometimes, with her husband and children. Not often, but all is nice when they do come. And Mister Thumper sees her when he goes to New York. But Miss Myrna coming to visit? Woof!"

She noticed Janey had stopped her prep work.

"Well, I will make things ready and we will see. And you will finish dicing onion, yes?"

Chapter 8

Smith Bondurant stood at the cinema screen-sized window in Cuyler Corley's office. Perched on the top floor of the Corley Enterprises headquarters building, the view encompassed an endless horizon of gleaming multi-story structures. The mid-morning sun reflected off acres of dark, angled glass fronts. Single level strip malls sat between the office complexes, connected via a web of spiraling highways fed by spokes of access roads. Even now, two hours after the last commuter had pulled into a distant parking spot on this Thursday morning, the traffic still moved in a thick flow, gurgling forward in spurts of metallic mass, only to stop after a few yards, wait, and heave forward again. At every intersection the frazzled traveler was enticed by the carnival colors of fast food eateries—oases of plastic pleasure in the concrete desert.

The window faced east, across Fairfax County toward Washington. On a clear day, such as this one, the spires of the National Cathedral could be seen on the horizon in northwest DC. Just beyond the commercial goldmine of central Fairfax, back toward Falls Church and Arlington, were hundreds of residential communities. They ranged from newly built mini-mansions selling for a million-plus to older homes dating back to the boom's beginning in the early fifties. Some of them, originally priced at around ten grand, now sold in the mid-to-upper six-figure range; brick ramblers barely bigger than a Crutchfield County tractor shed.

The spacious office was sprinkled with models of the Corleys' projects; sixty years of development history in miniature three-dimensional displays. The pine paneled walls held large framed renderings of office complexes, industrial parks, shopping centers, and a country club.

Bondurant turned from the window and took a seat in front of Corley's desk. "Have you had a chance to review the information I sent you?"

"I have."

"So you're up to speed on the concept, the acreage this will require, access from the major travel routes, target audience, and so forth?"

"I think so. Far enough out from the developed areas where land is cheaper, at least a good twenty years ahead of the growth curve."

Corley picked up the package of information Bondurant had sent in advance of his visit. The cover sheet showed an artist's rendering of a multi-story hotel surrounded by insets of an adjoining conference center, a golf course, water park, and hiking trails, with a panoramic view of the Blue Ridge Mountains in the background. "Very impressive," he said.

"We at Pymsdale envision this project to be much more than your typical resort facility. In addition to all the standard amenities, the overriding concept is to preserve and promote the history of this great country, to celebrate it you might say."

"I'm all for that."

Smith looked around the office. "I'm sure you are. It appears this country has been very good to you."

"Yes, it has. And I'm grateful. Glo works for you now, does she? I kinda lost track of her after she moved back to California. It was a pleasant surprise when she called and asked me to schedule a meeting with you. I've been an admirer of Pymsdale for many years. Y'all make our achievements here look like small potatoes by comparison. So what can little old Corley Enterprises do for you?"

"I'm here to look for possible sites. Virginia is definitely our first choice. But we'll be considering sites in Maryland and North Carolina as well if we can't work out an acceptable deal in Virginia."

"I can think of a few possibilities."

"There's one property in particular I'd like to consider. It's in Crutchfield County, just outside a place called Paradise Gap."

"Really?" Cuyler Corley assumed he knew every property that might be for sale, whether officially on the market or not, within at least a fifty mile radius of Paradise Gap. And he was not aware of any such property large enough to support Pymsdale's project.

"Yes," Smith continued, "it's owned by a woman named Myrna Billington, part of an estate called Montfair. Do you know it?"

"Know it? Hell, the Billingtons are my cousins. But selling part of Montfair? Especially for something like this? I don't see that happening. How did you hear about this?"

"Glo mentioned it. She said there might be some hurdles to get over, and wasn't sure if this particular property would be large enough or suitable for our plans, but suggested it would be worth taking a look at."

"Well, yes, you might say there are some hurdles involved. Like, for example, the current patriarch of the family, Thaddeus Augustus Billington the Fourth. Name ring a bell?"

"Can't say that it does. I don't keep up on who's who among the Virginia landed aristocracy."

"Well, if you're looking to pull off a major development deal somewhere in this state, particularly in Crutchfield County or the surrounding area, it might benefit you to have at least some handle on that aspect of our local culture. I can help fill you in on that sort of thing."

"I believe that's one of the reasons Miss Devereaux put us in touch."

"You do know *Miss* Devereaux is the former *Missus* Billington? As in Thaddeus Augustus the Fourth, more commonly known as Thumper."

"Well, no, I did not know that. I find it's best to not be too intrusive into the personal lives of coworkers. Especially females. Even a harmless question or comment, something as innocuous as asking about marital status, can be taken the wrong way and—Bam!—you're the target of a sexual harassment claim."

"Geez, damn shame where things have come to today. And poor us, two successful white guys. Pretty much have targets drawn on our foreheads."

"You just have to be mindful of how you conduct yourself."

"I reckon. So, look, about this piece of property. I don't know all the details, but it's my understanding that the parents left the Montfair estate to the three kids jointly—there's another sister—with each third marked out as to who owned which part. But they also included a restriction that none of them could sell their part without the other two agreeing. And, really Smith, I don't see any way that Thumper Billington would go along with that. Especially for a project like this."

"People can sometimes be persuaded to see things differently. It can just be a matter of presenting the offer the right way."

Cuyler felt a glimmer of unease at Bondurant's tone.

"But before we concern ourselves with that," Bondurant said, "perhaps it would be best if we had a look around the area first. If that spot doesn't match our criteria, then there won't be any need to concern ourselves with sticky family matters. When are you free to review some possible sites?"

"Would the first of next week be okay?" Cuyler asked. "I could block out a couple of days then, and have some options lined up for you to look at."

"Fine, I'm staying at a place out in Middleburg, the Salamander Resort."

"Excellent choice. Mmmm, a thought just occurred to me. The annual Crutchfield County Horse Show is this weekend. A major item on the local social calendar. Sunday is the big day, when everyone who's anyone, plus a few others, will be there. Might be a good opportunity for you to meet some of the folks you'll need to work with if that's where you end up deciding to go with this project."

Smith smiled warmly and nodded. "It's a date, m'friend. I appreciate your help."

Smith Bondurant was every bit the self-serving charmer as Cuyler Corley and his father Leeland. The only difference was the absence of the good-ole-boy demeanor and the presence of a much nicer suit.

Chapter 9

Thumper barely recognized his younger sister as he navigated his Jaguar through the pick-up lane at Dulles Airport. She seemed to have aged twice as much as he expected. Perhaps the lines under her eyes, slouching posture, and unkempt hair were the result of a tedious cross-country trip. But he could not dismiss the emaciated appearance of her body—frail arms, stick-like legs, and pencil-thin neck. Myrna had never been plump, not someone who would be called "voluptuous." But Thumper's first thought was she looked more like his aging aunt than his kid sister.

Their initial exchanges were forced pleasantries, neither making mention of their lengthy separation and the dispute that prompted it. Myrna maintained the charade that all was going well in her life. Sensing there were problems lurking behind her upbeat façade, Thumper downplayed how well things were going for him.

"So," she said, "I assume hunting has started by now."

"Yes, Saturday, had a good day. Tuesday was great, and another fine run this morning."

"Nice to know the family tradition continues, even if Claudette and I have abandoned it."

"It's never too late to come back."

"Maybe it is. For some anyway."

"Damn! Look at that." Thumper pointed to a site where ground was being cleared for new construction along one of the main arteries in Fairfax County. "I didn't think they could fit another building along this strip. Guess I was wrong."

"Somebody must be making a lot of money off all this."

"I'm sure. All this growth has certainly been good to our Uncle Leeland and Cousin Cuyler."

"How are they, by the way?"

"Leeland's not doing well. Suffered a stroke about a year ago. He's living at home but has full time care. Cuyler's running the business, and following in his old man's footsteps. He's even trying to buy Frank Worsham's farm, says he wants to build an assisted living facility there, something modest. But I don't really trust him. Once he gets title to that property, no telling what he might do with it."

Myrna noticed the edge in Thumper's voice and the rising flush on his face.

"And, as you know," he added, "Frank's farm is a major part of our hunting territory, right next to Montfair and the McKendricks' place."

It was slow going through the Thursday evening commuter traffic. As they passed from the suburban congestion to the outer fringes and then into the first arc of rural countryside, freed from the gravitational grip of the metroplex, the pace leveled off to a steady cruise toward a different universe.

The sun was setting as they crossed into Crutchfield County. The landscape began to look more familiar to Myrna, the part of Virginia she'd known since childhood. In the gauzy twilight she could make out the shapes of houses set far back from the road, lights inside just beginning to flicker. Shadowy barns, sheds, and other outbuildings—some large and solid, others small and decaying—stood in irregular patterns, placed for function rather than compliance with neighborhood uniformity. Cattle stood in fields, barely visible in the low-lying creases where the late summer grass was still moist.

The rigors of her journey and the pressures of her situation began to fade into a peaceful numbness. The familiar scenery, enveloping darkness, and smooth flow of the car lulled her along and before she could pull herself back from the brink, she had dropped into a deep slumber.

Thumper glanced over and saw that she was sleeping. Curled up on the passenger seat, she looked childlike, small and vulnerable. He remembered family trips in the backseat of his father's Ford sedan. Claudette, the eldest, always sat on the right, he on the left, and Myrna in the middle. The trips were often campaign stops for his father's reelection bids. The children would be trotted out to underscore Thad's role as a family man, an advocate for and unblemished example of traditional values.

On the way home from these tedious exhibitions, the three siblings often fell asleep; little Myrna first, then Claudette, and Thumper last. He remained awake longer, wondering how he could escape the obvious expectation that he would be the next Thaddeus Augustus Billington to seek public office.

Looking down again at Myrna, he wondered if he had failed her as a big brother. His sisters were very different people: Claudette serious and determined, Myrna sensitive and capricious. There was never any doubt that Claudette would find her way in the world. Should he have been more supportive of Myrna? More protective? More willing to accept her rejection of their enshrined family traditions?

So much time had passed, time that could never be recaptured. But now she had returned, and perhaps that signaled a willingness to see the value in those traditions and embrace them.

He slowed the car and turned into the entrance of Montfair. The movement stirred Myrna and she awoke as the Jag passed between the stone pillars and started up the long tree-lined drive toward the main house.

For a moment she thought her adult life had been a dream and she was still ten years old. The house looked exactly the same as it had when the family returned home from one of her father's campaign trips. The side porch light was on and one lamp cast a welcoming glow in the front sitting room. She expected to see Thad behind the wheel, her mother in the passenger seat, Claudette and Thumper flanking her in the backseat.

As the fog of sleep ebbed, she realized it was Thumper driving and the problems of her adult life were not a dream.

"Welcome home, kiddo," Thumper said.

****

Myrna's introduction to Janey was politely brief given the late hour and rigors of Myrna's trip.

With their visitor comfortably settled in her childhood bedroom, now used for guests, Thumper and Janey turned in for the night.

"That drive to and from Dulles gets worse every time I make it," Thumper said. "I'm beat."

"Good," Janey replied, "maybe you'll get a decent night's sleep for a change."

Chapter 10

It was nearly noon, East Coast time, when Myrna made her way downstairs. Ten hours of sleep had done little to improve her haggard appearance. She found Natasha in the kitchen preparing lunch.

Natasha tried to hide her shock at how much the youngest Billington sibling had aged since she last saw her. "Oh, Miss Myrna! It is so nice to be seeing you. You are looking wonderful."

"I'm looking anything but. Is there any coffee?"

"Yes, is fresh pot. And breakfast. I will make you breakfast. Sit. You are needing to eat. You are looking like bird."

Myrna recalled the portion sizes Natasha doled out. Her cooking was splendid, but after many years handling the food service duties for an itinerant circus troupe, she had never quite mastered adjusting the quantities to a much smaller audience. "Just coffee is fine for now. Are Thumper and Janey around?"

"I think they are in barn."

Myrna accepted the coffee Natasha poured for her and went to the barn.

She entered to find two horses clipped to cross-ties in the aisle and two people bustling around them. Another time warp flash struck as, for a moment, she thought it was her father and sister. Thumper resembled his father to some degree but his voice was virtually identical to Thad's. And although the woman neither looked nor sounded like Claudette, she was wearing her older sister's clothes: faded polo shirt, beige riding breeches, dusty paddock boots, and half-chaps.

Thumper was the first to notice Myrna's presence. "Hey, kiddo! Good morning! Sleep well?"

"Pretty well. You?"

"Like a rock," Thumper lied.

"You two coming or going?" Myrna asked.

"Already been," he replied. "Got in a good ride earlier before the heat set in. Now just doing some grooming prep for hunting tomorrow."

"Doing your own grooming these days?"

"We're between help. I had a really great couple from Argentina, but they got a better offer and moved on. Had a few interviews but haven't found the right match yet."

Myrna stepped up to the horse Thumper was brushing, Ozzy, a young gray Thoroughbred just starting his second season as a hunter. She stroked his neck and the horse turned his head toward her.

"Miss all this?" Thumper asked.

Myrna closed her eyes and took in the aromas of horse sweat, hay, manure, and the cool mist that rose from the concrete floor on this warm, humid morning. "Yes," she whispered.

"But, hell," Thumper said brightly, "an old barn can't compete with the glitz and glamour of Tinsel Town though. Right?"

She opened her eyes and forced a smile. "Right."

"Thumper said you mentioned you're in line for a new sitcom when you called," Janey remarked. "That sounds exciting."

Myrna had to think for a moment about the story she'd told Thumper on the phone, a small fib to make her life sound less desperate. "Oh, that. Well, it's not finalized yet. Auditions are coming up soon, but my agent thinks I'm a shoe-in for the part."

"I've spent so much time traveling, writing, and teaching," Janey said, "that I've never had much time to keep up on movies and TV shows."

"Just as well," Myrna said. "Sounds like you've been using your time for much better purposes."

Thumper and Janey caught the sour tone in Myrna's voice. But only Thumper understood the reason behind it. He did have time to keep up with movies and TV shows and the absence of his sister's presence in them as nothing more than an occasional background figure had not gone unnoticed.

"We're about done here," Thumper said, "and Natasha should have lunch ready soon. But I expect you're more in breakfast mode."

"Lunch will be fine," Myrna replied. "And then maybe I'll take a walk. I need to get some fresh air and stretch my legs."

****

After lunch, with Thumper and Janey back at work on their book projects, Myrna excused herself for a solo stroll around the old homestead. Her wanderings eventually led her to a rise along the northeast corner of the property that overlooked the McKendricks' Fair Enough Farm. Gazing down at the house, a much simpler structure than the grand Montfair, childhood memories began to flow.

On many late summer evenings, when Congress was in recess and the Washington social whirl paused for its warm weather hiatus, the Billington clan would decamp to the neighbor's home. Thad Billington sat on the porch with Fergus McKendrick where they discussed crop projections and speculated on temperature levels and rainfall—usually too much or not enough, rarely just right. One or the other would comment on the latest tractor models John Deere was coming out with and then both would whistle in amazement over the hi-tech marvels.

Their conversations encompassed tales of mounted exploits, obstinate horses, and incompetent riders. No member of the hunt was spared their acerbic insights.

One subject, however, was steadfastly off limits. The weighty concerns Congressman Billington was wrestling with in the national legislature were not allowed to intrude at the McKendrick's farm. This was Thad's refuge from the cares of Capitol Hill.

Fergus's wife and Myrna's mother positioned themselves at the opposite end of the small porch, maintaining the charade that men and women should congregate for casual conversation according to gender.

The bond between Rhetta McKendrick and Cyril Celeste (CeeCee) Billington had been a source of wonderment to Myrna from her early teens when she began to understand the chasm that separated their upbringings. Cyril Crutchfield: of the Richmond Crutchfields, formally debuted at sixteen, graduated from Hollins College at twenty-one, married the bright young Thad Billington, of the Montfair Billingtons. Rhetta Keane: of the no-town Keanes, one of eleven children, with no financial means but blessed with a fiery beauty and a spirit to match, married the handsome scion of the McKendrick Farm Implements empire (which consisted of one unassuming building in the tiny village of Paradise Gap).

Foxhunting and neighboring properties brought them together. But a union of spirits that went far deeper than a shared activity or a common property line joined them in an enduring sisterhood. Maybe Cyril needed Rhetta for relief from the expectations heaped upon the highly placed. Maybe Rhetta needed Cyril to prove the worth of just plain folks.

As their parents sat and talked, the two McKendrick boys and the three Billington children played in the yard and around the barn. The images of five children engaged in summer evening games while their parents sat and talked on the porch rumbled around in Myrna's mind. When the kids needed a break, they would repair to the porch, sit among the four adults, and sip lemonade. Myrna remembered Fergus's earthy scent of workman's sweat and diesel fuel, the smell of her father's Old Spice aftershave, and the tangy sharpness on both men's breath after a few beers. She saw Rhetta as she had been then—a thinly muscular woman with thick, curly brown hair and hypnotic pale blue eyes. She remembered Rhetta's arms, how they looked by late summer when she wore a sleeveless sundress, hard and tight, a deep brown speckled with flecks of white. She imagined, if bitten, that they would taste salty and crunch under her teeth, like a pretzel. That thought still made her giggle quietly to herself. She also heard her mother's voice, the only times it sounded relaxed and girlish, as she and Rhetta swapped gossip.

Myrna never spoke to anyone about the deep crush she had on Teedy McKendrick. He was the eldest of the five, a better pairing for Claudette than for her, the youngest. But such details didn't matter in her youthful fantasies. He exuded masculine appeal in his steady, no-nonsense manner. She felt safe and protected in his presence, even though he barely seemed to notice her. She had imagined their future life together in minute detail. She knew if she voiced any of that to her sister, the seriously mature Claudette would have dismissed such thoughts as mere foolishness. Her mother was an even less likely option for support. She'd already overheard CeeCee express her disappointment that her own younger sister had "married down." Leeland Corley may have had money, but he lacked "breeding." Tavish Dougal (Teedy) McKendrick lacked both.

None of that mattered to Myrna. She and Teedy were destined to be.

Decades later she still felt the sting from the news of his death. He was only twenty, she was fourteen. Life had seemed unfair ever since.

Chapter 11

Thumper's great-grandfather, Thaddeus the First, founded the Crutchfield County Horse Show. The inaugural event was held in 1898, ten years after Thaddeus started the Montfair Hunt. It had been held every September ever since (other than a few suspensions during war years), running for four days, always at the county fairgrounds. Sunday, the final day, was devoted to foxhunting classes: hunt-style jumping, ladies sidesaddle, hunt teams, horn blowing and whip cracking competitions. At the time of Smith Bondurant's visit, Virginia was home to 25 "recognized" hunt clubs (those awarded such status by the sport's governing body) plus a few "farmer" or "private" packs (smaller operations that either chose not to seek recognition or don't qualify for it). Most of those 30-plus clubs were within easy driving distance to Crutchfield County. Any hunt was welcome to participate, so it was not uncommon to see clubs from Maryland or Pennsylvania listed on the roster.

Hunt-sponsored tailgate spots ringed the arena and clubs competed for the trophy awarded to the best display. These ranged from simple potluck fare and basic settings to elaborate themes replete with formal service and decorated with artistic floral displays. Stuffed foxes in a variety of poses gazed out from tabletops and truck hoods.

Montfair's spot encompassed two spaces of prime real estate adjacent to the announcer's stand. Decades earlier Leeland Corley had secured an adjoining spot, forming a Billington family bastion at the focal point of the viewing area. Leeland was now too infirm to attend, but Cuyler upheld the tradition. As long as the Corleys' predations were focused on development projects far removed from Crutchfield County, a semblance of familial harmony was maintained. But now that Cuyler was angling to purchase Frank Worsham's farm, the pretense of civility was harder to maintain. Cuyler insisted that his vision for Worsham's property would not interfere with foxhunting or other local farming practices. But rather than helping appease such concerns, Smith Bondurant's presence as Corley's guest on this September Sunday only served to fuel suspicions that less benign motivations were at play.

A tall, elegant man, easily recognizable to everyone at the show, circulated among the attendees. He sported a well-tailored tweed jacket, silk tie imprinted with images of horses and hounds, and khaki slacks creased with military precision. His thick shock of steel-gray hair was worn in a casually calculated style and his craggy face was set off by sharp eyes and an avian nose. The combined effect gave him the appearance of an eagle swooping over the crowd, as if a taloned claw might descend at any second and snatch a slice of salmon from someone's plate.

As he made his way toward the Montfair tailgate spot, his attention zeroed in on a slight woman standing with Thumper and Janey.

"Myrna! My god! I haven't seen you since…well, you know, it's been quite awhile."

She turned to accept his outstretched hand. "Nate Plummer. You haven't changed a bit."

"A tad grayer and creakier since we last saw each other. You know better than most how the pressures of Congress can wear on someone."

"It's good to know you're still holding my father's seat."

"I hope I'm doing it justice. His legacy is a challenge to live up to." He turned to Thumper and Janey. "Thumper, good to see you too. And this lovely lady, I don't believe we've met."

Thumper provided the introduction. "Nate, this is Doctor Janey Musgrove. And this gangly, beak-faced fellow is Congressman Nathan Plummer, who inherited the local seat in the House when my father died and through bombast and subterfuge has held it ever since."

Plummer smiled at his longtime friend's jibe and extended a welcoming hand to Janey. "Doctor Musgrove, a pleasure to meet you. Call me Nate."

"A pleasure as well. And please call me Janey."

"Is Vangy here?" Thumper asked.

"Chatting with some other friends down the rail a bit. She'll be along directly." Back to Myrna, Plummer asked, "So what brings you home to Virginia after all this time?" His face instantly transformed from glowing joy to sincere concern, a well-practiced political skill. "I hope it's not anything like the last time."

"No, nothing like that. No one's died. I just had some time between my acting gigs and decided to come back for a short visit."

"Well, it's so good to see you." He pumped her hand and his earnest smile returned. "Here comes Vangy now. Evangeline! Come and say hello to an old friend of ours."

Evangeline Plummer glided along with patrician grace. Tall enough to be a proper match to Nate's six-four height without towering over other men of lesser stature, her slender frame allowed her to look elegant in whatever she chose to wear. On this day it was perfectly suited to a foxhunting-themed horse show in the Virginia countryside on a sunny September day: linen jacket in a muted brown plaid pattern accompanied by a silk scarf with intertwined hunting horns, mid-calf skirt in cinnamon, and tall rust leather boots.

"Myrna! So nice to see you. It's been too long."

Vangy leaned over to give the diminutive woman a light hug. Myrna had to rise on her toes to receive the polite embrace.

"You look lovely as ever," Myrna said.

"As do you," Vangy lied. "How are things in Hollywood? I'm afraid Nate and I don't have much time to keep up with what's going on in the entertainment world these days."

"Oh, Hollywood is pretty much the same as it's ever been I suppose. Powerful men, vulnerable women."

"I'm sorry to hear that. I hope you haven't had any problems with that sort of thing."

Myrna shrugged. "Nothing I couldn't handle."

Vangy's veneer of feigned concern cracked slightly as she saw the genuine sadness in Myrna's eyes.

Nate intervened. "Darling, Cuyler Corley is waving us over. It appears he has a guest with him."

A short bald man wearing a rumpled brown suit and striped tie stood next to a slightly younger man, nearly equal to Nate Plummer in height, wearing a navy blazer and gray trousers. His immaculate white button down shirt was a suitable canvas for the blue silk tie decorated with red and yellow horse show ribbons. On a tip from the Salamander Resort's gift shop manager, Bondurant had made a visit to Horse Country Saddlery in Warrenton. There he found the perfect neckwear for Sunday's event: equestrian themed but in a subtle pattern, absent any actual horses, that could just have easily related to any other ribbon-based event. Smith Bondurant believed strongly in the power of the proper tie.

"Yes, yes, of course." Evangeline regained her posture-perfect composure and a welcoming aura returned to her face. Preparing to take her leave from Myrna, she asked, "Will you be staying in Virginia long?"

"Probably not. Only here for a short visit. I'm up for a role in a new sitcom, just waiting for the word from my agent and then I'll be heading back."

"Well, best of luck with that. And I hope Nate and I have a chance to see you again before you go."

As she and Nate navigated their way through the crowd toward Corley and his guest, Vangy remarked, "Poor Myrna, she doesn't look well at all. So haggard, frail even. I have a feeling things aren't going well for her. Actually, for all the movies and TV shows we've seen, I can't recall ever seeing her in anything."

"There are so many more entertainment outlets these days," Nate replied. "Maybe she's making it big in some medium we're not up on. If you're concerned, I could have Elizabeth look into it." He mentioned Thumper's daughter who had spent the summer as an intern in Plummer's congressional office. "She's more in tune with all this new media stuff."

"Oh, I wouldn't bother Elizabeth with that. But what Myrna said about 'powerful men, vulnerable women,' it makes me wonder…"

"Nathan! Vangy!" Corley hollered. "Let me introduce you to someone you might find worth knowing."

Vangy glanced back once more at Myrna. Her protective radar was ablaze. But other duty called. "Cuyler, so nice to see you," she said as she leaned in for the obligatory embrace.

Many who attend horse-centered events—shows, races, polo—pay only modest attention to what's happening in the arena or on the course. Socializing is the main draw, interrupted sporadically to catch a few minutes of the action at hand. For this crowd, the hunt teams competition broke that pattern. Almost everyone present had, it might be said, a dog in the fight.

The Montfair Hunt was represented by Crispie O'Rourke and Patti Vestor, both professional staff, and Ryman McKendrick, honorary (i.e., volunteer) whipper-in. All three wore scarlet coats with the Montfair colors on their collars. Their horses were groomed to a gleaming finish, with manes elegantly braided and tack polished to a high gloss. Hunt whips in hand, they executed a series of jumps and turns, changing lead position as they went, and finishing the final fence three-abreast in perfect synchrony.

The crowd erupted in applause and everyone knew, as usual, the Montfair standard would be hard to beat.

Crispie would return for the huntsmen's class a little later. He faced a stiffer challenge against several long-serving professionals as well as some up-and-coming youngsters, women and men, carrying the horn for other clubs.

With two horses untacked and returned to the showground stalls, Patti stayed to help Crispie prepare for his solo performance while Ryman, accompanied by Nardell who had handled much of the grooming duty, ambled toward the Montfair/Corley tailgate spots. As Nardell veered toward the Montfair side, Cuyler waved Ryman over to his area.

"Ryman! What a great performance! C'mere. Let me introduce you to my guest, visiting all the way from California. Smith Bondurant, this is Ryman McKendrick, joint-master of the Montfair Hunt."

As Bondurant accepted the offered hand, the force of Ryman's grip took him by surprise.

"And the Apostle of Saint Hubert. May his name be praised!" Ryman exclaimed.

Bondurant cast a questioning eye at Corley, who simply shrugged in response. "Very impressive performance you put on out there," he said.

"All because of our dear Saint Hubert's blessings. You see, it's all about the chase. What are you chasing, Brother Smith?"

Bondurant wiggled his empty plastic cup. "Right now, I believe I'm chasing a refill of my drink."

"Hah! Good man! But to have come all the way from California, you must be chasing some bigger quarry than that." Ryman gave Smith a studied look. His ebullient manner ebbed and his tone turned serious. "And it's not a fox. Perhaps your chase does not align with Saint Hubert's purposes."

Corley interrupted. "Smith is here on some mutual business matters. But, I assure you, nothing that should cause you or Saint Hubert any concerns."

Ryman maintained his skeptical stance.

Cuyler put his hand on Ryman's arm. "How about a drink? The Corley bar always has the best stuff."

"No. Thanks. I need to touch base with Thumper on some things."

Bondurant lit up his brightest, most innocent smile. "Well, nice to meet you. I hope to see you again before I leave."

Ryman returned a curt nod, swung on his booted heels, and left.

"There's an odd bird," Bondurant said.

"He has been lately," Corley replied. "He had a nasty fall from a young horse about a year ago, right around the same time his old man died. Might have been some concussion-related symptoms, along with the shock of seeing his father drop dead right in front of him. Anyway, now he thinks Saint Hubert, the patron saint of hunters, has called him to turn foxhunting into some kind of a religion."

"Really? I don't suppose there's any way he could know the real reason I'm here."

"Not a chance."

"And yet…it seemed like…" Bondurant shook his head, then looked down at his empty cup. "Well, he was right about one thing. I need to chase down another drink."

Ryman's thoughts were still troubled as he walked over to the Montfair enclosure. He didn't notice the couple approaching him from behind, heading in the same direction.

The young woman took his arm and, his concentration broken, he turned to find Elizabeth Billington standing next to him. "Lizziebits," he said with a faint smile. "Did you see us in the hunt staff class?"

"Sorry, but we missed it. Tobias had a late night on the beat so we didn't get on the road in time to catch that. But I'm sure y'all did the old hunt club proud."

"Tobias?" Ryman looked at the young man standing with his goddaughter.

"Oh, right," Elizabeth said. "You two haven't met. Tobias, this is Ryman McKendrick, our next-door neighbor, joint-master of the hunt along with my father, and sort of my unofficial uncle."

Tobias extended his hand and Ryman took it. The force was much less than the vice-like squeeze he'd given Smith Bondurant. "Tobias Johnson. A pleasure to meet you, sir."

"And you two are...?" Ryman flipped a finger back and forth between the young couple.

"Friends," Elizabeth replied. "Well, sort of more like...dating."

"Ah." Ryman got the implication. "*Dating*."

"Tobias is a UVA alum, and a Kappa Sig." She mentioned her father's fraternity, founded at the University of Virginia in 1869 and rarely without at least one Billington as a member ever since. "We met this summer when I was interning for Uncle Nate." Another reference to an "unofficial" uncle.

Tobias Johnson, mid-twenties with a gymnast's build, was jacketless as the September afternoon heat rose. But he looked crisp and composed in a pale yellow Brooks Brothers dress shirt, the muted pattern of his perfectly knotted tie a balanced blend of designer flair and business-like gravitas. The face above was squarely handsome, with glowing chocolate skin stretched over prominent cheekbones. A meticulously groomed mustache formed a dividing line between his nose and lips.

"'A late night on the beat'?" Ryman asked. "You a cop?"

"Reporter. I cover Capitol Hill. A late session last night, budget wrangling in a frenzy."

"An annual event, from what I recall of Elizabeth's grandfather's tales."

"Yes, a DC tradition going back even farther than the Crutchfield County Horse Show."

Ryman's mood lightened. A sharp young man, he thought. And about time Elizabeth found someone capable of keeping up with her.

The threesome continued on into the heart of the tailgate action. Ryman noticed Myrna was engaged in conversation with Reverend Daniel Davenport, pastor of Paradise Gap's Saint-Cuthbert's-in-the-Woods Episcopal Church. Despite his humble Mid-West origins, the good reverend cultivated the image of a vicar from the English Shires. Stoop-shouldered with a rounded paunch, his aquiline nose protruded between pale, sunken cheeks. His graying beard and hair were at least a month past a good trim, as were his bushy eyebrows that curled up at the ends like tiny horns. The eyes beneath were a languid brown that looked out at the world with weary resolve.

"So you took over after Father Herb died?" Myrna asked, a reference to Reverend Herbert Laudermilk who served as St. Cuthbert's pastor for nearly forty years. He was the only clergyman Myrna had ever known and she'd last heard his gentle, thoughtful, reassuring voice when he officiated at her parents' funeral. The not-so-gentle aftermath had sent her packing back to the West Coast where she'd remained till now, self-exiled from her family roots.

"Yes, I have been privileged to serve our local congregation these past few years." Davenport waved a limp hand toward the show arena. "It's been quite an experience adapting to the local culture."

"Shouldn't you be doing church things? I mean, it is Sunday, right?"

"Oh, we had our regular service this morning, but wrapped up in time for everyone to get here for the show, at least the major classes anyway. I find that the only way I can spend time with some of my parishioners outside the church is to attend their social functions." He held up the glass of wine in his hand, pointed toward a hefty plate of hors d'oeuvres on the table beside him, and added with a wry grin, "It is a policy not without some notable benefits."

"I have very happy memories of Saint Cuthbert's. And of Father Herb."

"Well, while Father Herb has gone on to be with the Lord, the old church is still standing. Perhaps you can join us for a service or two before you leave."

The suggestion caused a warm sensation to flow over Myrna. Even as a child her affection for the church stemmed more from the peaceful atmosphere within the small, historic structure than from any sense of God's presence. Father Herb's sermons, rather than rousing her to spiritual passion, had a hypnotic effect that left her with the feeling all was well, even if the words themselves did not register. During her tumultuous teen years, Sunday mornings were a haven of calm in an otherwise stormy sea.

"I just might do that."

"Nice sermon, Reverend." The compliment came from Bing Sensabaugh. "And thanks for keeping it short."

The interruption gave Myrna the chance to slip away unnoticed. With everyone else focused on the staff class contest in the ring, she made her way over to Corley's section. She'd never met Smith Bondurant but she'd seen his image in various industry publications. Gloriana, as the keeper of her boss's schedule, had tipped Myrna off that he'd be attending the show.

"Cuyler," she said quietly, drawing his attention away from the threesome cantering their horses around the ring.

"Cousin Myrna!" he said, with more enthusiasm than she would have preferred. "So great to see you! What a surprise. How's everything going?"

"Fine. All fine."

"I had no idea you were back. Hey, let me introduce you to my friend. Smith Bondurant, this is Myrna Billington. Or maybe better known as Lola Leeland."

"A pleasure." Smith offered a gentle hand and ramped up the charm-o-meter. "Lola Leeland?"

"My stage name."

"Oh, of course. Now I recognize it. You were in…?"

"Probably nothing you've seen or heard of."

"Myrna borrowed my father's name," Cuyler explained, "and added the 'Lola' part because she liked the Kinks' song. Isn't that right?"

"Yes. Plus I thought the alliteration would be helpful. Of course, that was back when real names weren't in fashion."

"Well," Smith said, "whatever the moniker, I'm sure you were an asset to any troupe you've acted with. Anything I should be tuning into now?"

"Not at the moment. Maybe soon."

"I'll be on the lookout for your name at the top of the cast list."

Myrna moved in closer to the two men. "Um, look, we can drop the crap. We all know why I'm here. But this isn't the time or place." To Smith she said, "Could we meet somewhere soon to, y'know, talk about…things?"

"Certainly," he replied, maintaining the conspiratorial tone. "First, though, Cuyler and I plan to look at a few properties, just drive-bys for now, to get a better lay of the land, see if there's a reasonable possibility of something suitable to our purposes. Maybe one day next week?"

"Fine. How can I contact you?"

Cuyler spoke up. "Call me." He slipped his business card to Myrna. "And I'll put you in touch."

Summoning her thespian skills to conceal her desperation, she smiled pleasantly and walked away with a confident stride. Rather than returning to Montfair's area, she opted for a detour to the port-a-potties and a chance to compose herself. As she approached the row of toilets, she noticed a large man leaning against a tree on the hill just above them. He gave her a subtle wave and flashed a leering grin. Any chance of self-composure disappeared.

Chapter 12

Cuyler Corley collected Smith Bondurant from the Salamander resort early Monday morning and they headed to Crutchfield County. He piloted his Cadillac Escalade past the main entrance to Montfair. About a half mile farther down the road he turned right onto Fair Enough Lane. The winding gravel road took them south, with the Billington property to the west and the McKendrick farm to the east. Located in the central part of the county, the terrain was gently rolling pastures leading to steeper wooded elevations farther back from the road. Peaks of the Blue Ridge Mountains formed a scenic backdrop behind the Montfair estate.

Corley stopped the car and pointed to a spot along the road's edge. "As best as I can tell, Myrna's property starts about here." He traced his finger toward a far distant hilltop. "Goes to about there." His finger then moved straight from right to left. "And runs along that ridge south for about a mile and a half, where it abuts the northeast edge of Worsham's farm. A little shy of a thousand acres."

"It has potential," Smith Bondurant said. "And here on the left, this is McKendrick's land?"

"Right, about seven hundred acres."

"And Worsham's?"

"His runs five hundred and eighty two acres. But he's been leasing most of McKendricks' land for many years. The McKendricks focused more on their farm implement business rather than the actual farming, so Frank's been running cattle and growing some crops, mostly corn and soybeans, on some of their land."

As Corley resumed a slow cruise down the road, Bondurant sat silently and formed the possible images in his mind. The main resort building here, adjoining conference center there, recreation facility and waterpark nestled at the base of that hillside. Scanning the farther horizons on both sides, he saw ample space for hiking trails and nature centers. And perhaps an equestrian facility somewhere. That hadn't been part of the original plans, but after his visit to the horse show, he thought it might be worth considering, a way to distinguish the Pymsdale resort from the competition.

"It could work," he said. "If the price is right, and if the sellers are willing."

"Just a matter of putting the best deal together. With the right information, there's always a way to get to 'yes.'" Corley looked at his watch. "And now we need to get on to our next agenda item."

****

There have always been a few Washington restaurants— rarely more than two or three at any one time—where the powerful congregate. These places achieve an ephemeral quality; an unofficial though undeniable sanctification immediately sensed upon walking through the door that the air is somehow different. The mighty can rest easy. Partisans agree to meet on neutral ground. Offhand remarks will not appear as tomorrow's headlines. Such is the atmosphere at The Palm.

A mere congressman from a mostly rural Virginia district sitting with two unknowns caused no heads to turn. The majority of other diners tucking into the high-priced fare were instantly recognizable to anyone who followed the national news media, whether liberal or conservative.

"This project will put Crutchfield County on the map," Corley said, addressing Plummer. "You know as well as I that the lack of industry has been a drain on the area's economy for decades now. The younger generation leaves at their first chance. No one wants to keep farming, there's no future in it. This could change all that."

"Speaking of the future, and of change," Bondurant said, "Cuyler tells me you may be considering a change for your own future."

"Not official yet," Plummer replied, "but it's no secret I'm considering a run for the Senate next year."

"And I think I can speak on behalf of Pymsdale Development that we wish you well in that endeavor."

Plummer clearly understood the implication.

Corley continued. "For all the obvious positives, we know this isn't going to be an easy sell. The preservationists will be up in arms at the first hint something might be afoot. And the fiscal conservatives will go apoplectic over the infrastructure costs. Zoning approval alone will make the Battle of Paradise Gap look like a Sunday picnic." He cited a small scrimmage between Union troops and Confederate guerillas that took place close to the village in 1863 and had since taken on legendary proportions far beyond its actual consequences.

"Congressman, your influence in these matters will be crucial," Bondurant said.

Plummer took a sip of his favorite cocktail, a special of the house, an Old Fashioned made with exclusive small-batch bourbon. "I have no doubt my influence could be helpful with the state and county issues. But there's one obstacle you fellows haven't mentioned."

He paused for another sip as Bondurant and Corley waited.

"And that, gentlemen, is Thaddeus Augustus Billington the Fourth. Even if it were just the neighboring properties, possibly anywhere in the county, he'd marshal every resource and connection to stop it. But do you really think he'd agree to let his sister sell her share of Montfair for something like this?"

"Perhaps there's some way," Bondurant said, "some leverage point, that might help him see the larger benefits of this project. You know, for the good of the community."

"A leverage point?" Plummer swirled the ice in his cocktail and stared into the glass as if studying a crystal ball. "You mean dirt."

"I prefer 'leverage.' A bargaining tool."

Plummer turned to Corley. "There is that one thing."

Corley thought for moment. "Oh, right. But nothing was ever proven. Just rumors."

"Rumors can be as damaging as facts," Plummer said. "Sometimes more so." He leaned back and addressed Bondurant. "Dirt. I remember one thing Thumper's father, my old mentor, used to say. 'There is always dirt.'"

Bondurant smiled. "I'm listening."

Chapter 13

Abel, Rhetta's ever-present Boxer, bounded out the front door to greet the man coming up the walkway.

"There's a good boy!" The dog wiggled his stub of a tail and leaned in to accept a vigorous rub behind his ears from Cuyler Corley. Looking up at Rhetta standing on the porch, her visitor said, "I think he remembers me."

"Ain't much he don't remember. So what is you wanted to talk about?"

"I assume you've heard about the deal I'm working on with Frank Worsham."

"Anyone who's been to the General Store in the past few weeks knows about that."

"The reason I called and asked if I could stop by is because I know it will have some impact on you if the deal goes through."

Rhetta stepped down from the porch. She patted her thigh and the dog went to her side. "Mighty thoughtful of you," she said, sarcasm dripping from her tone. Her mood then softened. "Oh, hell, Cuyler, I reckon it may not have all that much impact either way. Frank's looking to get out of farming one way or t'other. Sheltie Lou told me he was in the shop on Saturday asking Bar about the resale value on that tractor he bought last year. If you or somebody else don't buy his land right off, he probably won't keep up the lease on my land much longer anyways."

"And I suppose that's going to put a serious dent in your income."

"Mebbe. Might be somebody else interested in leasing those acres. They've been right productive for Frank. Plenty of grazing for his cattle, and enough level areas with good soil for some decent crops. Tell you the truth, Frank's been getting a pretty sweet deal all these years, being a friend and neighbor, and someone we knew could be trusted to be good on his word."

"Trust is important in any relationship."

Rhetta could not stifle an amused snort. Cuyer Corley was not someone most people associated with the word "trust."

"Might be someone else willing to take up the lease if Frank drops it," she said. "Or we could just let that go."

"And give up that extra income?"

"Not like I need much to live on. And the shop's doing much better since Sheltie Lou came back and took over after Fergus died."

"I guess that's been about a year now. I was here for the memorial service." He pointed over toward the Montfair estate where the service had been held. "Quite an event. Fergus was well liked and highly respected."

"I reckon."

Corley thought for a moment. "Now that I think about it, I remember Ryman had an incident. Passed out and fell off his horse in the middle of the vicar's eulogy. Is he okay?"

She snorted again. "Okay? That boy ain't been okay in a long damn time. And he's been getting less okay every day since his daddy died. Keeps blabbing on about his Saint Hubert crap and his silly-ass Church of Foxhunting. He's no use to anyone. Thank God Sheltie Lou's running things. And as much as I hate to admit it, Bar's been a big help too. If it hadn't been for him, the shop would have gone under for sure."

"I saw Ryman at the show the other day. He did seem…odd."

"Odd don't do it justice. More like bat shit crazy. Matter of fact, given his mental state, I decided to change my will." She waved her arm toward the surrounding countryside. "I ain't leaving none of this to him. It's all going straight to Sheltie Lou when I'm gone."

"I'm sure she'll be a good steward of it."

"I don't know what she'll do with it. She won't be taking up farming, I'm sure of that. Anyway, better it go to her than her shit-for-brains father." She turned toward the barn. "I gotta get some chores done. If you want to stick around, you can come along with me. I don't get many visitors out here in the sticks." She gave Corley a playful jab. "You ain't the best company I could hope for, but I reckon you're better than nothing. You do look kinda puny though. But mebbe you can still toss a hay bale, hoist a feed bag, and swing a muck rake."

Corley chuckled and they strolled over toward the old barn. An old gray horse stood in a paddock beside the building. His ribs and hipbones protruded distinctly under his sagging hide. He walked slowly, stiffly, in short steps, grazing on what few traces of grass could be found within his enclosure. The absence of lush vegetation didn't seem to matter much. He looked to be going through the grazing motions more out of habit than hunger. A large pile of fresh hay in one corner assured he wouldn't starve for lack of forage.

"Is that Minstrel's Delight?" Corley asked.

The horse lifted his head, pricked his ears forward, and gazed toward the humans. Senility showed in his clouded eyes—the confused stare of a nursing home resident, as if he sensed that the surroundings were pleasant but a little uncertain of where he was, why he was there, or the identity of the people approaching him. After a few seconds, he returned to his pantomime of snatching at grass blades.

"Yep, that's Minnie Dee."

"I remember Ivan hunting on him all those years back." Corley mentioned the late Ivan Mooney, the long-serving Montfair huntsman prior to Crispie. "They were quite a pair. But he's gotta be…what?…well into his thirties by now."

"Around thirty-four as best we can figure. Ivan retired him when he was in his late teens. We took him in, gave him a good home, turned him out with the youngsters Fergus and Ryman brought in off the track. He let 'em know what's what and taught 'em some manners. But he's too old and feeble now."

"Good of you to give him such great care all these years."

"Likely won't be much longer. But I do what I can to keep him comfortable."

"Old age." Corley stood silently and reflected on that inevitability. "I don't mean to lessen the loss of Fergus, but if I had the choice, that would be the way to go. Living life full on then—whammo!—a heart attack takes you down on the spot. Not like the way my father's going."

"Not doing well?"

"I guess you know he had a stroke, right around the same time Fergus died. And there's been a series of others since. He's in pretty bad shape, needs a wheelchair, barely able to speak. I've set up a full care facility at home and arranged for round the clock help."

"Good of you to do all that."

"Least I can do. I wouldn't be where I am today without him." He turned his attention back to the ancient horse. "That's why I'd like to do something for others in his name, a lasting legacy. 'The Leeland Corley Retirement Home.' And Worsham's farm would be just the place for it. Plenty of space, lovely views, peaceful and quiet."

"Bah! Plenty of time for peace and quiet when you're dead. I figure to keep on living to the fullest right up to the end, just like Fergus did."

"Well, you never know, do you?"

"No, I reckon not, but us Keanes are known to be a hardy stock. Most everyone's lived to a ripe old age. Only exception was my daddy, but that was his own doing."

"But don't you ever think it might be nice to not be tied down to all the work to keep this old place up? Especially with Fergus gone, Ryman off doing his crazy church thing, Sheltie Lou and Bar so busy keeping the shop going?"

"What the hell would I do if I didn't have this place to keep me busy?"

"Well, you could sell it, pass most of the money along to Sheltie Lou now, use some of it for your retirement fund. Maybe buy yourself a nice condominium somewhere, and enjoy yourself for a change."

Rhetta looked at him with a bemused smile as she reached for a muck rake leaning against the barn wall. "Cuyler Corley, could you really see me living in some damn con-DO-minium?"

He thought about that for a few seconds, then sighed. "No, I don't reckon I can."

Chapter 14

"Are you sure you don't want to come along and car follow?" Thumper asked Myrna as he and Janey prepared to leave for Tuesday's hunt.

Myrna sat at the kitchen table, wearing a bathrobe, coffee mug in hand. "I'm still adjusting to the time change. And you two get up so damn early. It's still the middle of the night in LA. Besides, I'd really like to get to Middleburg for some shopping while I have the chance. I could be flying back any day now if my agent calls."

"Okay. Well, have fun. We'll see you later."

"Thanks for letting me use your car."

"Not a problem. The old Jag knows its way to Middleburg pretty much on autopilot."

Thumper and Janey dashed out the kitchen door to the barn where Voytek, Natasha's husband and Montfair's farm manager, had their horses ready to load on the trailer.

****

Driving through Middleburg around noontime, Myrna recalled her teen years as a student at the exclusive Foxcroft School just north of the village. She had chafed under the prim and proper strictures of the elite academy for young ladies. Regardless of her academic record, a degree from Foxcroft, plus the legacy of Billington and Crutchfield women before her, including her mother, assured her acceptance to Hollins College. She lasted less than two years there before hitching a ride to the Golden State where she was certain Hollywood stardom awaited.

With not a dime of Glo's money to spare, she could only drive past the tempting shops in Middleburg. She parked Thumper's Jag in the main lot of the Salamander Resort and Spa and then waited in the cavernous lobby for Smith Bondurant to appear. As she sat nervously on the edge of a plush chair, she noticed a familiar face in the bar area. Despite the passage of many years, her Foxcroft roommate was unmistakable, thanks mostly to a few rounds of excellent cosmetic surgery. Jealousy was her first reaction, wondering what her old friend would look like without such subterfuge. Fear then took over. Was she part of the local horsey set? Possibly a member of a local hunt club? The membership roles were filled with Foxcroft grads. If so, she'd probably know Thumper. What if word got back to him that she'd been seen with Bondurant? That would be difficult, impossible really, to explain. Maybe Salamander wasn't the best choice for a meeting place. But she'd been so eager that when he suggested the resort, she quickly agreed without thinking it through.

The elevator doors opened and Bondurant stepped out into the lobby. He saw Myrna, cranked up his welcoming smile, and strode toward her. She leaped up, intercepted him mid-stride, and guided him away from the bar area down a hallway toward the salon and fitness center. The aroma of herbal scents and bath steam from the spa mingled in the corridor.

"This was a mistake," she said. "I'm so sorry. I should have thought better."

"So you've decided you don't want to sell? And you've come here to tell me in person?"

"No, no! Yes, I want to sell. I need to make that happen. But, you see, I can't let my brother know about it. Not yet. I'll need time to work that part out." She had no idea how she could achieve that, but the first step was to assure

Bondurant she was serious about making a deal. Once she had that lined up, she'd figure out some way to convince Thumper.

"Okay. I won't tell if you won't."

"It's not that easy. Middleburg is a tight community. Everybody knows everybody, and word gets around quickly. If someone sees me here with you, someone who knows my brother, that could be a problem."

As they walked along the winding hallway, Myrna kept her head down in case they passed anyone else who might recognize her.

"So let's go someplace else," Bondurant suggested. "You know the area. I don't."

"That's just it. There isn't any place around here where it would be safe to be seen together."

"Well, there is one place nearby where we wouldn't be seen at all."

"Where?"

"My room."

Myrna considered that. It could work. Better to have his undivided attention to make her pitch. "Good idea. There's no problem if anyone sees me alone. So if we split up, you go back up to your room, and I meet you there, we should be okay."

He gave her his room number, turned around, and walked casually back to the lobby.

****

An hour later Bondurant stood at the window of his suite and watched Myrna walk to the parking lot. His phone rang.

"I paid a visit to Rhetta McKendrick," Cuyler Corley said. "Nothing specific, will take some time to bring her along to the idea of selling. But I think I planted a seed, something for her to think about. How'd it go with Myrna?"

"Fine. I think I planted a seed or two as well. But it's a complicated situation with that damn will. If she had clear title, she'd do the deal today. And probably for half what that acreage is actually worth. But as it stands, we're looking at some ongoing negotiations, a good bit of back-and-forth ahead between her and me."

As Myrna reached the car, Bondurant saw a large man leaning against it.

"But I'm confident she'll find a way to make things work out."

****

Myrna, her thoughts distracted, was almost to the car before she noticed the man.

"Enjoy your 'lunch'?" He added finger quotes and raised an eyebrow.

It took a moment for Myrna to regain her focus. How was he able to follow her all the way across the country? First the horse show, and now here. She thought he was just a smalltime hoodlum working for a local LA loan shark. Surely he had other deadbeats to pursue, some who were probably much deeper in debt to his boss than she was. So why her? And why here? But she knew better than to ask him such questions.

"Look," she said, "I told you the truth back in California, and I'm telling you the truth here. I just had a meeting with someone interested in buying my property. We have to work out some complications but I'll make it happen. Whatever it takes, I'll make it happen."

"That's the attitude." He gave her an encouraging chuck on the shoulder, an odd departure from his usual threatening manner. "Whatever it takes. We're counting on you to do whatever it takes."

He stepped aside and opened the door for her.

"Damn," she said, "I must have forgotten to lock the car."

He cocked his head, smiled innocently, and waved his hand toward the driver's seat.

****

Thumper and Janey were in the study when Myrna returned. She tried to get to her room without being confronted but as she started down the hallway from the kitchen Thumper stepped out and greeted her.

"Hey, kiddo! How'd the shopping trip go? Need some help carrying in the bags?"

"Oh, well, y'know, I just didn't see anything that I liked. Certainly nothing I needed. My closets are already filled with vintage clothing and it turns out most of the stuff in Middleburg still looks 'vintage.' Silly me."

"You okay? You look a little…out of sorts."

"Do I? Oh, well, I…I almost hit a deer. Ran right in front of me. Had to slam on the brakes and swerve. I was so scared I'd damaged your car. But no harm done. Just left me rattled. No deer running around in LA." She forced a smile. "Guess my wildlife radar is out of practice."

"Yeah, they're thick this time of year. Glad you're okay. Sorry the trip was a blank."

"Not completely. I ran into an old friend from Foxcroft. No one you'd remember. She invited me to join her and some others for lunch. Didn't set a date, but we'll line something up. Hope it's okay to use the car again."

"Sure, any time. At least till your agent calls with the good news and you have to jet off back to LaLa Land."

"Right, at least till then."

Chapter 15

A dark bay horse stood in the Montfair barn aisle. Its leather halter, clipped to the rope cross-ties, bore a brass plaque with the name "Leonard Slye" engraved in ornate script. The gelding, just over sixteen hands tall, was well-muscled and in prime weight. Seven years had passed since the end of Lenny's modestly successful career as a steeplechaser, specializing in three-mile races over timber fences. He now earned his keep carrying Thumper Billington across the Virginia countryside.

The horse stood calmly for the familiar shoeing routine as Ansel Hart flitted around his feet. The rough concrete floor was littered with hoof shavings and spent horseshoe nails. The heady odors of hay, horse hair, sawdust, weathered wood, and manure mixed with the hot scent of the farrier's portable gas-fired furnace.

"No luck finding a replacement for the Ledesmas?" Ansel asked.

"Not yet," Thumper replied.

"Hard to find good barn help these days. Speaking of help, I gotta ask you a question. Would you have any problem with Miles coming along for the next shoeing session?"

Thumper had to think about that before replying. "You know there's been some bad blood between us."

"I know. But that was a while back. I thought things might have got smoothed over by now. He's living at my place and he's been helping me some mornings and evenings in addition to his hours at the shop. The more he's kept busy, the less likely he is to get into trouble. I think he's settled down a good bit. And he's a handy helper to have around."

"Well, I guess he can't cause much trouble as long as he's just helping you with shoeing work. I'd never put him on one of my horses again. Not after that incident...well, you know it got pretty ugly."

"As I recall, it was mostly Natasha he got mixed up with."

"Yeah, if I hadn't intervened, Miles would have been flattened like a bug." He reached up and stroked Lenny's glossy neck. "All right, we can try it. I'll give Natasha a heads up before he comes, and we'd best make sure they stay well away from each other."

"Um, well, something else is coming up sooner than that. Y'know, this Friday and Saturday..."

"The reenactment? Is he part of that now?"

"He started riding with the 43rd after he moved into my barn apartment. I've loaned him a bunch of my gear, and he's riding one of my horses. He's really getting into it, and I think it's good for him. Better he stay busy, plenty of work and an interesting hobby. The last thing we want him to do is sit around thinking up crazy shit that causes trouble."

"Maybe some good meds wouldn't be a bad idea either."

"Yeah, well, good luck convincing him of that. Anyway, if it's okay with you, I'd like to bring him along. It's hard to find new recruits for the Rangers and some of the older guys are likely to be phasing out soon."

"Oh, all right then. As a favor to you. Just keep an eye on him, will you?"

"You bet. Thanks."

****

As Ansel approached the Montfair entrance on his way out, he noticed Cuyler's car driving by. Two men he didn't recognize were in the car with Corley. He watched as the massive SUV cruised by and turned down Fair Enough Lane. *Odd*, he thought to himself, *but nothing that concerns me*. He turned the other way and headed to his next shoeing appointment.

Cuyler continued along the rough road and stopped at the point where the McKendrick, Worsham, and Billington properties met.

The three men, one wearing a rumpled brown suit and the other two in elegantly tailored attired, step out of the car.

"This is our first choice," Bondurant said. "There's one other possibility outside Richmond and one in North Carolina near Charlotte. I've found nothing worth considering in Maryland so far."

Maurice Pymsdale scanned the terrain. He remained silent as he walked around, assessing the land from every angle.

Bondurant remarked quietly to Corley, "Mr. P. is a legend for picking resort sites. Like you and your old man, it's in his genes, learning how his father took a small land speculation deal and turned it into an international empire."

"I reckon those Pymsdale genes have a lot more going for them than my Corley genes. My father and I haven't done too bad, but nothing near the Pymsdale scale."

"The rest of us have to do detailed studies and even then it can be a crap shoot. But Maurice can see things others miss. And he hasn't been wrong yet."

Maurice stood still, closed his eyes, and inhaled deeply. He then opened his eyes and turned to Bondurant. "Smith, you've found the spot. Keep those other two on the line so it looks like we have choices. But this is where we need to make the deal." He took one more panoramic view of the land—gentle slopes, wooded patches, mountains beyond. "Whatever it takes, make this happen."

Chapter 16

Voytek held Lenny and Bee at the mounting stone by the front entrance to the Montfair barn as Thumper and Janey emerged from the mudroom door. The morning air tingled as the temperature transitioned from the coolness of a dewy night to the rapid surge of daylight warmth. The resulting fog lingered over the fields in a smoky shroud. Shards of faint sunlight slipped through the mist, knifing between the leafy lattice of the woods behind the main house and caretaker's cottage.

Janey inhaled the odors of damp soil and oiled leather that blended into a pungent concoction she found both exciting and comforting. She was falling easily into the rhythm of her new life, accompanying Thumper three days a week to follow hounds around the local countryside, riding in the ring and on the farm's trails most other days to keep herself and the horses in shape.

On this Thursday the hunt was meeting at the kennels. Completing the short hack from Thumper's backdoor, they arrived to find the usual crew—Crispie, Patti, Ryman, Mildred Preston, Bing Sensabaugh, and Marie Hardesty. Nardell, who made a modest living as an equine massage therapist, had appointments that morning and could not turn down the income. The Ancient and Venerable Church of Ars Venatica had yet to receive its first dime in donations.

Others present included a builder of custom homes, a high school English teacher, an insurance agent, a lobbyist, a small animal vet, a mortgage broker, and two ladies whose late husbands had been kind enough to endow them with sufficient resources to enjoy foxhunting and long lunches. Occupations and personal wealth, or lack thereof, did not matter once hounds were off and sport was afoot. As Thumper's father often reminded his fellow hunters: *Persequere aut redi domum*—Keep up or go home!

"Ah, Brother Thumper!" Ryman called out, holding up a slim book. "Author of *The Foxhunter's Guide to Life & Love*, created under the guidance of our beloved Saint Hubert." He stood up in his stirrups and showed the book to those gathered around. "The Seven Principles of the Foxhunter Model: Primal Urges, Pageantry, Preparation, Practice, Patience, Persistence, and Payoff. You are all wonderful examples of those principles. And the world needs to hear that message. I encourage y'all to..."

"That's enough," Thumper said sharply. He noticed Janey was smiling and she looked disappointed when he cut Ryman off. His tone softened. "I appreciate your eagerness to spread the word, Ry. But this isn't the best time. Hounds are ready and we need to move off before the heat rises."

"I was just going to tell everyone they need to get a copy of your book, read it for themselves, so they can see how Saint Hubert is working through you."

"Fine." He addressed the group of riders. "Whether or not Saint Hubert is working through me or anyone else, you all might find this a fun read. If you'd like a copy, see me after the hunt." He turned back to Ryman. "Now, with Saint Hubert's permission, may we move off?"

"Absolutely. And may I say that, thanks to all the preparation, practice, patience, and persistence exhibited by everyone here, he has assured me that there will be a glorious payoff as our reward. So let's go hunting! I'll see you all at the rocks."

"What? What rocks? What do you mean?" Thumper asked. But Ryman quickly took up his whipper-in position as Crispie signaled the hounds to attention.

They stayed in a cohesive pack around and behind Crispie as they moved away from the kennels. Ten riders followed Thumper in the jumping field, five non-jumpers rode behind Mildred. The pace was leisurely and the riders chatted quietly. But they were cautious to not invoke a look of rebuke from the master for "coffeehousing"—talking loudly and to excess during a hunt, a breach of etiquette.

Crispie moved toward the first jump in the fence line along the west edge of the Montfair territory. Referred to in hunt country as a "coop," based on its resemblance to an old-fashioned chicken coop, the jump consisted of a wooden A-frame structure about twelve feet across by three feet high. Most of the jumps in the Montfair territory were of this style, with some post-and-rail barways and a few stone walls. Hounds followed their leader into the open field at the base of the foothills marking the property's edge. The wooded hillside offered good prospects for rousting up a fox.

Hounds worked diligently just inside the woods' edge while the riders stayed back and watched. Several minutes passed and then Warwick, an experienced and reliable hound, opened with a long, deep note, signaling his detection of hot scent. Several others honored their pack mate, ran to the scent, and voiced their agreement. Noses to the ground, sterns aloft, they darted about like dodge-em cars, sorting out the evidence before deciding which way to go.

Crispie sat quietly and let his hounds work out the line.

The mystery of scent was solved and Warwick took off on the line. The pack followed. About twenty or thirty feet into the woods, they fanned out and moved through the trees in a southerly route, toward the riders' left.

Patti rode into the woods and made her way up a rarely used trail—a "huntsman's trail"—to stay above the pack. Ryman headed back the way they had come and took a position to the east in case the fox turned in that direction.

Crispie waited a few more beats to assure hounds were solidly on the scent, then turned and cantered back toward the coop.

Thumper held his followers until the huntsman had a sufficient lead. Then he too moved off to the coop, his followers coming along at a brisk canter.

The hounds' collective cry echoed off the hillside. A tingle shot down every rider's spine.

Once over the jump, Crispie turned hard to the right and accelerated to a gallop to keep up with the screaming hounds.

The rest of the jumping field followed.

Mildred and her non-jumpers had just finished entering through and then closing a gate farther down the fence line. They now had to reopen the gate, come back through the other way, and then close the gate again. They would quickly fall far behind the fast-moving fox and hounds.

The jumpers were now in a field that curved into the woods edge at the base of what in Crutchfield County is considered a "minor mountain": not officially part of the Blue Ridge chain but more than just a "foothill."

A small, dark red creature burst forth from the woods, just ahead of the pack, and made a straight dash across the open expanse.

Several hounds emerged in hot pursuit.

The fox covered the grassy stretch in seconds and disappeared into the woods on the far side of the clearing, hounds in close pursuit. Another trail began along the mountain's base at this point. A three-rail barway guarded the entrance. Hounds swarmed over and around, baying loudly. Crispie sailed over the rails and headed down the trail. Thumper and the rest followed, transitioning down to a canter as they took the jump into the woods.

The next section of open ground lay directly behind Fair Enough Farm. Thumper knew they would soon reach the point where the trail ended in another coop and they would emerge into a clearing that rolled gently away from the Fair Enough barn toward the juncture where the McKendrick, Billington, and Worsham properties met more than a mile into the heart of the Montfair Hunt country.

The fox persisted in moving that way. Patti was now cantering along the Montfair driveway and her presence may have discouraged him from swinging to the right. A crafty fox might have turned sharply enough to pass behind the whipper-in, crossing his scent with that of the whip's horse, causing hounds to hesitate while they sorted out the mixed signals. But this fellow had other plans and wasn't going to be deterred.

Thumper guessed the fox was playing with them. The quick glimpse he'd seen in the open field revealed a young, healthy, well-muscled critter. The size indicated it was a male, a "dog fox," with a thick tail, or "brush," and a fine coat with no trace of mange.

The fox did not seem to be much concerned about staying ahead of the pack. Despite the hard work to keep hounds exercised over the summer, they are never as fit in the early days of a new season as they will become after a few months of regular hunting. In contrast, the fox was in top form after an active summer of hunting mice, voles, rabbits, the occasional duck or goose, and raiding any henhouse that wasn't sufficiently secured.

His straight-on path took the chase past the retirement paddock of Minstrel's Delight. As if taunting the aged horse along with the unfit hounds, the fox ran within ten feet of Minnie Dee's enclosure.

When the riders reached the paddock, the horse was prancing along his fence line. The music of the hounds inspired him to arch his neck, toss his head, snort loudly, and paw the ground. As Thumper cantered past, he could easily envision Ivan Mooney seated on the gray horse, back when both of them could handle a five-hour hunt.

He knew that, once the last rider went past, Minnie Dee would stand at the end of his enclosure for a few minutes, his eyes wide, head aloft, nostrils flaring, blood pumping, adrenalin flowing, eager to be off with the hounds, wondering why he was not able to follow the action. After a bit, the blood would settle, the eyes would cloud over, and the stiffness would return to his joints, providing the answer to his question.

Memories of the hunt would again fade to a hazy dream.

For the rest of the horses and their riders, the heat of the chase was real. Creamy white lather formed on the horses' necks, shoulders, and chests where the reins and breastplates laid against them. Bodies sweated heavily under tweed jackets and buttoned collars as the morning air took on a sauna-like thickness. Thumper's hair—what was left of it—was wet and matted under his hunt cap.

The fox knew where he was going. Worsham's cattle had been grazing the southern acreage of Fair Enough Farm for the past two weeks, on rotation from other fields depending on where there was still enough forage. Their droppings would allow the fox to conceal his scent just enough to throw hounds off the line. He knew they'd regain it, but the distraction would be sufficient for him to reach his den, a rock outcropping on the hillside where the land rose again to another "minor mountain." Once safely tucked inside, the hounds could swarm around the rocks and scratch away at will with no bother to him.

The plan worked perfectly. The pack hesitated at the cow foil. Then Hempstead, an up-and-coming second year hound, regained the line and led his mates to the rocky den.

Crispie rode to the base of the mountain and dismounted. Thumper rode forward and took the horse's reins. The huntsman scrambled up the steep hillside and reached the den where he blew the wavering notes of "Gone to Ground."

"Good hounds," he called out, cheering his team for a job well done. "That's me good lads and lasses!"

He let the hounds enjoy a few minutes to savor their victory and then called them down off the hillside.

Ryman rode in from his patrol position on the left, Patti arrived from the right. Flasks appeared from pockets and saddle cases and everyone enjoyed a toast to a successful morning.

Ryman looked at Thumper, a bright grin illuminating his face, and said, "Didn't I tell you Saint Hubert promised a payoff today? His name, and your Seven Principles, be praised!"

Thumper scowled and started to reply but he caught the subtle headshake Janey gave him. He handed the reins back to Crispie and said, "A good run. Let's work back toward kennels. Hounds and horses have had enough work for one morning."

****

As Thumper and Janey rode back to the barn, they saw Myrna driving away in Thumper's car.

"Off to meet her old friends for lunch in Middleburg, I reckon," Thumper said. "Sorry we missed her."

Janey reined Bee to a gentle stop. She watched the Jag pass through the front gates and turn onto the road. "Has she seemed distracted to you the past couple of days?"

"Distracted? She's always been kind of like that. Flaky, flighty. She's probably ADD. That just wasn't a diagnosed thing when we were kids."

"That's not what I mean. The past couple of days, her thoughts seem to be somewhere else. And not a happy somewhere."

"Geez, maybe she heard from her agent, didn't get the sitcom gig, and she doesn't want to tell us."

"Yeah, maybe that's it. We should try to cheer her up when she gets back."

"Oh, I expect a long boozy, gossipy lunch with her old girlfriends will help with that. C'mon, we gotta get the horses put up, and Natasha will have lunch ready soon."

Janey took a few more seconds to gaze down the driveway, then turned Bee and followed Thumper to the barn.

****

It was late afternoon when Myrna returned to Montfair. Natasha was in the kitchen starting dinner preparations.

"Ah, you are home! I am making one of Mister Thumper's favorites for tonight."

"That's nice," Myrna replied in a weak voice. "I may not be very hungry. I had…I had a big lunch…y'know, with my friends."

Natasha turned from her food prep chores to study Myrna. "You are not looking well. Maybe you are eating too much at this lunch. Or something is not agreeing with you."

"Yeah, that might be it. I should probably go lie down."

"Yes, go and rest. When you are feeling better, come down and I will make you something. And some tea. Tea would be good."

"Thanks. I didn't see Thumper's truck. Is he not home?"

"He and Miss Janey are in the north field with Voytek making sure all is ready for tomorrow when the pretend people are coming."

"Pretend people? Oh, right, the reenactors."

"Yes, them. I am never remembering that word, 'reenactors.' Is an odd word."

"I suppose so. Please tell him I'm okay, just going to rest for a bit. I'll be down when I feel better."

Natasha watched her walk down the hallway, head down and her steps shaky.

Chapter 17

Myrna spent most of Friday in her room. Janey and Natasha checked on her periodically, taking her tea and some light lunch. She told them she must have eaten something in Middleburg that disagreed with her, just needed to rest, was sure she'd be fine for tomorrow. She didn't want to miss the Paradise Gap Day festivities. She had fond memories of that from childhood.

By late afternoon the north field was abuzz with activity: trailers pulling in, ramps dropping as horses were unloaded, equipment pulled from the beds of pickup trucks. Myrna watched from her bedroom window.

The sun was tickling the crests of the foothills behind Montfair when Thumper walked out to the north field to check on his guests.

The reenactors, under the leadership of Ansel Hart, were setting up their camp with practiced precision. Once the trucks and trailers were parked along the wood's edge at the base of the mountain, all traces of modernity vanished. Sixteen horses stood close to the old cemetery plot, tied to a picket line strung between two trees. Well-trained for this discipline, the animals calmly ate the hay piled on the ground before them. Some troopers had set up shebangs—the one-man tents used during the Civil War—while others spread their McClellan saddles and rough woolen blankets out on the ground. Pieces of wood—branches and old deadfall—had been hauled over to the campfire, a pit ringed with rocks.

The troopers of the Forty-third Battalion of Virginia Cavalry—Mosby's Partisan Rangers—maintained a high standard of authenticity. If an item of clothing or equipment was not an actual period piece, it was a fully faithful replica. Being both Confederates and guerilla fighters, the concept of "uniform" was observed loosely. Most wore predominantly gray garb but there were several coats of butternut and even a couple that approached a shade of Union blue. Styling ranged from trim shell jackets to long field coats. Some wore only billowy white blouses with dark vests. Headwear included felt slouch hats with wide brims, short billed kepis, and a couple of stiff military hats with one side turned upward and plumage added for a dash of flair. The most consistently similar items were the tall black boots. Some stopped just below the knee while others continued up to provide more protection for the cavalryman's vulnerable legs.

The two elements that fell short in the authentic display were the age and, to varying degrees, the size of the men themselves.

The average weight of a Civil War-era cavalry trooper was around one hundred thirty five pounds. Only Miles Flanagan, former steeplechase jockey, could maintain such a low, and by today's standards unhealthy, weight. Most of Ansel's men were at least reasonably fit and trim, if not as tight and wiry as an 1860s horse soldier. A few, however, showed sizeable paunches unbefitting a mounted guerilla fighter.

There was, though, no getting around the age issue. John Singleton Mosby, born in December of 1833, was just thirty-one years old when the war ended in April of '65. Likewise, most of his men were of similar age or younger. The men assembled in Thumper's field were more likely candidates to portray the fathers of the Partisan Rangers. Older men were not uncommon among the ranks of the infantry, particularly toward the latter stages of the war as the South began to run low on manpower. But Mosby's men were the Green Berets or the SEALs of their day. It was a young man's game.

As Thumper roamed through the camp, he came upon Miles arranging his gear. Trooper Flanagan had no intention of shielding himself under a canvas shebang. A coarse woolen blanket, dark blue with rust-red lines around the edges, was laid out on the damp grass. His saddle would serve as a pillow and his equipment was neatly placed at the head of his bivouac.

He was just setting down his gun belt when Thumper arrived.

"A two gun rig?" Thumper commented, noticing the double holster arrangement.

"Lots of troopers carried two pistols," Miles explained. "Some even more if they had 'em. Hard to reload one of these things from the back of a horse. So if you got into some mischief and had to keep firing, you'd unload one pistol at the Yanks then grab another and keep blasting." He pointed to his left-hand holster. "I got mine rigged up so I can reach over with my right hand and grab this one straight across. Can't shoot for shit with my left hand. Besides, I gotta use that hand to hold the reins."

Miles unsnapped the flap on one of the holsters and withdrew a large pistol. It looked even bigger in his small hand. "This here's a replica of a 1863 Navy Colt Revolver," Miles said, holding the weapon out for Thumper to see. "Black powder, cap and ball, .44 caliber. Makes a helluva hole. Lotta noise and smoke too."

"I'm familiar with the breed," Thumper said. "We have Uncle Josiah's pistols mounted on the living room wall." He nodded back toward his house. "Of course, they haven't been fired since the war ended. Least not that I know of."

"Ooooo-weeee!" Miles exclaimed. "You got any idea what them guns is worth?"

"Not really. I'd never consider selling them anyway."

"Well, hell, I hope you at least got 'em insured. They're probably worth around, oh, maybe three grand each." He looked back at his replica, for which he'd paid less than two hundred dollars. And even that was a stretch for him.

"It must have been a real pain dealing with these black powder weapons," Thumper remarked, taking the pistol as Miles held it out to him.

"Still is," Miles replied. "'Course, we use blank loads for our living history demonstrations. Sometimes, though, Ansel and me get together and do some target practice with real round balls. Like I said, a .44 caliber ball coming at you can do some serious damage."

"I reckon so," Thumper said. He handed the pistol back to Miles and wandered off to check out some more of the camp arrangements.

The campfire, started earlier by the first arrivals, was now smoldering with a warm red glow beneath a layer of white ash. One of the men began dropping thick steaks onto an iron grill positioned above the flames. A crackling sizzle sounded as each piece of meat hit the grill and the juicy smell of prime beef started to swirl around the camp.

Three of the troopers lit cigars.

Thumper began to understand the appeal of this hobby.

"Got time to join us for a snort?" Ansel asked, pulling a flask from his pocket.

"It would sully my reputation if I ever refused such a gracious gesture," Thumper replied.

He was offered a seat by the fire and joined the men for a spot of refreshment and conversation. The trooper next to him offered a cigar. Thumper hesitated for moment, then accepted the small cheroot.

"You guys look great," he said. "My compliments to all of you."

Several nods and thanks were returned.

"Any of your people fight in the war?" one of the troopers asked.

"A few Billingtons, in one way or another, participated in the War of Northern Aggression." Thumper's accent took on a deeper Southern twang. "My great-great-grandfather, Archibald, was too old and infirm to fight and his only son, Thaddeus the First, was too young. Family legend has it that Archie kept trying and, after six daughters, finally had the son he needed to keep the family name going. By that time, and after living with seven females, he was too worn out to fight the Yankees."

Chuckles sounded among the troopers.

"But his younger brother, Josiah, rode with General Forrest. Now there was a cavalryman for you."

Grunts of agreement came from the men.

"And although Archie wasn't able to fight, he did what he could to help The Cause: food, horses, weapons, ammunition, and a place to hide when the Yanks came snooping." Thumper's finger now swung over toward his own home.

"Rebs hid in your house?" one of the Rangers asked.

"So it's said. You can still see where a hiding place used to be between two of the upstairs bedrooms. Archibald had a fake wall put in that left a small space between the rooms, just enough for a thin man to hide in." He glanced around at a couple of the heftier troopers. "If you looked in one room, and then the other, you wouldn't be able to tell anything was there. And if the Yanks got to snooping too close, there was a way to shinny up into the attic and then slip out a window, climb down the trellis, and skeedaddle into the mountains." He jerked his thumb toward the wooded hillside, now a dark, irregular shadow in the fading light.

Miles Flanagan, his eyes sparkling with fascination in the dancing firelight, asked, "Think Mosby ever hid out in the house? Or camped out in this field?"

"Waaall," Thumper drawled, "some say the Colonel himself did take advantage of Billington hospitality a time or two. Don't know for sure, but yeah, it's quite possible that

Mosby could have used that hiding place. Pretty certain some of his men did if not him personally."

"How come Josiah rode with Forrest and not Mosby?" Miles asked.

"Archie figured it would be better if his little brother wasn't fighting right around here, especially with a guerilla unit. Could have gone hard on the family, and the farm, if he'd been captured. Unlikely Montfair would have survived. It was less risky for him to be fighting with Forrest down in the Mississippi and Alabama campaigns where no one knew him."

One of the troopers pointed toward the private cemetery. "Any of those guys buried over there?"

Thumper took offense at the casual reference to his revered ancestors as "those guys." But he said simply, "Nope. No family members buried there."

"Who then?" the trooper asked.

"Oh, some other folks who used to live around here," Thumper replied. "Some special people who worked for the family. But no Billingtons. They're all in the Episcopal church cemetery down in the village."

The trooper handling the steak grilling duty turned the meat over with an expert hand. The sizzle flared up and the aroma merged with the scents of fresh hay, strong cigars, and rough wool.

Thumper flicked his cigar butt into the fire and stood up. "Y'all have a pleasant evening and a good night. Big day tomorrow. If you need anything, don't hesitate to ask."

As he headed toward his house, some of the troopers pulled out instruments—guitar, banjo, mandolin, and fiddle—and began playing a soft bluegrass tune. He paused and looked back. The sun was now fully below the crest of the mountains and the camp began to take on an apparitional haze. The men moved in a spectral mist, their features indistinct in the fading light. The music's gentle syncopation matched the crackle of the open fire. The fiddler's mournful solo sounded long and low across the darkening land.

For a brief moment, Thumper thought he felt Archibald's phantom hand resting on his shoulder.

Chapter 18

"The Battle of Paradise Gap" was more bungle than battle. A small band of partisan Rebel guerillas (known as Rangers, irregular troops loosely under the command of the Confederate army) was camped on the outskirts of the village in early autumn of 1863. A Union cavalry captain, eager to make a name for himself, received a scout's report on the location of the camp. Cartography being an inexact art in those days, combined with the scout's affinity for distilled spirits, the report was off by about a half mile.

Intending to surprise the Rangers at daybreak, navigating the rough unfamiliar country in the dark of night added a further complication. As a misty dawn broke, the Union troopers found themselves facing a large barn, owned by a Quaker family. Avowed pacifists and strong anti-slavery advocates, the Quakers were considered neutral and off limits to any depredations by the invading troops. Unable to see the Quaker symbol on the barn in the morning fog and trusting the scout's insistence that the Rangers must be holed up inside, the captain ordered his men to dismount and surround the building. Once in position, rifles aimed, one of the men discharged his weapon—whether accidentally or intentionally was never determined. The other troopers, thinking an attack had begun, followed suit, despite the captain's shouts to hold their fire.

The Quaker farmer's pacifism took a backseat to his anger over this assault on his property. He stormed out of the barn, where he'd been milking his cows, and expressed his displeasure in terms ill suited to a member of the Society of Friends.

Meanwhile, the Rangers, aroused by the sound of gunfire, quickly broke their camp and mounted up. Not ones to run from a fight, but also not knowing the situation they might be facing, they spread out and approached cautiously. As the powder smoke and mist cleared, they saw the enemy gathered in a farmyard, an irate Quaker berating a humiliated Union captain. The Rangers were outnumbered by more than two-to-one. But given their inclination toward bravado, combined with holding the home field advantage, they felt the odds were in their favor. One of the Union troopers noticed the enemy looking on and sounded the alarm. Still apologizing to the farmer, the captain backed away and ordered his men to remount and engage the Secessionists.

The Rangers found this all very amusing and decided the better course was to have a little fun with these hapless fellows, surely no match for the best mounted guerilla fighters engaged in the national conflict. They were not bloodthirsty marauders out to kill anyone wearing a blue uniform. Their mission was to sow havoc among the invaders, make them expend resources and manpower in an effort to track them down, hijack payrolls, cause embarrassment by capturing high ranking officers, and other diversionary tactics. They relied on the cooperation of the local populace, people like the Billingtons as well as those of lesser means. Had the Rangers engaged in unbridled brutality, their protectors would have suffered the consequences.

So they feigned an attack, whooping and hollering, as the panicked Union men scrambled back to their horses. But at the wood's edge where the horses were being held, the Rangers veered off and galloped away, back toward the mountains behind Montfair. The captain and his men gave chase, but the pursuit was hopeless and, realizing they had no chance to catch up with the Rangers and were only getting more lost in the unfamiliar country, gave up and withdrew.

Over time the accounts of the "battle" were embroidered with a variety of overstatements and outright falsehoods, mostly made by those who had no firsthand knowledge of the event.

In the final tally, the death toll consisted of one cow (for which the farmer was paid ample compensation).

****

Paradise Gap Day started as an expression of local pride at a time when those in and around the village needed something to celebrate. The years following the war saw a prolonged period of economic hardship with the sting made sharper by martial law. Around 1900, as conditions were beginning to improve, the owner of the general store, an enterprising and visionary merchant, came up with the idea. He employed a greatly embellished version of the "Battle of 1863" as the central theme for the day. Those in and around the village welcomed the diversion and the event became an annual fixture. As Sunday was reserved for worshipping the Lord, Saturday was the default day to remember the "Battle," whichever Saturday fell closest to the date recorded in the Union captain's report (which may or not have been the correct date). As a gesture of village solidarity, the leaders of the Montfair Hunt agreed to skip hunting that one Saturday each year.

More than a hundred years later the veracity of the event's history was of little concern to anyone. It was mostly a chance for the few merchants in town to promote their businesses and for locals to enjoy a day of socializing.

The main attraction that drew visitors from outside the limited orbit of Paradise Gap was the "living history" encampment. Reenacting the "battle" itself was not part of the program, given the logistical difficulties. But the devoted members of the 43rd Battalion of Virginia Cavalry put on a pretty good show. The public was invited to tour the encampment and learn about the life and adventures of a Partisan Ranger. At three hour intervals the troopers mounted their horses and assembled in a large open section of Montfair's north field. Watching from behind a roped off viewing section, the spectators were treated to a display of precision cavalry drills: forming a line of two abreast, then four abreast, then all in one line doing a wheel-about where the rider at one end pivots in place while the one at the opposite end moves at a brisk trot and each rider in the line adjusts his pace to keep the line straight. From there they reformed four lines of four each for saber drills, flashing their blades in a series of precision moves.

The finale of the show was a simulated skirmish. Absent any actual Yankee counterparts, eight of the Rangers donned blue coats and formed a line across the field facing the other eight members of the unit. At a signal from Ansel Hart, the opposing units charged each other, firing the blank loads in their black powder pistols, accompanied by hoots and hollers. When they met in the middle, sabers were drawn and, positioned in pairs of two, the clang of metal on metal rang out across the field.

Ansel took the part of a Yankee to assure he was the one who engaged in sword-to-sword combat with Miles Flanagan. Miles had knocked two other troopers from the saddle by overplaying his role in practice drills. Ansel was the only one who could match him for horsemanship. But not even Ansel, the embodiment of the legendary Gray Ghost himself, could equal Miles' fanatic commitment to "The Cause." In a life with neither plan nor purpose, he had found his calling.

****

Myrna watched the show from the audience enclosure. The quality of the performance and the size of the cast had improved from the last time she'd attended, several years earlier. The spectacle was a much-needed distraction from other matters on her mind.

As the troopers rode back to the picket line and dismounted, the spectators were free to leave the roped off area and resume browsing through the encampment. Roaming along aimlessly, Myrna came upon Shelton.

"Aunt Myrna!" Shelton said, using another unofficial familial title. She pulled Myrna into a powerful hug, nearly lifting the much smaller woman off the ground.

"Well, look at you," Myrna said when released. "You're all grown up."

"A little too grown up," Sheltie Lou replied, conscious of her hefty six-foot frame that dwarfed her diminutive "aunt."

"I hear you're running the shop now, gave up your other job to take over after Fergus died. So why aren't you at the shop now? Aren't there streams of customers in the place on the big celebration day?"

"Not that many people looking to buy tractors or other equipment. The tourists are all hitting the antique shops and the general store, places like that. And the locals are either partying or staying out of town to avoid all the traffic. Besides, Bar's got the shop covered. He has no interest in this sort of thing." She gestured toward the encampment. "Says he's seen enough real war, doesn't need to see the fake stuff."

Myrna couldn't suppress a shudder at the mention of Bar and his war experience. His disfigured face creeped her out when she was young. His size added to her fear, as if he was an evil ogre living deep in the woods on the farm right next door.

Shelton continued, "I'll drop by the shop later, got some paperwork to catch up on."

They strolled along through the encampment as they talked.

Shelton's face brightened and she asked, "How long are you back for? Maybe we can meet for lunch sometime."

"Hard to say. I'm waiting to hear from my agent about a new gig. When I get the call, I'll have to beat it back to LA. But, sure, if I'm still here, lunch sometime would be great."

"How about Tuesday? That's the slowest day at the shop."

"Oh, well, Tuesdays aren't good. I met some old friends when I was in Middleburg a few days ago. They invited me to join their lunch group. It's a regular Tuesday thing, sometimes Thursdays too." She made a floppy wave of her hand. "Y'know, the ladies who lunch. Married well, or inherited some wealth, or both. We were all classmates at Foxcroft and Pony Clubbers together. Now I'm catching up on decades of gossip since I left. It's lots of fun."

"Sounds like it. Well, maybe we can find another day that works for both of us."

"I hope we can."

"It was so cool of you to get out of here and make your own way in show biz. I know my grandma's always envied you. You remember how she and your mother used to go on and on about the movies?"

Recollections of summer evenings on the Fair Enough front porch came back. A shared love of movies was the spark that launched the friendship between Rhetta and CeeCee, a subject that bridged the gap between their social standings. "Yes, I remember. Mother named my sister and me for her two favorite stars, Claudette Colbert and Myrna Loy."

"Oh, right. I'd forgotten about that."

"Thumper claims Mother wanted to name him Clark Humphrey Billington, but Father wouldn't allow it. His son was going to be The Fourth, and that was that. And if I'd been a boy, I'd have been Archibald. So I guess I got off easy."

"But then you dropped it and became 'Lola Leeland.'"

"I arrived in Hollywood just before the stage name thing started to fade and people began using their real names, even if long and clunky. And too late to change it back by then."

"Well, I'll be looking to see 'Starring Lola Leeland' when the press releases come out about your new gig."

Myrna turned toward Shelton and, as her line of sight landed at mid-chest on the taller woman, noticed she was wearing two matching medallions around her neck. "Are those both Saint Hubert medals?" she asked.

"Oh, these? Yes." She held one up. It was dark from decades of wear, the images rubbed smooth. "This one was given to me by Father Herb at the Blessing of the Hounds when I was eight." She lifted the other one, which looked shiny and new. "And my father gave me this one last year after the memorial service for my grandfather. They both have special meaning, sort of a way to remember who I am no matter where I am or what I'm doing."

"That's so sweet. I'm sure I had one when I was a child, back when the whole family used to hunt together. No idea where it is now."

"Do you miss it?"

"The medal?"

"No, I mean hunting."

"Yeah, maybe, sometimes. I don't know. I haven't thought about it for so long, it hasn't been part of my life. But now that I'm back here, it seems that hardly anything has changed." She looked around at the Rangers' camp. "Talk about a time warp. The family always took a lot of pride in our history, going back even way before all this." She gestured toward the shebangs and campfires. "Sure, Claudette moved away, our parents are dead. Old Ivan Mooney's gone, and now your grandfather. But Natasha and Voytek are still here. And Thumper hasn't changed a bit.

Everything for him still revolves around horses, hounds, and hunting."

"It was like that for me, too. I didn't know life was any different when I was growing up. Hunting with my father and grandfather, Pony Club. Wasn't till I went off to college that I discovered there was a whole world out there that had no idea about any of that stuff."

"So what about you? I'm just here for a short visit. But you're back to stay. Are you going to get back into the hunting world?"

"Hah! Look at me. Do I look fit enough to get back on a horse? At my size I'd crush the poor thing."

"Well, I remember seeing some pretty big men riding with the hunt. Most of them rode heavier drafty type horses, not the light Thoroughbreds."

"Yeah, maybe some day. For now I'm too busy with the shop. Although I have gotten out on a couple of mornings to car follow, just for a bit before going in to work. Hey! Why don't you come with me? We could do that Tuesday morning, before you go meet your friends for lunch."

"Oh, well, I don't know. It's a long drive into Middleburg. And we start around noonish."

"Not a problem. The meet's at 8:00. We could just follow for an hour or so, give you plenty of time to get back and head into town."

Myrna took a deep breath. "All right. It's a date. Am I allowed to follow even if I'm not wearing my Saint Hubert medal? Even two of them?"

Shelton chuckled then reached for her two medals, fondling them between her thick fingers, a reflex action akin to handling prayer beads. "I think it's important to honor your roots, to keep the family bonds strong. Don't you?"

She looked away from Shelton, back toward the Montfair house and the section of property that lay beyond it in the distance, along the edge of the McKendricks' land. Somewhere on that side of the road was an old trailer deep in the woods where a scary ogre, who kept vultures for pets, lived. "Yes, of course, very important."

Myrna turned her attention back to Shelton. "Your grandmother's getting on in years. Your grandfather's gone. So I assume your father's next in line to inherit the family farm."

"Actually, Grandma told me recently she's changed her will, skipping my father, and leaving everything to me, both the farm and her interest in the shop."

"Really? That's a shock. She and Ryman have a falling out?"

"Yeah, a pretty big one. She thinks he's lost his marbles with this Saint Hubert thing."

"Thumper was telling me about that, how he's trying to turn foxhunting in a religion. Does sound pretty crazy."

"It's been going on about a year now, and doesn't look like he's going to give it up anytime soon. So maybe Grandma's right to not trust him with the farm and everything. No telling what he might do with it."

"What about you? What would you do with it?"

Shelton stopped walking. "Y'know, I hadn't really thought about that. I mean, I guess I just figure Grandma's gonna live forever. Or at least a good while longer, tough as she is." She took some time to consider the inevitable. "I honestly don't know. I'm not a farmer, I know that much. It's a lot of land to pay taxes on, try to keep it up. But, gosh, that land has meant so much to my family for generations. It's where our roots are."

Myrna placed a gentle hand on Shelton's arm. "Maybe family roots are about more than just a few acres of dirt."

Chapter 19

Shelton was in the shop's office later that afternoon at the desk where her grandfather had sat for more than forty years. Hunched over the computer keyboard, she didn't notice Muriel Hudkins' entrance.

"I thought you were taking the day off," Muriel said.

Without looking up, Shelton replied, "I need to get these sales projections finished. Mister Sensabaugh wants our updated financials on his desk first thing Monday to be sure our line of credit with the bank keeps flowing."

"Can I help you with that? I've been handling the books here for a few years, you know."

Muriel Hudkins had shared the small office space for all but the first few months that Fergus McKendrick ran the business after taking over from his father. Fergus was a natural salesman, and wise enough to know numbers were not his strong suit. So he advertised for help and of the few candidates who applied, Muriel was the best qualified. And so began a four decade working partnership between "Mister McKendrick"—a large white man, proud former Marine, with a contagious enthusiasm for life—and "Missus Hudkins"—a small, prim, African American woman who managed equal devotion to her husband and four children, Paradise Gap's AME church, and the McKendricks' business.

Shelton broke her focus away from the computer. "Yes, of course you have. And we couldn't keep it going without you. These are just some additional numbers the bank needs. With some of the changes we're making, the old sales figures aren't relevant any more. I have to justify the estimates to keep the bank happy." She took a deep breath and let it out slowly. "And I need to have this done and get going."

"Saturday," Muriel noted. "I assume you're going to visit your friend."

"Um, yes." She looked at her watch. "We're meeting for dinner."

"When are we going to meet this person? You're spending a lot of time driving back and forth to Arlington. Why doesn't she come out here for a change?" Muriel wanted to ask if Shelton was embarrassed by folks like her, Bar, Rhetta, and especially her father. But she was too polite to raise such a question. And while her deep faith in traditional Christian values still made her uneasy about Shelton's orientation, that reality had been clearly evident for many years. Muriel came to accept it and still loved "little Sheltie Lou" as she'd done since the day Shelton was born.

"Oh, well, she's really busy," Shelton replied. "Really demanding job. Hard enough to get a few hours for dinner and a little time together." She looked at her watch again. "I'd better get going." She shut down her computer, wished Muriel a good evening, and dashed out the door.

****

Several hours later, after dinner at Astrid's favorite Thai restaurant followed by an exhilaratingly athletic session in Astrid's bed, the two women sat snuggled together on the sofa in Astrid's apartment vaguely watching an old movie.

Astrid reached for the remote control. "Let's see what else is on." She changed the channel and another late-night movie appeared—*Auntie Mame*. "Oh! I love this movie," she said.

She had clicked in at the point where Mame is in South

Carolina meeting the family of her most recent love interest, Beauregard Jackson Pickett Burnside. The visit features a foxhunt to be held in Mame's honor.

"Well, maybe not this part," Astrid said.

"What?" Shelton remarked. "This is one of the funniest parts in the movie." Shelton sat up, her attention focused on the screen. "Oh, my God! When she's trying to get on the horse, every time I see that I nearly wet my pants."

"Then perhaps you should get off my sofa before you have an accident." There was a chill in Astrid's voice.

"You don't think that's funny?"

"I don't think setting a pack of hounds on a poor, defenseless creature is funny."

Shelton suddenly remembered who she was with, what Astrid did for a living, and why she'd been so cautious to keep her family's foxhunting lifestyle from the founder and head of People Against Cruelty to Animals. "Oh, well, sure. Of course, I agree about that. But, I mean, this is just a comedy, a parody. It's not how foxhunting really is."

"It's not? And how would you know?" Astrid sat up in a rigid posture, arms crossed, head cocked, an accusatory stare leveled at Shelton.

Shelton knew she'd stepped in it. "Oh, well, some folks out where I grew up do that sort of thing. Not me, of course. But, you know, to some people it's just a way of life. And they hardly ever actually kill a fox, they just chase it around for awhile."

"Really? So it's okay if they only *occasionally* kill an innocent fox? And the ones who aren't killed, do you think they enjoy being 'chased around for awhile?'" She added finger quotes for emphasis.

"Gee, I don't know. Who can say what an animal is really thinking or feeling? Especially a wild animal."

"You don't think an animal, wild or domesticated, can feel pain, sense fear, suffer anxiety when it's being chased and is running for its life?" Astrid leaned farther away from

Shelton and the ice in her voice grew colder.

Meanwhile, the movie played on, Rosalind Russell in full formal hunting attire walking to the waiting horse, her boots only halfway on and sticking out to the sides, flopping clumsily as she tried to look dignified.

Shelton attempted to use that as a dodge. "C'mon," she said, pointing to the screen. "Now *that's* funny. Doesn't that tell you this is just a parody? It's a complete send-up of Old South society, slapstick humor."

"Okay, fine. The movie's a parody, slapstick. But I'm frankly shocked that you know people who treat animals that way and don't condemn them for it."

Condemn her father, and her late grandfather? Condemn all her old friends who still rode to hounds? Perhaps she shouldn't have tried to conceal her country girl upbringing. "Look, I'm not part of that world anymore. Okay, so maybe I haven't taken up the cause against that sort of thing the way you have. But I left all that behind me years ago. Like I've told you, I'm a city girl now." She moved along the sofa closer to Astrid and tried to affect a tender smile. "With city girl tastes."

Astrid stood up, her arms still folded. "This is one city girl you might not be tasting for awhile. I'm going to bed. The sofa's all yours. And if you're going to watch the rest of that movie, please don't pee on my furniture." She strode off to her bedroom and closed the door with an authoritative smack.

****

Shelton awoke early the next morning. She'd hardly slept as her dilemma with Astrid kept tumbling in her mind. She couldn't continue this double life much longer. It had been hard enough to keep a relationship going when their jobs were on opposite coasts. But at least it was easier to avoid the reality of her family and friends back home in

Crutchfield County with their foxhunting lifestyle. A clash of cultures was now inevitable.

Groggy, distraught over her looming choice, she arose from the sofa in the near dark and quietly left the apartment.

Driving through the vacant streets as dawn broke on Sunday morning, she absently reached for the small metal objects she wore around her neck. But instead of two chains and two medals, there was only one. She lifted the single medallion and gave it a quick glance. It was not the one Father Herb had placed around her neck twenty-five years earlier at her first Blessing of the Hounds. This one, its engraved face still bright and sharp, was the one her father had given her at the memorial service for her grandfather the previous year. She always took them off at night and she now remembered that she'd placed them in the drawer of the end table beside the sofa before trying to sleep. In her distracted haste to leave the apartment, she had retrieved the new one, slipped it around her neck, and left the old one—the one that meant so much to her—at Astrid's.

Her need to deal with this situation took on much greater urgency.

Chapter 20

Bar was pleased to see Miles arrive for work on time Monday morning. He was not pleased when he saw Miles get out of his scratched and dented Chevy S10 pickup wearing most of his Ranger uniform. Bar's ire rose even farther when a saber and scabbard tumbled out of the truck. Miles picked it up and tossed it back in the cab before continuing on into the shop.

"I thought I told you not to wear that shit to work," Bar barked.

Miles stopped, put a hand on his hip, and looked his boss up and down. "You're a fine one to talk about wearing shit to work. So you finally had to start wearing a shirt, after...what?...like forty years of coming to work half-fucking-naked."

"That didn't matter when all I did was repair work in the back. But I'm with customers now, and so are you. Sheltie Lou wants us to set a proper image. And if I tell you not to wear your goddamn Civil War play clothes, you'll damn well do what I say."

"So show me the company dress code."

Bar's anger rose as Miles became more defiant. "I don't need to show you anything but this!" He lifted a foot and pointed at his size 13 Redwing boot. "Which will be up your goddamn ass if you don't..." He stopped as the front door opened and a customer entered the showroom. Lowering his voice, he said, "So you get the message. Show up here like this tomorrow, and I'll rip the damn clothes off your sorry ass. Got it?"

Miles sneered at the big man's threat, turned and sauntered back to the parts department to begin his workday.

****

Later that afternoon, Shelton found Bar in the service bay going over a tricky repair job with Conway Purvis, former assistant service tech now in training to become the chief mechanic.

"I just got a call from Cecelia. She thinks the clutch has gone out on her mower deck. At least that's what Charlie, her farm guy, told her."

Still crouched over the disassembled piece of equipment he was helping Conway repair, Bar replied. "Charlie knows his shit. If he says it's the clutch, pretty sure that's what it is." He rose up and considered the situation. "I reckon it'll have to be picked up and brought in."

"Yes, it will."

He caught the expectant look in Shelton's eyes. "And...let me guess...that needs to happen right away."

Shelton nodded.

"And Miles is already out with a shitload of deliveries to make." He turned to Conway. "Think you can finish this up on your own?"

"Yeah, I think so."

Turning back to Shelton, Bar said, "Tell Cecelia I'll be there in thirty minutes."

****

An hour and a half later, Bar was pulling out of Cecelia's Kimber Farm with a disabled mower deck strapped to the flatbed of the company's service truck. As he approached the stone pillars at the exit, he saw a car blocking his way. *Some stupid ass tourist stopping to take in the scenery*, he thought.

He laid on the horn and waited. The car did not move. He couldn't see anyone in it.

"What the fuck?" he mumbled, climbing out of the truck and stomping toward the vehicle. As he walked around to the driver's side, he heard a voice behind him.

"Hello, Barstow."

He spun around to see a man, as large as himself, leaning casually against the stone wall at the farm's entrance. Bar tried to sound nonchalant as he replied, "Well, I'll be damned. Look who's here."

Dragomir Korth pushed himself away from the wall. "Damn, Bar, you look like you've just seen a ghost."

"Tell you the truth, Drago, I figured you probably were dead by now. Or doing hard time somewhere. Sure as shit didn't expect to see you pop up here."

Korth walked over to Bar. "Oh, you never know where I might pop up. You look like you've done okay for yourself since we parted ways." He assessed Bar up and down. "Even wearing an eye patch now. I guess you don't want to scare the locals. As I recall, that missing eye came in handy for making a point to some of the assholes we had to deal with back in the day. How many different stories did we have for how you lost it? Each one more grisly than the last. Scared the shit out of those poor sumbitches." His gruesome chuckle brought back memories Bar thought were long forgotten.

"All that's behind me now. A long damn time ago."

"Yeah, a long time by some measures. Maybe not so long by others. You know, that pesky statute of limitations thing."

"What the fuck do you want from me? I'm just a working stiff now, selling tractor parts, living in a trailer, keeping to myself. All that crazy-ass shit we did together? Yeah, I remember some of the things we did. And I ain't proud of it. But that was a different time and I was a different person. That war fucked me up. But I ain't that person any more."

Korth smiled. Bar recalled that the sight of Dragomir Korth smiling was never a good thing. "Oh, lighten up, Barstow. I'm not here to drag you back into anything like we did in the old days. I just need you to help out an old friend. That's not too much to ask, is it?"

"Whatever it is you tracked me down for, it can't be anything good."

"C'mon, gimme a break. Y'see, I'm here on an assignment for a client. Well, two clients actually. It's all legit, has to do with the same person. One client is owed some money, another might be able to figure out a way to get that money paid back. But there are complications. One fellow in particular who could squash the whole deal."

"And if I don't want to play this game?"

Korth's manner turned serious. "It's not a game, Reinhardt. These people want things to happen, and it's my job to see that they do. And there are some other people who might like to know where you disappeared to. So let's just say it would be good for both of us if you pitched in here."

Bar tried to summon up the cold, uncaring person he had been decades earlier when he and Dragomir Korth were a feared pair among the shady denizens of southern California. In his best attempt at an emotionless voice, he said, "Fine. Whatcha need?"

"Just some info, that's all. I need to know the lay of the land around here, to get up to speed on who's who and what's what. Where the pressure points might be, where the skeletons are buried. You know a few things about buried skeletons, right?"

****

Astrid Stevenson's preferred private meeting spot was the cocktail lounge in the Arlington Hyatt, just across the Key

Bridge from DC's swanky Georgetown neighborhood. The businesses in the area known as Rosslyn had consisted mostly of pawn shops and shady bars until an aggressive development campaign launched in the 1970s converted it into a tightly packed wedge of gleaming high rise office buildings and trendy apartment towers. The Hyatt's location three blocks from the headquarters of PACA—People Against Cruelty to Animals—afforded Astrid a handy respite from the pressures of running a nationwide nonprofit organization.

Seated at a small cocktail table with Smith Bondurant, the two blended easily into the business-friendly environment.

"I can't thank you enough for the generous contributions from Pymsdale," Astrid said.

"You know as well as I that it's all just for PR. The Pymsdales don't give a crap about animal welfare. But it helps offset the accusations from tree huggers that we're raping the land by promoting the image of helping you take care of poor little puppies and kitties."

Astrid smiled and raised her glass. "That's what I like about you, Smith. Always the straightforward type."

He raised his glass in return. "But only with those who share my jaundiced view of the world."

They clinked glasses as Astrid said, "Here's to being straightforwardly jaundiced."

"Hear, hear!"

"It's always good to see you," she said, "even if it's just to maintain that cherished public relations image."

"You too. So how's the 13th Amendment case going? Pretty damn interesting hook you came up with."

"It's moving along favorably. We have a pretty sympathetic judge who's hearing the case. So far I think he may agree with our position that since the amendment only says no 'party' can be held in involuntary servitude and doesn't say 'person,' the amendment could apply to animals as well as humans."

"I'm pretty sure that's not what the creators of the amendment had in mind."

"I'm sure they didn't. But it's proving to be a good fundraising tool. We're getting all kinds of free publicity thanks to people arguing about both sides."

"And is some of that money going toward the Costa Rica project?"

Astrid Stevenson rarely blushed, but her cheeks showed a slight flash of pink. "It's being allocated across a range of our projects, just like the money Pymsdale donates."

"So, in other words, yes."

She nodded slightly. "So how about you? To what do I owe the honor of this rare face time?"

"As I was going to be spending some time in your neck of the woods, Mister P. suggested I swing by for a personal meeting, something we can log into the record to show our ongoing support for PACA."

"Okay, so now that we've met that obligation, what is it that brings you all the way here from California? Surely it wasn't just to have a quick drink with me on a Monday afternoon."

"We've targeted the Mid-Atlantic area for our next resort project. Virginia, Maryland, or North Carolina. Virginia's our first choice, so this is where I'm based. Working on a possible site out west of here, in Crutchfield County, near some little place called Paradise Gap. Doubt you've ever heard of it."

"Paradise Gap doesn't ring a bell, but I do know someone who lives in Crutchfield County."

"Really? Who's that?"

"Oh, probably no one you'd know if you're working on a big land deal. A young woman named Shelton McKendrick."

"McKendrick? I've met someone by that name, a fellow named Ryman. And the local developer I'm working with has mentioned the guy's mother, Rhetta. Think they might be related to the woman you know?"

"Well, she hasn't mentioned anything about her family, seems to get kind of uneasy when I ask. But with all the inbreeding that goes on out in those places, there are probably a whole bunch of McKendricks running around, with big ears, sloping foreheads, and low IQs." Astrid caught herself and dropped the mocking tone. "Actually, that's unfair of me. The McKendrick I know is a lovely young woman. Very intelligent, well educated, and accomplished. We met when she working as a veterinary pharmaceuticals rep on the West Coast. She gave that up to come back to Virginia to help run the family business."

Bondurant caught the gleam in Astrid's eye. "So you two are friends, really good friends?"

"Yes, really good."

"Ah, I see."

"But it's not just that. She's been making some nice contributions to PACA, designated for the Costa Rica project."

"I'm certainly looking forward to making a visit there once everything's ready."

"I'm sure all the little furry creatures will be happy to see you."

Chapter 21

TUESDAY'S MEET WAS at Mildred and Josh Preston's BoSox farm. Transplants from Massachusetts and ardent Red Sox fans, Josh wanted to name their Virginia property Green Monster Acres. He considered it a brilliant play on both the storied left field wall at Boston's Fenway Park, known as the Green Monster, and the classic '60s TV show about a city couple who move to the country. Mildred nixed the name out of concern that too many locals would not get the first reference and could be offended by the second one. So they struck a compromise with BoSox Farm.

Thumper and Janey, along with several others, were already at the Prestons' preparing for the morning's sport when Shelton pulled up to the mudroom door at Montfair. Myrna, coffee mug in hand, shuffled out, plopped into the car, and let out a dramatic yawn.

"Still too early for you?" Shelton asked.

"Between the time change and the fact that even on West Coast time I never got up before ten o'clock, yeah, it feels pretty early."

"It took me a while to adjust when I moved back last year. But with all the traveling I did and the long hours, I was used to getting up early, hitting the road, and working late."

"I'm fine with the working late part. The other two? Not so much."

It was only a fifteen-minute drive to BoSox Farm. Shelton let Myrna have some quiet time to drink her coffee and revive herself. The farm was along the eastern edge of the hunt's territory, where the ground was gently rolling, more open and less steep than the land around Montfair and adjoining fixtures. This, plus a network of farm roads that crisscrossed the fields and wooded sections, made it well suited to watch the hunting action from the comfort of a truck or car.

Myrna perked up when they pulled into the field where a dozen trailers were parked. Horses were secured with lead lines along trailer sides as the hunters bustled about with final preparations: brushing manes and tails, tightening girths, spraying fly repellent, buckling helmet chin straps, setting up mounting blocks.

Shelton noticed the brightness in Myrna's eyes when they stepped out of the car. "Bring back some memories?"

"Sure does." She scanned the scene before her. "A few things have changed. Nobody wore safety helmets when I was a kid. It was all hunt caps, bowlers, and top hats. The trucks and trailers are a lot nicer. I remember some folks pulled rickety old trailers behind station wagons. Of course, the cars were sturdier and had bigger engines back then. But..." She paused, inhaled, and let out a long breath. "...the feel of it, the smell of it, the way it gives you a little shiver, that anticipation that something exciting is about to start. That's still the same."

"I remember that feeling too. And there was, like, a sense that you were part of something. You had your family around you, and everyone was part of this community. I hadn't really thought about it since I came back. But now that you mention it, I kinda miss it.

"Yeah, me too."

They walked over to where the riders had assembled to hear Thumper's opening announcements.

"It's good to see so many of you here this morning. And I'm especially glad to see some guests are out with us." He waved at Myrna and Shelton. "Most of you know my kid sister, Myrna. And I'm sure everyone knows Sheltie Lou.

I'm so happy you got up early and will be following along. I'd also like to thank our hosts, Mildred and Josh, for allowing us to hunt from their farm. As y'all know, but I can never say it enough, without our gracious landowners, we would not be able to do this. So we always need to be mindful to thank those who keep their land open, resist the temptation to sell out to the developers, and allow us to follow hounds across their property."

A chorus of "Hear, hear!" sounded across the field.

Myrna tried to maintain a poker face, but Shelton noticed her smile faded to a forced grimace.

Thumper continued. "I'll be leading first field, Mildred will take the second field. So let's get..."

"Brother Thumper," Ryman interrupted, "may I share a few words?"

Thumper sighed. "Oh, all right. But keep it short, okay?"

"Certainly." Addressing the riders, he said, "As I've been sharing the inspiring words from our dear Brother Thumper that Saint Hubert guided him to write, let me just pass along a quick thought before we move off. The fourth of his twenty-four Tally-Ho Tips is about the Creature Connection. We, more than most folks, have developed a strong sensitivity toward animals. Not just pampered house pets that don't get to act like the animals they are, but the horses we ride and the hounds we follow, animals in their natural state, running across open land, hunting together as a pack, living the life denied to so many of their kin. And that's taught us how to think like they think, to understand how they feel, how to relate to them as part of the pack or herd. Now, of course it's a different type of relationship with horses than it is with hounds, the prey animal versus the predator animal thing. But that makes it even more important to sense how a horse thinks and feels, as the horse sees the world differently than humans and hounds do.

"And Saint Hubert would have us use that ability to

relate to our fellow humans as well, especially with those who, you might say, see the world differently than we do." He smiled, reached over and took Nardell's hand. "Like, say, how women and men relate to each other. As Nardell and I know, following the guidance of Saint Hubert can do wonders for a couple's relationship. And guys, let me tell you, the sensitivity you've developed from working with horses, the need for non-verbal communication, to respond to those subtle physical cues, to understand that it's not about coercion by mass and muscle, well, that, my friends, is sexy. Am I right, ladies?"

A choir of female voices sang out another "Hear, hear!"

"And so, as our beloved Saint Hubert inspired Brother Thumper to write as his fourth Tally-Ho Tip, 'When a man whispers to an animal, a woman listens.' " Turning back to Thumper, he said, "And now, let's go hunting!"

Myrna and Shelton watched as Crispie moved off with hounds and the riders followed. They then got back in the car and Shelton pulled onto the farm road to follow at a safe distance.

"Everyone's been calling Ryman's Saint Hubert stuff crazy," Myrna said, "that he's lost his marbles. What he said kind of made sense, didn't it?"

"Yeah, it made sense, I suppose. Of course, my relational perspective is a little different. But you have to remember he was quoting your brother's words. The crazy part is that my father thinks the spirit of some guy who died thirteen hundred years ago and became the patron saint of hunters inspired your brother to write his book about foxhunting as a metaphor for life."

"And yet you wear two of that saint's medals every day."

"Oh, well, that's more about family and tradition. Not that I really think there's any magical power to them." Shelton's hand touched the one medal she was wearing and Myrna noticed the other was absent.

"You're only wearing one today. What happened to the other one?"

Shelton did not have the emotional energy to explain the real reason. "I must have forgotten to put it on this morning. It's probably just on my bureau back home." The mention of the medallions served to remind Shelton that she had to quit stalling and make her decision: it had to be either Astrid or her family. She couldn't conceive of any workable way to have both.

She brought the car to a stop when Crispie cast hounds into the woods and the riders paused in the field between the woods and farm road. Myrna tried to recall the last time she'd hunted with Montfair. It was probably on a weekend or a holiday when she was home from school at Hollins College. At that point in her life she was convinced that Hollywood stardom was her destiny and she couldn't wait to leave Virginia. Her parents were friends with David Wendler, the huntsman for West Hills Hunt, where several film industry luminaries, as well as a future US president, rode to hounds. While skeptical of her chances for success in show biz, Thad and CeeCee also knew that the right connections could make all the difference. So they told her to take her hunting kit with her, introduce herself to Wendler when she got to California, and join the hunt. Riding alongside famous actors, producers, and directors would give her an advantage other aspiring starlets lacked.

It was sound advice. In hindsight, she should have taken it. But youthful pride led her to reject her parents' counsel, certain she could succeed on her own merits without the help of family connections. Never mind that the Billingons and Crutchfields had achieved most of their success over the generations aided considerably by family connections.

Hounds opened and the followers all snapped to attention. The pack, in full voice, took off up the wooded hillside as Crispie cantered along the edge, turned left at the entrance to a well-groomed trail, and paralleled his hounds as the chase quickened. Thumper followed with his first-fielders, Mildred's group close behind.

"I think I know where they're going," Shelton said. "If we follow this around to the next road, it bends left along the other side of the woods. I'd bet money the fox will come out there and we might get a good view."

The hounds' cry reverberated through the trees as the car rattled down the rough farm road. The sound of the pack and the sight of the woods and fields rushing past rekindled memories for both women: the feel of being on a well-muscled horse, eager for the chase, the wind buffeting them as they sped along in joyful pursuit of the quarry, every muscle attuned to the challenge, every thought focused solely on the moment.

Shelton alternated between keeping her eyes on the road and watching the woods for any hint of a small red creature darting out into the open field. Myrna, unburdened by the distraction of driving, was able to concentrate on where the fox might appear.

She was the first to shout, "Tally ho!"

Shelton looked to where Myrna, with a sparkling smile on her face, was pointing. The fox was sprinting into the field right where Shelton predicted. There was a culvert under the road just ahead and Shelton had seen this trick before. The fox could fit easily through the culvert without losing a step. Hounds, though, would be foiled as the culvert was too narrow for them. Once through the pipe, the fox had only to slip under the fence that ran along the right side of the road, one more open field to navigate, and then a quick sprint to another wooded area on a low hill where a safe den awaited his return. Hounds would regain the line on the other end of the culvert but the ruse would give the fox an ample lead. Riders would have to wait while hounds sorted out the question, then give them time to get through or over the three-board wooden fence. There was a coop in the fence line that the first field could jump and then follow close behind hounds. A gate was to the right of the coop, closer to where Shelton had stopped the car.

"I'll get the gate," she said, and both women jumped out of the car.

Mildred saw them and was relieved that she and her followers would be able to get through easily without having to open and close the gate.

Shelton waited until hounds had recovered the line and the first field riders had all cleared the jump, then swung the gate open. Every one of the riders said "Thank you" as they rode past Shelton and Myrna and took off at a gallop to be in on the culmination of the chase when the fox went to ground.

If the sound of hounds and the sight of the countryside flying past had roused old memories of mounted days afield, standing next to the horses and riders heightened the sense of being part of the chase once again. There was a blend of joy and determination on the face of every rider. The horses were fully in the game, nostrils pulsing, bound in the unity of the herd as they surged forward. The scent of oiled leather and equine sweat rolled over the two gate-getters, carried on the swirling dust as dozens of steel-shod hooves churned over the ground.

The two women stood at the gate and watched until the last rider had galloped up the hill and disappeared into the woods at the top.

"Aren't you glad you came along this morning?" Shelton asked.

Myrna stood silently, looking up the hill to the trail's entrance into the woods. It seemed familiar to her, a hazy memory from childhood. Had she ridden that trail before, all those years ago? Probably. The hunting country had changed little since her youth, when her father and Shelton's grandfather were the joint masters. She looked out toward the left and took in the panoramic view of open rolling fields, fenced pastures, a few farmhouses and outbuildings.

Was she glad she'd gone along with Shelton? Or would it have been better to have left all those ancient memories of a life she'd long since abandoned tucked safely away somewhere out of mind?

"Oh, yes, of course," she said, trying to sound convincing, "very glad I came."

Shelton picked up on the glimmer of hesitation. "Maybe we should be getting on back. I've got some things I need to take of care."

"Yeah, so do I."

On the drive back to Montfair, Shelton asked, "I don't mean to pry, and if it's none of my business, just tell me to leave it alone. But I've never heard much about your life out there in Hollywood. Y'know, like were you married? Are you married now? Kids? A partner?"

"No, you're not prying. I guess I've been the mysterious 'Aunt Myrna.' Not really an aunt, just some odd figure who breezes in once in a great while and then flits off again. Yes, I was married. Typical Hollywood union, which means stormy and brief. He was a stunt man, not a very good one. No idea where he is now. He's probably a carpenter somewhere in Oregon with a vegan wife and a bunch of kids." She chuckled at her imagined vision of her ex. "Sure, some boyfriends have come and gone. Mostly gone. No kids."

"Was your family background ever an issue?"

Myrna cocked her head. "Why would it have been?"

"Y'know, foxhunting and all that? Some people don't approve."

"My family background never came up much. Has that been an issue for you?"

"Not so far. But, y'know, just wondering. The foxhunting thing could be a turn off to someone who's not familiar with how things are around here. I mean, some members of my family might seem a bit odd."

They turned into Montfair's entrance.

"Family," Myrna said quietly. "I guess I rejected mine. That was probably a mistake. And now it's too late to do anything about it."

"That can't be true. Okay, so your parents are dead. You can't do anything about that. But you and Thumper are getting along pretty well, aren't you?"

"Yeah, Thumper and me. Big brother and little sister. Just like old times."

The tone of cynicism took Shelton by surprise. "You two are all right, aren't you?"

"Oh, sure. We're just fine."

They reached the mudroom entrance and Shelton stopped the car.

Myrna turned to her and said, "Look, never be ashamed of your family. Hold onto them no matter what. If you let that go, you may never be able to get it back." She glanced at her watch. "I have to get going. Middleburg lunch group. Thanks for this morning. It was great."

As Myrna entered the mudroom door, Shelton sat and thought about what she'd said. *Hold on to them no matter what.*

Chapter 22

Cuyler Corley turned his Escalade off Paradise Turnpike onto Montfair Lane. A large flatbed truck was coming the other way, piled high and wide with round bales of hay.

Smith Bondurant gripped the passenger door armrest as the two vehicles rolled toward each other, neither one slowing down. Corley took his left hand off the steering wheel and waved at the driver of the truck, which caused Bondurant to grip the armrest even harder.

When the truck had safely passed, Bondurant relaxed his grip, let out a breath, and said, "I don't know how everyone around here handles these damn country roads. You've got no curbs, just rough edges, and no lane markings. And they keep winding this way and that, so you never know what's around the next curve. But nobody slows down when someone's coming the other way. It's like a perpetual game of chicken."

"Just seems that way to you city folk. The roads are as wide as any of those with curbs and centerlines. You hardly ever hear about head-on crashes. The accidents that do happen are more likely because the driver had a few too many, ran off the road, and hit a tree. Or swerved to miss a deer."

"But why are they so curvy? Sure, there's a poetic appeal to the 'winding country road.' But couldn't they have been made straighter?"

"My father started his working life as a highway engineer. That's what got him interested in land speculation. The job allowed him to see where future development opportunities would be before others found out. He used to say that the Indian trails followed the deer trails, the cattle trails followed the Indian trails, and the roads followed the cattle trails. The roads around here were all originally designed for horse-drawn traffic. And it was easier to just make the existing trails wider than try to move large natural obstacles or level the ground."

"That's going to need to change if we move forward on our plans."

"And that's where Nate Plummer comes in. He served in the state legislature before taking over Thad Billington's seat in the House. And he's well positioned to win next year's Senate race. Lots of connections, and lots of favors owed. Nate can make things happen. State money and federal money, plenty of dough for all the infrastructure needs."

Corley cruised past the entrance to Montfair and turned into Fair Enough Farm. "Don't let Rhetta McKendrick fool you," he said. "She'll play the simple country girl, the old 'I ain't got much book learning' ruse. But behind all that crap she's sharp as a tack. And she can be one hard-ass old broad."

Having agreed to Corley's request for a meeting and an introduction to Smith Bondurant, Rhetta opened the front door and let Abel out just as the men were getting out of the car.

"C'mere, boy!" Corley called out. "There's a good boy."

Abel bounded to him, barking loudly, and leaned into Corley's legs for the customary rubbing. His joyful expression changed when Bondurant stepped around from the other side of the car. He stared at the man and uttered a low growl.

Bondurant stopped in his tracks. "Does he bite?"

"He ain't never bit yet," Rhetta replied from the porch. "But there's always a first time."

"He just doesn't know you," Corley said. "He'll be fine. Best to not make any sudden moves though. Walk on up nice and casual."

As Bondurant began to walk toward the house as calmly as he could, Abel escalated from a growl to a full blown barking fit. He kept his distance from the strange intruder, but made sure his threat was understood.

Rhetta allowed the dog to make his point, then called him to her. "You boys come on in. Got some coffee on in the kitchen."

The two men followed her into the house, down the cluttered hallway to the kitchen. Little had changed there over the decades. A row of windows fitted with faded curtains provided a view of the woods behind the house. The countertops were mismatched, stained and scarred. A dinette table stood in the middle of the room atop a dingy linoleum floor.

To Bondurant's refined nose, the room smelled like stale cereal and flea powder.

"Have a seat. I'll pour you some coffee."

As Rhetta reached for the grimy brown plastic percolator, Bondurant pulled out a chair and saw that gashes in its vinyl-covered seat and back were patched over with multicolored strips of electrical tape. He hesitated and looked at Corley, who nodded and gestured for him to sit.

"Cuyler tells me you boys are kicking around plans for some kind of resort," Rhetta said as she joined them at the table. "Don't know why you'd want to do something like that way out here. Paradise Gap ain't exactly a tourist hotspot."

"This will be a destination center," Bondurant replied. "Pymsdale operates several such facilities, most of them located in similar places, away from congested cities, where our guests can relax. We also offer convention facilities for professional groups and associations. There's a great appeal to gathering in one central location, with a variety of planned activities for the participants. We think Crutchfield County is well-positioned to offer those amenities."

Rhetta smirked. "Amenities. *Amen*-ities. Sounds like you've preached this sermon a few times before. But I expect you're preaching to the wrong audience here. Now, I ain't exactly the sentimental type, but, still, I feel some obligation to the McKendrick legacy. This farm has been in the family for a century and a half. And there are two more generations around after me. So if you boys are thinking about building this resort of yours around here, I'm afraid you've got another 'think' coming."

Corley added his input. "It's all just early stages still, Rhetta. Smith's looking at several properties, not only around here but some in North Carolina and a couple in Maryland. So we're testing the waters at this point. Wherever it happens, it's going to be a real class operation. Here…" He reached into a notebook he'd brought with him, pulled out a large brochure, and laid it before Rhetta. "…let me show you how it's going to look, wherever it ends up."

She took the brochure and flipped through the pages. "Quite an operation. And you really believe lots of people will come to a place like this, way out here?"

"They already do in many similar places," Bondurant said. "We offer convenient transportation from multiple airports and we look for locations within easy driving distance from major metropolitan areas."

Rhetta flipped another page of the brochure. "What's this thing here?"

"That's the heliport."

"What?"

"It's a place where helicopters can land."

"Helicopters? People come to these places in helicopters?"

"Some do."

"I'll be damned." Rhetta looked out the kitchen window to where her bright orange International Harvester Scout was parked. "People flying to places like this in helicopters. Things sure have changed."

Corley put in his two cents. "They have, Rhetta. And changes will be coming to Crutchfield County at some point, like it or not. I know how much this old farm means to you, and that you'd like it to stay in the family for generations to come. But we can't stop progress forever. Maybe it's better to take advantage of the opportunities we have while we can still enjoy them, and then pass those resources along to those who come after us."

She sat quietly for a long moment. "This farm ain't all that big, at least not by Crutchfield County standards. You think there's enough land here for all this stuff you're planning to build?"

"You have a good eye for land use," Bondurant said. "You're right. There will be additional acreage required. Cuyler, show her the map you've had drawn up."

Corley pulled a folded piece of paper from his notebook and laid it out on the table. It showed the planned resort centered at Fair Enough Farm but extending out to other bordering properties, including Worsham's and part of Montfair.

Rhetta studied the map carefully and then pointed to one area. "This part here. Looks like it's on Billington property. That can't be right. Thumper would never sell off one square foot of Montfair, especially for something like this."

"Technically," Corley explained, "that part of the family property doesn't belong to Thumper. He's just the caretaker, you might say. It's a complicated arrangement, no need to bore you with the details. But Smith here is in the process of negotiating a deal with the actual owner, and those talks are moving forward nicely."

"Well, if Thumper doesn't own the whole place, who the hell is this other owner? I thought it all went to him when his folks died."

"Like I said, it's a complicated situation. And because

of the sensitivity of the ongoing negotiations, we can't share any of the details just yet."

Bondurant reached into the pocket of his suit coat and pulled out a piece of paper. "We can, though, give you a rough estimate of what we think your property might go for if this project moves forward and you decide to take advantage of this opportunity." He slid the paper toward Rhetta.

She studied the figure written on it. "That's quite a heap of change. You boys must really be serious about this."

"As I said, it's just a rough estimate," Bondurant explained, "not a firm offer yet. But we wanted to give you some general idea of what we're talking about, something you can mull over on your own time. We don't want you to feel pressured or rushed. Like Cuyler said, I'm considering other properties, so nothing's definite yet. To be honest, this area is our first choice. But if it's not in the best interest of everyone involved, we'd rather move on to another option, even if it's less appealing, than risk creating hard feelings."

Smith's sincerity was almost believable. But Rhetta McKendrick knew slick when she saw it. She looked at the figure on the paper again. "Well, this kinda cash could go a long way to smoothing any ruffled feathers."

Bondurant stood up and Corley took the cue to join him.

"We won't take up any more of your time, Mrs. McKendrick. We appreciate you giving us the opportunity to chat. Just so you know, if you think this is something you'd like to move forward with, all we need at this stage is a signed letter of intent. As I'm sure you understand, a project of this scale requires a multitude of approvals and permits before anything can get started. Being able to show serious commitment that the current landowners support the project and wish to see it happen is always a big help in that effort."

Rhetta paid only partial attention to what Bondurant said. Her thoughts were on two things: the amount of money on that piece of paper and the clock on the wall, which showed how much time remained before Shelton arrived home from the shop.

****

Rhetta had become accustomed to Shelton's late hours. Dinner was waiting and the two women sat down at the kitchen table.

"You realize I ain't gonna be around forever," Rhetta said with her usual bluntness.

As well as she knew her grandmother, the statement still took Shelton by surprise. "Yes, of course. Is there something you need to tell me?"

"Oh, I ain't saying I'm sick or anything. Everything seems to still be working just fine. But, y'know, I'm getting on in years. You're still so young, got so much life ahead of you. I was just wondering if I'm putting you in a bad spot by skipping over your crazy-ass daddy and leaving the farm directly to you when I'm gone. Gotta face that reality at some point, don't we?"

"So who else would you leave it to? And why would passing it on to me put me in a bad place?"

"Just that it takes a lot to keep the place up. And you're so busy with the shop. I don't expect you're going to have time for farming on the side. Your granddaddy tried to do both, plus all the time he wasted with his foxhunting foolishness. And look how that ended up. The damn place would have gone under if you and Bar hadn't bailed it out. And your daddy sure wasn't any help either."

Shelton put down her fork and took a breath. "I haven't really given it much thought. It's been such a whirlwind since I came back, there hasn't been time to think about much other than how to keep the shop afloat. But would I want to take on farming in addition to the shop? No, I can't see trying to do both. Foxhunting? Probably not that either. Or even if I did, not like how it was with Fergus, so much a part of his life that it took away from handling business. And this is a pretty big place for one person to live alone."

"So you might—what?—just sell it and move somewhere smaller?"

"Geez, Grandma, I don't know. You've kind of hit me by surprise with this. It really means a lot to me that you've made me your sole heir, skipped over Daddy to do that. But that also raises a bunch of questions, doesn't it?"

"Maybe I could make that easier on you if I just left you a pile of cash instead of a rundown old house and a bunch of useless land."

"Are you thinking about selling the farm?"

"Not in any serious way just yet. But this thing with Frank Worsham wanting to sell his place got me thinking."

"Yeah, I've heard about that."

"It's tough making a living from farming around here these days. Might be awhile longer yet but sooner or later all that development's gonna start creeping out this way."

"To be honest, I've been looking into long term forecasts for this area, what's predicted in terms of population growth, housing, commercial development, and stuff like that. How it's all likely to affect our business."

"I don't reckon it's gonna look good for selling tractors like the one Worsham bought."

"No, it's not. That's already starting to change and we're repositioning the shop because of it. The market's going to move toward equipment like riding mowers, weedeaters, smaller chainsaws, that sort of stuff, things people need to keep up residential properties, maybe on a few acres or less. That's going to mean smaller dollar value per sale so we'll need to increase the volume to stay afloat. And that means more people will need to find their way to Paradise Gap to buy those things from us."

"I'm guessing you've already got some ideas about how to make that happen."

Shelton smiled. "I do. I've been placing ads in small

newspapers promoting our lower prices. The theme line is, 'Drive a little, save a lot.' "

"Catchy. And how's it working?"

"Pretty well so far."

"Then I reckon you'll be okay no matter what I decide to do with this old place."

"What I'd be okay with is you sticking around for many more years, with or without this old farm."

****

The following morning Rhetta placed a call to Cecelia Broadhurst.

"Can you swing by for a chat? Got a possible real estate deal I could use some help with."

Cecelia was skeptical. "Look, if it's about trying to sell the part of the farm where Bar lives, I already told you the restrictions on the property won't allow that."

"No, it ain't that. This time it's about selling the whole place—lock, stock, and rotting old barrel. Ain't no restriction on that, is there?"

"I can be there in an hour."

Chapter 23

"I hope I'm not interfering with your important church duties," Myrna said as she took a seat in front of Reverend Davenport's desk.

The cramped office was littered with piles of books and papers that appeared to be arranged in no particular order. A small wooden stand on the desktop held an assortment of pipes with a humidor and ashtray beside it. Reverend Dan wore his white clerical collar with a lavender shirt. His suitably threadbare tweed jacket was draped over the back of his chair.

The Reverend Doctor Daniel T. Davenport had spent decades cultivating his image to appear as a country vicar from the English Shires. He never openly suggested that was true, he simply allowed his appearance and manner of speaking to imply he was something other than a kid from Portage, Illinois, the son of blue-collar parents, who found life as an Episcopal priest a workable way to recreate himself in an image more to his own liking.

Visions of a prominent leadership position in the church hierarchy had long since faded. After more than two decades in the priesthood, his career consisted of brief assignments in more than a dozen dioceses, peppered with short stints subbing for fellow clerics on sabbatical. His posting to Saint Cuthbert's-in-the-Woods, with its fading membership and remote location in the tiny village of Paradise Gap, seemed to be his final exile from the church's mainstream life.

At first he resigned himself to the situation's futility. And then Ryman McKendrick felt called to start the Ancient and Venerable Church of Ars Venatica. What Dan Davenport had been lacking all those years was a challenge worthy of his mettle, not the theoretical concept of Satan and evil in general but a real, flesh-and-blood opponent.

His newfound mission was to convince his parishioners that, while foxhunting itself was an acceptable practice for those who wished to maintain the tradition, elevating this arcane pastime to the status of a structured religion was an abomination. His sermons, once burdensome lectures on the more esoteric and arcane nuances of Episcopal theology, took on more practical and relatable themes, delivered with passion, humor, and humility. Hints of his native Mid-Western accent replaced his long-practiced efforts to sound vaguely British.

Church attendance began to increase, as did the offerings, and the fortunes of Saint Cuthbert's, although still teetering on failure, had taken a modest turn for the better.

"Certainly not," Dan replied. "No interruption at all. I was actually hoping you might have a chance to stop by before you fly back to Hollywood. At least for a visit if not for a Sunday service."

"The church hasn't changed much. Brings back a lot of memories. Father Herb was a wonderful man. He helped me through some difficult times when I was young."

"I wish I'd had a chance to know him. I've heard countless remarks like that since I came here. I know I'm no match for his legacy, but I do hope I'm able to provide some help for those in need as well."

"Oh, I'm sure you are. I didn't mean to imply...it's just that, well, that was a long time ago. Looking back, I suppose my teen years weren't all that different from a lot of kids. Maybe better than many. But when you're young, you think any problem in life is a major catastrophe. It takes the perspective of adulthood to see what the real catastrophes are."

Dan caught a note of resignation in Myrna's remark. "I

truly hope you're not going through anything like that now."

"I wouldn't call it a catastrophe exactly. But, to be honest, there is something I'm struggling with. Something I can't talk to anyone else about. I was thinking, maybe, y'know, since a priest has to keep everything confidential, I could talk to you."

"Yes, certainly. You can share anything within these walls and it will definitely stay between only you, God, and me."

For the next thirty minutes Myrna unburdened herself. Dan did little more than nod, maintain an air of compassion, and express non-judgmental agreement at the appropriate moments.

When she was done, Dan said, "Yes, I can see that you're in a very difficult situation. I can't tell you what to do. And suggesting you pray for the Lord's guidance isn't what you need to hear. But I'll pray on your behalf that you find the right path to take, the path that will give you peace. And know that you can come to me at any time if you need someone to listen and bear the struggle with you. I can't lift your burden, but maybe I can help lighten it if only a little."

It was all Myrna needed to hear.

Chapter 24

The town of Middleburg is an anachronistic oasis in the midst of Virginia horse country. It's one of the few places around where a person can pop into the Safeway grocery store in full foxhunting attire and no one stares, wondering if perhaps the local theater is performing an Oscar Wilde play. The post office has a ten-page list of people waiting for a box to open up so they can put a Middleburg address on their stationery, even if they live five towns away.

The commercial section is only six blocks long and two blocks wide. The businesses consist mostly of restaurants ranging from the quickie sandwich nook to the upscale eatery, clothing shops that cater to conventional East Coast preferences along with designer boutiques for trendy party-goers, antique and art shops, and tack stores specializing in English-style riding equipment. Ads taped in the windows of half a dozen realty offices display aerial photos of country estates with price tags starting in the low millions.

Many of the town's buildings are historical landmarks, complete with plaques attesting to construction dates from the 1700s. Middleburg was a pivotal point of action during the Civil War, occupied by one side or the other as the balance of power shifted with the tides of battle.

It was shortly past eight o'clock when Thumper, Janey, and Myrna stepped into the dark paneled, candle-lit dining room of the Red Fox Inn. Only the modern attire of the patrons weakened the impression that one had been carried back two centuries in time. A large fieldstone fireplace adorned one wall, though it sat dormant on this warm

October night. The slate floor and rough timber ceiling supports created a subterranean feel. Heavy oak tables and ladder-backed chairs dominated the room.

The Red Fox billed itself as the "oldest original inn in America," boasting a founding date of 1728. Colonel John Singleton Mosby, the Confederacy's legendary Gray Ghost, and his Partisan Rangers were occasional patrons. Officially the Forty-third Battalion of Virginia Cavalry, the guerillas enjoyed the tavern's hospitality when the fortunes of the Recent Unpleasantness surged in their favor. More than once their respite was cut short when the Yankees rolled in with superior force and retook the village.

A century later the President's press secretary held media conferences in the Jeb Stuart Room of the Red Fox. It was a handy spot when the entourage of Salinger's boss, including the President's wife and young children, were relaxing at a farm located not far outside of town.

The hostess escorted the threesome to a table in the back dining room where the other members of the dinner party awaited—Nathan and Evangeline Plummer, Cuyler Corley, and Smith Bondurant. Myrna kept her head bowed and tried to look even smaller between Thumper and Janey.

"I believe you three met Smith at the horse show last month," Nate Plummer said.

Smith Bondurant stood, shook hands with Thumper, and nodded to the two ladies. "Yes, it was a pleasure meeting all of you. But we didn't have much of a chance to talk then, and I've been pretty busy since. Cuyler has been running me ragged from one state to the next."

With dinner concluded and small talk out of the way, Plummer touched on the evening's first agenda item. Addressing Thumper, he said, "You've probably heard rumors of what Smith's doing here."

Thumper nodded dismissively.

"And I'm sure you're familiar with Pymsdale's facilities. Maybe been to some yourself?"

139

"One or two. Bar Association meetings, a couple of academic conferences."

Smith interjected. "I trust you found them satisfactory."

"Yes, nice places. You all do a very fine job."

Plummer resumed. "How would you feel about a similar facility coming to Virginia?"

"Well, that's not really my area of expertise, is it? If you need legal counsel, you'll want to talk to someone who specializes in development issues, not a crusty old historian."

"You underestimate yourself," Plummer said. "It's precisely your role as a historian, and specifically a Constitutional scholar, that we're interested in."

"What would that have to do with a Pymsdale resort?"

"Each of our facilities is based on a theme," Bondurant explained. "The one in the works now, ideally to be located somewhere in Virginia, will be built on a historical concept. This state has played such a pivotal role in so much of our nation's development, from Jamestown on. The Revolution, Civil War, birthplace of presidents. I don't have to tell you. Most of that is just Billington family history. We're looking at sites in Maryland and North Carolina as well. But our first choice, far and away, is Virginia."

"I still don't see what that has to do with me."

"Two things," Plummer said. "One, Pymsdale will need a well-known, highly credentialed historical expert to oversee that aspect of the project, make sure everything is done correctly, that all details are presented honestly and accurately. Now, really, who could possibly fit that bill better than Professor Thaddeus Augustus Billington the Fourth, JD, PhD?"

Plummer allowed that to set in for a few seconds. Then said, "I'll let your cousin Cuyler fill you in on the second thing."

Corley leaned forward. "As you know, Thumper, every Pymsdale facility features a conference center. Like you said, you've attended some meetings at them yourself. Pretty nice operations, right?"

"I had no complaints."

"And I'm sure you won't have any about this new one either. Especially as it will be named for your father and my uncle, the Thaddeus A. Billington the Third Conference Center."

"Quite a mouthful."

"How about 'TAB-3' for short?" Corley joked. "Seriously, Thumper, think what this would mean for your father's legacy. A permanent tribute to his accomplishments and the opportunity for you to share the inspirational stories of this country with a far greater audience."

"And where do you see this place being built?" Thumper asked.

Bondurant took over. "We have a few possible sites in mind, but all still in the early stages of discussion. So we have to respect the landowners' privacy until everyone's ready to go public."

Myrna noticed a couple seated at a small table in the corner of the dimly lit dining room. She didn't recognize the man, but the woman looked familiar. He was signing the credit card slip and she was gathering her purse and jacket as they prepared to leave. Their path would take them right past Myrna's seat. She thought about fleeing to the ladies' room, but it was too late.

As the couple passed by, the woman stopped. "Myrna? Myrna Billington? Is that you?"

The voice brought back ancient memories. She looked up and realized she was facing an old Foxcroft classmate.

"My goodness," the woman said, "I haven't seen you since we left school. Where have you been all these years?"

"Oh, um, California mostly. Just back for a quick family visit. Nice to see you." She looked down, hoping the woman would take the cue and just walk on.

But the woman persisted. "How long are you staying?

Maybe we could meet for lunch sometime. A few of us get together every week or so. We have our own special table at Salamander. We'd love to have you join us."

The chatter at the table fell silent.

"Oh, well, I may be leaving any day now. But, sure, if I have some time…"

The woman reached into her purse. "Here's my card. Call me any time. So nice to see you."

Thumper and Janey looked at each other with questioning expressions. Corley and Bondurant remained stone-faced. Evangeline simply maintained her beatific patrician aura.

"Excuse me," Myrna said, "I have to visit the ladies' room."

She rose and quick-timed away before anyone could say a word. She needed time to rehearse her story before the questions began.

Bondurant restarted the discussion. "Well, Professor, what do you think?"

Thumper took a breath. "It's something to consider. I trust you don't need a commitment right here tonight."

"No, of course not," Bondurant replied. "Plenty of time to mull it over. We wouldn't expect anything less than your complete comfort with the project and your role in fulfilling the vision we have for it."

Nate Plummer spoke up. "I have another vision for a role you might be interested in."

"And what would that be?"

"It's no secret I'll be making a bid for the Senate next year. I'm going to need someone to spearhead that effort, someone familiar with campaign strategy."

"So you'd like me to help you find someone for that job?"

"Don't be coy, Thumper. You know as well as I that you miss being in the game. There's no way your father would have hung on to his seat those last few terms without your savvy and behind-the-scenes counsel. I know his passing hit you hard, but it's time to get off the sidelines and return to the fight. There's a lot at stake here and I'm offering you the chance to help make a difference in the fortunes of our state. And the whole country for that matter."

Thumper looked at Smith Bondurant, then back at Nate Plummer. "You fellows seem intent on keeping me pretty busy. Maybe way too busy. How would I have time to consult on the Pymsdale project while also helping with a Senate campaign? And don't forget, I have an estate to run and a hunt club I'm mostly responsible for."

"I'm sure you could find the time," Plummer replied. "The Pymsdale project is still a good ways off. Smith has to decide on a site, then work out the land acquisition, permitting, design, so much to do before the first shovel of dirt gets turned. It'll be awhile before your input on the historical stuff is needed. Meantime, most of what I'll need your help with will be next spring and summer, shouldn't interrupt much with your hunting routine."

"I don't know, Nate. Tempting. It's all very tempting. Give me some time to think it over." He turned to Janey. "And discuss it with my own strategist. I'm not just making life changing decisions on my own now."

The remark surprised Janey. If she had any doubts about how serious their relationship was, that one remark went a long way to settle her mind.

The group's attention was distracted again when Myrna reentered the room. As she retook her seat at the table, Thumper turned to her and said, "Is there more than one lunch group of old Foxcroft gals?"

Myrna tried to remain nonchalant, and avoided eye contact with Bondurant. "I suppose there is. You remember the tradition at the school, where the girls are divided into two teams, Foxes and Hounds? Kind of like the Hogwarts houses, like Gryffindor and Hufflepuff." She looked to Evangeline for support. "You went to Foxcroft, right?

Where you a Fox or a Hound?"

"That was quite a long time ago, before you or Claudette were there. But, yes, I remember. I was a Fox."

"And so was this woman." She held up the card she'd been given. "I was a Hound. The group I've been meeting for lunch are all fellow Hounds. They call themselves the Lunch Pack. I didn't know there was a Fox lunch group too. They must meet on different days."

"Oh, I see," Thumper said. "Maybe y'all should get together sometime for a big group lunch."

"Yes, maybe so. But it's not really my place. I'm just joining in while I'm here, a little distraction while I'm waiting for my agent to call."

"Oh, right." He turned to the rest of the group. "As much as I'd like to hang around with you good folks all night, Janey and I have an early flight to catch in the morning. Her niece back in Minnesota is getting married this weekend. So if y'all will excuse us..."

As the group moved toward the exit, Bondurant touched Myrna's arm and the two of them dropped back behind the others.

Without looking directly at her, he said, "You're a better actress than you give yourself credit for. And very good at improv too. That Fox and Hound thing was brilliant."

"I was afraid something like this would happen. I told you I didn't want to come, too much chance I'd run into someone like her. But you insisted."

"I wanted you to be here when Cuyler and I made the pitch to your brother. After all, unless we can get him on board, your deal can't happen. So now you can work your magic on him at home. We're all on the same team here, right? No Foxes or Hounds, just all after the same thing at the end of the chase."

The main street of Middleburg was ghostly quiet as the group stepped out of the three-centuries-old building. The autumn night breeze carried a perfumed reminder that they were just a few blocks away from open pastures and thick woods. Forty miles to the east the heat island effect around Washington produced temperatures ten degrees warmer. There the atmosphere was filled with the aroma of more than half a million people and their collective detritus packed into a confined space. Here they inhaled the pungent smell of a small Virginia town at the close of a fruitful harvest season, like the sharp tang of apple cider freshly squeezed from an old oaken press.

Janey, Myrna, and Evangline chatted about the weekend's wedding plans for Janey's niece as they walked to the cars.

Nate Plummer placed a hand on Thumper's shoulder and led him aside. "Give this all some serious thought," he said. "I'm really thinking about your best interest. I owe that to you, and to your father's memory. I wouldn't be where I am had it not been for his help. And his career would have ended much sooner had it not been for yours. We'd make a helluva team, Thumper. And this Pymsdale thing, I think that's worth considering too. Also for both your father's legacy and your own best interests."

"I need some time, Nate. But, yes, I'll give it some thought and let you know."

As Plummer rejoined Corley and Bondurant, Thumper stood alone between the two threesomes; ladies on one side, men on the other. He looked up and down the quiet streets of Middleburg. Here the rhythms of country life promised a dependable consistency. Government administrations came and went. Senatorial campaigns were won and lost. But Middleburg, and a diminishing number of other old Virginia villages, Paradise Gap among them, still remained largely unchanged.

But for how much longer? *His best interest.* Is that what Nate Plummer was really concerned about? Or was he just using his persuasive skills to bolster the chances of approval for Pymsdale's project, wherever they chose to build it? And was Nate's offer of a spot on his senatorial campaign sincere? Or was it a ploy to help pave the way for Thumper to sign on with Pymsdale?

Pave! Ah, yes. Pavement. Macadam. Asphalt. Tarmac. If Bondurant succeeds, some part of Virginia will be paved with hundreds, possibly thousands, of acres of the stuff, entombing the once verdant fields of someone's property beneath a suffocating crust of black death.

The steamroller nightmare flashed in his mind.

"I think we've laid some solid foundation tonight," Plummer said to Corley and Bondurant. "But it's possible we might still need that extra incentive."

"My man is working on that," Bondurant said. "His contacts assure him there's sufficient evidence to be had and arrangements are being laid to get that to him, and then on to me."

Plummer turned to Corley. "Are you good with this, Cuyler? Personally, I hope we don't have to use it. It would come at quite a cost to our friendship with Thumper."

"My dear cousin could use a wake up call about the realities of life. He's been living in his little bubble of wealth and peace for too damn long. A dose of hard bargaining might do him good."

****

Back at Montfair, Janey and Myrna went straight upstairs to bed. Thumper told Janey he'd join her shortly, needed a little more time to unwind. Yes, he knew they had to be up early to get to the airport. He wouldn't be long.

He poured three fingers of Wasmund's Copper Fox single malt Virginia whiskey and stood in his study looking at the family photos mounted on the wall. One of them showed his father presenting a large, ornate trophy to a short man wearing a rumpled brown suit and a striped tie. Bright sunlight gleamed off Leeland Corley's bald head. A blanketed racehorse stood behind them. Jockey, trainer, and wives flanked them, two much younger men—Thumper and Cuyler—stood at opposite ends.

Thumper's gaze moved to the imposing portrait of his great-grandfather, Thaddeus the First, hung at the room's focal point above the large fieldstone fireplace. On the thick oak mantel was a framed five-by-seven of three lean teenage boys standing in front of a towering pile of hay bales stacked on an old flatbed trailer. The boys were wearing sweat-soaked tee shirts, jeans, and cowboy boots. Their pose—arms around each other's shoulders—spoke of the camaraderie born of shared labor.

The boy in the middle, between Thumper and Ryman, was older and taller, broad shouldered, with a charismatic smile and a playful tuft of hair curled over his forehead. He looked to be a blend of James Dean's lovable rebel and John Wayne's rugged manliness.

Two years after that shot was taken on a hot August day during haying operations at Fair Enough Farm, Teedy McKendrick shipped out with his Marine unit to a distant country with an odd-sounding name. He did not come back.

The McKenricks arrived later than the Billingtons into what was then undeveloped frontier. They did not participate in the "peculiar institution" that allowed one group of people to own other human beings as chattel property. They farmed the land themselves and were beholden to no one. When invaders marched down from the North, they took up arms to defend themselves, their land, all they worked so hard to create out of rough, untamed country.

How, Thumper thought, could the new invaders, a bunch of Californians, capture the true spirit of these local stories in their resort project? Who was he kidding? They weren't interested in capturing any of it, only in profiting off the repackaging of history for popular consumption. The struggles of conscience his ancestors faced over such gargantuan issues as rebelling against the most powerful empire in the world, determining how to create a new nation and governmental system in the aftermath of their improbable victory, what do about the abhorrent but entrenched problem of slavery, and then a devastating conflict that divided families, cost more than half a million American lives, and left a substantial part of the country in ruins from which recovery took decades—these tales defied storybook packaging. The result would more likely be a puerile distortion; the grisly meat of history ground up into a pabulum of easily swallowed mush.

But with his knowledge and family lineage, could he make a difference? If he agreed to serve as Pymsdale's consultant, could he make sure the historical theme of this resort embodied an accurate, unbiased account of the truth? Or would he find his counsel overridden by the corporate higher-ups unwilling to sacrifice profitability for truth?

He looked at his watch. Only a few short hours before he had to be up and on the road to Dulles Airport. Maybe he could catch a nap on the flight to Minnesota. He slurped down the remains of his single malt and dragged himself upstairs to bed.

****

Barstow Reinhardt was still awake. He sat in his habitual spot for contemplative thought, a rumpled lawn chair parked in front of the small trailer he'd called home for much of his adult life. Shirtless and with one strap of his bib overalls loosened, the cool night air felt refreshing on his bare flesh. The laces of his Red Wing boots were unfastened and he was two cans into the six-pack of Budweiser on the ground beside him.

A black vulture, part of the flock he fed and considered his friends and pets, stirred in a nearby tree.

"Are you Reggie or Heathcliffe?" he said to the bird. "Hard to tell in the dark. Well, guess what. My old pal Drago showed up here. Never thought I'd see him again. I don't think you guys would like him much. Hell, y'all don't really like me that much. Probably just waiting for me to kick off for your next meal." He raised his beer can toward the bird. "But I respect you for that. You guys get a bad rap, but you're not killers. Your job is to clean up everyone else's mess. Can't say the same for people like Drago and me. We were the ones creating the mess."

He took a long swig of beer, shook his head, and went on. "I gotta tell you, we did some stupid shit back in the day. But, y'know, the people we were dealing with were bad dudes. They pretty much got what they deserved. Most of them I guess. Besides, it wasn't like blowing up villages with innocent women and children in a country we shouldn't have been in anyway. I paid my price, watched my buddies get shot to pieces and blown up all around me. Left part of my face there. What did it matter if I skirted around some rules when I got home? Figured I was entitled to some slack. Right?"

He finished the beer in his hand and reached for another.

"But I gotta tell you, Reggie old boy, that Drago, he was a different sort. Said he was Special Ops but I was never sure that was for real. Never answered any questions about where he was or what he did. Sure, lots of guys were like that, too painful to talk about that crazy shit. But, still, something about him just didn't seem right. And the more we did, the worse he got, like he was enjoying every bit of it, and needed more.

"I didn't tell him I was leaving, just split from the coast and snuck off, ended up here. Seemed like a good place to hide out for a while. Never thought I'd still be here after all these years. Lucky for you guys, though."

He looked around at the thick woods that encircled his trailer. "My own little oasis, just me and my birds. Besides, I figured Drago was probably dead or serving life without parole somewhere, San Quentin or maybe even Pelican Bay. This place may not be the Ritz, but it sure beats the shit out of an eight-by-ten concrete cell.

"And now that son-of-a-bitch shows up here and wants to make like it's old times. Dragomir-Fucking-Korth! How the hell did he know where I was? How long has he known? Probably just sitting on that intel all these years, just waiting for a time he might need to use me for something. I gotta tell, you, Reg, I damn near shit my overalls when I heard that voice. So what do I do? Says he just wants my help for details about the local residents, who's who, where their weak points are, where some leverage could be applied to help them see things the way certain people would like them to be seen.

"'Certain people.' Haven't heard that for a long damn time. But I know what he meant and it ain't a good thing. Figured I was done with 'certain people.' But it appears I ain't, not quite yet. What the fuck is going on around here that he'd be involved in? Tell you what, Reg, you and the rest of the flock keep your ears open. When you're munching on a deer carcass along the road somewhere, if you hear anything, let me know, will you? Meanwhile, I reckon I got no choice but to play along. For now anyway."

Chapter 25

Gloriana was awakened early Saturday morning by a ringtone she knew too well. She grabbed the phone from the nightstand, silenced the ringer, slipped out of bed and ducked into the bathroom. With the door closed, her finger hovered over the "Accept" button. She did not want to answer the call, but knew she had no choice. "Yes?"

"I have some information for you to pass along to our friend," Drago said. "Tell him the circus will soon be in town after making a stop in Costa Rica."

He could read the tension in Glo's jaw as she replied with a curt, "Fine."

"You got a problem with this?"

"No. I'll do as I'm told. As always."

"Good. You're well compensated for your service, are you not? For this and other duties our friend entrusts you with?"

"Yes, I am. It's just that…I mean, things seem to be getting…sort of…deeper. All this cloak-and-dagger stuff, coded messages. Calling me at home. It wasn't like that when we started."

Drago's voice was calm and sounded reassuring. "Perhaps the way our friend prefers to handle these communications, that we channel the information through you rather than directly between ourselves, is causing you too much stress. If you're no longer comfortable with the arrangement, I'm sure you could be relieved of your involvement in these activities." A hint of threat infused his next remark. "And relieved of a few other things as well."

Glo knew what that could mean, and the consequences were more than she could face. "No, I'm okay. You know you can count on me."

"Good. Now, here are some of the details our friend needs to know."

With the call finished, she returned to bed.

Half-asleep, her husband asked who that was.

"Just something from work, about the East Coast project. The site agent helping Mr. Bondurant seems to have trouble remembering what day it is or that he's three hours ahead of us. You go back to sleep."

He grunted and drifted off. Glo remained wide-awake.

****

Two thousand miles away and two hours ahead, Thumper and Janey were enjoying a leisurely morning at a motel in Clara City, Minnesota, before heading off to the Lutheran church for her niece's wedding. The accommodations were adequate but no comparison to the service and luxury of a typical Pymsdale property or the Salamander Resort. Facilities of that caliber were scarce in southwestern Minnesota. For Janey, who had slept in thatch huts and under the open sky of the Kalahari, the comforts of the Quality Inn were more than sufficient.

Another thousand miles to the east, and one more hour ahead, the Montfair Hunt was enjoying a spirited morning of sport under the leadership of Elizabeth Billington subbing for her absent father. Myrna had accepted Reverend Davenport's offer to ride with him as a car follower. He was still learning his way around the unmarked, crisscrossing network of unpaved lanes and barely visible farm roads, and his Mini Cooper was ill suited for much of the terrain compared to the trucks and SUVs others drove. But he managed to keep positioned well enough for some decent views of the hounds and hunters.

With the action concluded, members gathered around the tailgate table.

Cecelia Broadhurst glided in beside Elizabeth. "When you have a minute, there's something I need to tell you," she said with a note of urgency.

Elizabeth nodded and the two women walked off a short distance from the crowd.

"Rhetta asked me to come to her place the other day," Cecelia began. "At first I thought she was trying to come up with another plan to get Bar off her property. But this time she was talking about selling the entire farm."

"You're kidding. Why would she do that?"

"Simple. Money. A whole lot of it."

"Someone's offered to buy the place?"

"Seems so. Not a firm offer yet, just in the discussion stage at this point, she says. She wanted to get my take on what I thought the farm is worth, see if the figure the prospective buyer tossed out is fair."

"And?"

"If it turns into a legitimate offer, it's more than fair. In fact, so much more than I think the property would be worth on the open market, it makes me wonder if the offer is legit."

"Did she tell you who's making the offer?"

"She did. It's your cousin Cuyler and his new best friend, Smith Bondurant."

"The Pymsdale guy! He and Cuyler want to build their resort on Fair Enough Farm?"

"Part of it anyway. They need more than just the Fair Enough acreage. Rhetta says Cuyler showed her a map of the planned facility. It includes her property, Worsham's place, and part of Montfair."

"What? How could that be? My father would never sell any part of our property. Certainly not for something like this. And even if he was thinking about it, he'd surely have told me."

"Rhetta said Cuyler and this Bondurant fellow told her the portion of Montfair they're looking at doesn't technically belong to Thumper. They said he's just the 'caretaker' they called it. The actual owner is someone else, but they wouldn't tell her who."

Elizabeth knew who. Her father had gone over the estate planning details with her in case something happened to him. Lawyerly prudence. She knew how her grandparents had divided the Montfair property and the restrictions they placed on it.

She looked over at Myrna, happily chatting with the good vicar.

Cecelia continued. "Rhetta said they told her the offer was contingent on the adjoining property owners agreeing to sell. Had to be a package deal."

"Thanks for letting me know."

Elizabeth's first impulse was to grab Myrna by the arm, drag her away from Reverend Dan, and have it out with her right there. But she took a breath, decided not make a scene in front of the members of the hunt, and did her best to maintain her composure. The confrontation would have to wait until she had Myrna alone back at Montfair.

****

Elizabeth rushed through her post-hunt chores. With her horse turned out and her tack put away, she stormed through the mudroom door and into the kitchen.

"Where's Myrna?" she asked Natasha.

Taken aback by the young woman's angry tone, Natasha hesitated for a moment, then replied, "I am thinking she is in her room. There is problem?"

"Oh, yes, there is problem." She marched down the hallway, sprinted up the stairs, and barged into the guest room where she found Myrna curled up in an oversized chair reading *People* magazine. "What the hell are you up to?"

"What are you talking about?" Myrna's gut tightened as she sensed she'd been found out, but she drew on her acting skills to sound sweetly innocent. "What could I possibly be up to?"

"Trying to make a deal to sell your part of Montfair, that's what. And to that Pymsdale guy of all people, for some monstrous resort. On our family land! And the McKendricks' too! Are you out of your mind?"

"Who told you that? I haven't made any such deal." Maybe there was some way to wiggle out of this. She'd been careful to leave no record of her discussions with Bondurant, no paper trail that could link her to any negotiations. What was the term she'd heard her father and brother use about crafty politicians? *Plausible deniability.* She cranked up the glow of confused innocence.

"Maybe not yet," Elizabeth countered, "but you're definitely working on something. Tell me the truth, are you or are not trying to cut some kind of a deal with Bondurant and your cousin Cuyler?"

"Well, yes, they mentioned something about that. But I didn't think they were serious, just asking around about possible land deals, wondering if there was any way I might consider selling my part of Montfair."

"And did you know they've made a tentative offer to Rhetta for all of her farm?"

"No, I had no idea."

"Well, according to Cecelia, they're waving a huge amount of money in front of her. And they showed her a map of their planned project, a large chunk of which just happens to align with the part of Montfair my grandparents assigned to you. They told Rhetta my father is just the 'caretaker' and they're negotiating with the 'real owner.' That could only be you."

Sensing her wiggling chances were narrowing, Myrna tried another tactic. "I guess it depends on how you define 'negotiations.' I thought it was just a passing thought. You know how those types are. Always looking to make a deal, lining up as many possibilities as they can to see which one works out best."

Elizabeth paused and an ugly realization struck her. "Wait a minute. Why would they say something to you about this? And why are you just conveniently back in Virginia, after all this time of basically disowning us? There's no sitcom role coming up, is there? And Cuyler and this Bondurant guy didn't approach you. You brought up the idea to them. You've been going behind my father's back, trying to pull off some kind of deal that would destroy Montfair. How could you?"

Myrna threw the magazine to the floor and stood up to defend herself. "You have no idea what I've been through. You and your perfect, privileged life! You don't know what it's like to struggle, years of rejection, dead broke, no one to count on." She sneered at Elizabeth. "Look at you. Daddy's girl. The best schools, everything paid for, a nice car, clothes, horses, a secure future thanks to your father's connections. You have no right to interfere in what I'm trying to do. What I *have* to do."

"I have every right. Yes, I'm a privileged white girl. But you don't know me, what I think, what I stand for. You've never been a part of my life. So, okay, I don't know what you've had to struggle through, or are dealing with now. But whose fault is that? You chose to leave us out of your life after my grandparents died. And now you show up giving us a bunch of BS about a role in some new sitcom, when all along the real reason for you being here is to try to sell your part of the family property, and for some huge resort that will ruin this whole place. If you think I'm upset, what do you think my father is going to say when he hears about this?"

"I hope he'll understand. I'm desperate. I have to make this work. You have no idea."

"I think I know my father well enough that, no, he's not going to understand. In fact, it's probably best you not be here when he gets home. Get your stuff together and get out of here."

"What! You're kicking me out?"

"Damn right I am."

"But…but where will I go? I don't have a car, I have nowhere else to stay. You can't just throw me out. I'm family!"

"You haven't acted like family, going behind my father's back like this, lying to everyone about why you're here. So you don't deserve to be treated like family. But maybe there's one family member you can count on. Why don't you call cousin Cuyler? I'm sure he'd be happy to help you out. After all, he's got a lot riding on what you're trying to do." She picked up Myrna's phone and handed it to her. "Here. I'm sure you have his number at the top of your favorites. Give him a call."

Myrna reached out defiantly and took the phone. "Fine. If that's how you want it, I will." She punched in the number and he answered quickly.

Elizabeth stood listening to Myrna's side of the conversation.

When the call ended, Myrna said, "Cuyler says he has a cabin not far from here, a place his father used on hunting weekends. He says he's kept it up and I can stay there. But he's in meetings and won't be able to drive me there till much later."

"I know the place. I'll have Voytek take you. Get your stuff together. You're out of here in ten minutes."

Elizabeth stomped out of the room, reached for her phone, and started to call her father. But she stopped, considered where he probably was at that moment, and thought better. If the wedding hadn't already started, it would begin soon, followed by the reception well into the evening. The next day would be more visiting with Janey's family. He didn't need a distraction like this in the middle of all that. No, better to wait till he got home Sunday night.

****

Voytek knew to stay out of Billington family squabbles. He made no inquiry about why his passenger was crying or the reason for her ejection from the main house. He carried her bags into the cabin, nodded politely, and left.

Myrna called Cuyler. "What will I do now? Elizabeth has probably already told Thumper. Or at least he'll find out soon. There's no way he'll let me sell now. I'm screwed, Cuyler. My life is over."

"Now, hold on. Don't do anything drastic. Smith and I are working on another angle that could give your brother an incentive to go along with the deal."

"Naming the conference center after our father and making him the historical consultant isn't going to work now. He might have gone for that if it was in some other part of the state. But on Billington land? Right next to the family home? Not a chance."

"Oh, I agree. But we sort of figured that already. It was just a little teaser to warm him up before we started the real squeeze."

"What are you talking about? Thumper hasn't lived a perfect life, but he's never hidden anything about it. You couldn't possibly have any dirt on him."

"My dear, sweet cousin. If you dig deep enough, there is always dirt somewhere."

The coolness in his voice was both reassuring and unsettling.

"Look," he said, "you just sit tight. I know the cabin isn't as luxurious as Montfair. But it's cozy and livable. There's an old truck around back that still runs. The larder has a few canned goods. You can run into town for anything else you need. Do you have any money?"

"Some left from what Glo loaned me."

"Good. Now just try to stay calm and leave everything to Smith and me. We knew we'd have to deal with Thumper seriously at some point. This comes a little sooner than we'd expected, but it's not going to throw everything off track. So, are you okay now? Not going to do anything foolish?"

"No, I'll be all right."

"Feel free to call me any time, day or night, if you need to talk. I'll keep you posted on how things are going. Maybe Smith and I can stop by sometime to give you some company."

She clicked off the call and immediately punched in Glo's number. She told her what had happened and the desperation in her voice made Glo fear her friend might do something rash.

"Maybe it's not as bad as it looks," Glo said. "I've been working for Mister Bondurant for several years and I've seen him make some deals that everyone else thought were impossible. I don't know how he does it, but he always seems to come through for the Pymsdale cause. And we both know how the Corleys work. Cuyler's shown himself to be every bit as sly and cunning as his old man when it comes to making land deals. I know Thumper's going to be pissed, beyond pissed really, volcanic probably. But you knew this was never going to be an easy sell, right?"

"No, I guess so. Maybe I just wasn't prepared for what would happen when I had to face up to my real reason for being here. That's me, always trying to avoid reality until it walks up and slaps me in the face."

"So you've been slapped. It's not the end of the mission, just part of the challenge. I don't know all the details, but I've picked up some information that makes me think Cuyler and Smith have something in their pocket that might help swing the deal."

"Cuyler said something like that too. But you know Thumper as well as anyone. He's no perfect angel, but I can't imagine there's anything in his past they could use against him now."

"It doesn't have to be *his* past. It could be someone else's past, someone he cares about deeply."

"I hadn't thought about that. You don't suppose it might have something to do with…"

"Look, there's no point in us speculating. My suggestion is you take a breath, sit tight, let Cuyler and Smith do their thing, and see where this goes. Can you do that?"

"I'll try."

"Good. Call me any time you need to talk. You know I'll always be here for you."

Myrna looked around at the cabin's interior. It was, as Cuyler said, cozy and livable. She'd be fine there for now, at least physically. Mentally was going to be a challenge.

Chapter 26

"Good talking to you, too, cousin," Cuyler said with a sarcastic smile as he clicked off his phone.

"Went well, did it?" Bondurant asked with an amused grin.

"Cousin Thumper is not happy with us. He made some unpleasant remarks regarding what he considers our outlandish duplicity and dishonesty, and tossed in some references to our maternal lineage for good measure."

"Not surprised. A shame that the old McKendrick bitch couldn't keep her mouth shut, even though we told her not to say anything."

"That's Rhetta. No one's ever been able to get her saddle broke. She's always gone her own way and never gave a damn about what anyone else thought. But on the upside, if she took the time to have Cecelia come out and give her an estimate on what she thinks the place is worth, that suggests she's seriously considering our offer."

"Won't mean a damn thing though if we can't get the Billington acreage too. I was hoping we'd have some more time to work on that angle. Mr. P. is getting anxious for us to wrap this up. I've never let him down before and I don't intend to start now. He wants this deal to happen, no matter what we have to do."

"Ah, shit, we knew Thumper wasn't going to go for that crap about making him the history director and naming the conference center after his old man. That was just what you'd call a diversionary tactic. We've still got the secret weapon your site agent is working on. And tomorrow we lay some groundwork for the squeeze on Rhetta."

"What time's he coming?"

"Two o'clock. Said he won't stick around for the tailgate after the Tuesday morning hunt, but can't miss the hunting part. Saint Hubert wouldn't approve."

Both men chuckled and shook their heads.

****

By Monday afternoon cabin fever was setting in on Myrna. Leeland Corley had put in a substantial stock of nice Virginia red wines, which was now down to a couple of dusty bottles. A bookshelf held a small collection of paperback novels, mostly there for decoration. (The Corleys were not known as avid readers of anything other than land sales contracts.) The wine and dog-eared books had kept Myrna distracted to a degree. But the food supply was running low and solitude was getting to her.

She fired up the old truck and drove to the Paradise Gap General Store. She hoped the floppy hat and large sunglasses would provide enough cover for her to grab a few things and get out of there before being recognized. She almost made it, but just as she finished paying and was about to leave, Luella Starret, proprietor of the store and local grapevine administrator, saw a glimmer of something familiar in this mysterious customer.

"Myrna? Myrna Billington? Or should I say Lola Leeland? Is that you?" Luella took Myrna's silence as confirmation. "I'd heard you'd made a guest appearance back in little old Paradise Gap. But we hadn't seen you here at the store. So glad you finally dropped by. How's everything going?"

Luella knew exactly how everything was going. She always did.

And Myrna knew, despite Luella's feigned ignorance and genial manner, that Luella knew every detail of how things were going. "Everything's fine. Nice to see you." She grabbed her groceries and hustled out the door.

Head down and walking fast, she almost slammed into Dragomir Korth who was leaning against the front of the old truck. Several canned items and a bottle of wine fell to the ground. Fortunately the wine bottle did not break.

Drago reached down to pick up the groceries as Myrna stood shaking, trying to hold back the tears. She was kicking herself for not driving the extra distance into a larger town where it was unlikely she'd be recognized. Nobody's radar could compare to Luella's perceptive skills.

Except perhaps Drago, who had the most disturbing ability to show up out of nowhere at inopportune times. But as he gathered up the fallen goods and put them back in the bag, he gently took Myrna's hand and said in a soothing voice, "Now, now, no need to be upset about dropping a few things. My fault for being in your way. I should have given you a heads-up."

A faint semblance of a smile attempted to break through his customary scowl. Myrna found it more creepy than comforting.

"So your plans have taken an unexpected turn," he said. "These things happen. Not to worry. Others are working on your behalf to achieve the result we all want. For now you must just be patient. Enjoy the solitude of your new residence, and appreciate whatever company shows up."

"And if that desired result doesn't happen?"

The creepy smile faded and the rigid scowl returned. "The consequences will not be pleasant. So I suggest you take whatever comfort comes along in the meantime."

Chapter 27

"Wish I could stay for the tailgate, but I've got an important meeting to get to," Ryman said as he hustled his horse onto the trailer.

"Saint Hubert sending you off on another wild goose chase?" Thumper asked.

"His name be praised! This could be the biggest thing to ever come along for the Church of Foxhunting. But I'm sworn to secrecy."

"Considering your wacky church thing is barely more than a year old, 'ever' covers a pretty short time span."

"Go ahead. Scoff like you always do. But I believe Saint Hubert will one day open your eyes and you'll see the truth."

"The only thing I'm seeing now is you ignoring some of your duties as joint-master of this hunt to go chasing some idiotic pseudo-religious mission."

"I did my duty as a whip this morning. And did we not have another great day, thanks to the blessings of our beloved Saint Hubert?"

"We had a great day thanks to a variety of factors like good scenting conditions, an excellent pack of hounds, a topnotch huntsman, and an ample population of foxes willing to oblige us with some harmless chases. Whether or not a little known figure who died thirteen hundred years ago had anything to do with it is highly questionable."

"Was it just this morning? Or has every hunting day been like this since Saint Hubert sent his message to me over a year ago? And yet you still refuse to see the light."

Thumper shook his head. "It's no use arguing with you. Go, get to your mysterious meeting. I hope you and Saint Humpty-Bump have a good time."

****

A few hours later Ryman was seated in Cuyler Corley's Fairfax office. Cuyler sat behind his desk with Ryman and Smith Bondurant in the two guest chairs.

"We're hearing a lot of good things about what you're doing," Cuyler said. "I suppose foxhunting was kind of a religion for my father, as it was for yours. You're just taking that a step further."

Ryman was excited to have such a receptive audience. "It's all about Saint Hubert, you see. His name be praised. He sent me the vision and I've just been following his lead ever since."

"And where," Smith asked, "do you see that vision going?"

"Well, to tell you the truth, I don't really know at this point. I know Saint Hubert wants me to spread the word. I went on a mission last year, visited several other hunts and shared the good news. Most folks received the message happily. And, of course, everywhere Nardell and I went the sport was excellent. But, well, I kinda ran out of money. So we had to come back home sooner than I'd hoped. But Saint Hubert has kept me busy working on other things. And then Thumper came up with his book, *The Foxhunter's Guide to Life and Love*, with his seven principles of the foxhunter model. It's the perfect next step to show people what a great example foxhunting is for how to live your life, to always be chasing something. Saint Hubert certainly guided Thumper's hand in writing it, even though he won't admit that."

"It sounds like you need a platform to work from, a way to get your message—Saint Hubert's message—to a wider audience," Smith said.

"Exactly. I haven't figured out how to make that happen yet, but I'm sure Saint Hubert will show me the way when the time is right."

Cuyler leaned forward across this desk and said, "Perhaps that time has just arrived."

****

Twenty minutes later Ryman praised Saint Hubert and pumped the other men's hands as they escorted him to the door.

"Just leave everything to us," Cuyler said. "Of course, if the opportunity comes up for you to put in a word or two where it's needed, I reckon that couldn't hurt."

"Oh, I will. I certainly will!" Ryman paused halfway out the door, turned back to Bondurant, and said, "I guess I misjudged you when we met at the horse show. Something didn't feel right then. But now I see how Saint Hubert was just preparing you for a role in his larger plan."

"And we're happy we can be part of that," Bondurant replied, as he pushed Ryman gently through the doorway. With the door closed, he turned to Cuyler and said, "Now there's a whack job if I've ever seen one."

"He's always been a bit of an odd bird," Cuyler replied. "But that bump on the head last year must have pushed him over the edge. Anyone who's been riding and hunting as long as Ryman has—like his whole damn life since he was a kid—probably can't count the number of concussions they've had over the years. I guess sometimes all it takes is just one too many and that's what you get."

"Seems like he took our offer seriously."

"Probably another result of his head bump. Anyone who thinks we're actually going to allow him to use our resort as a base for his crazy-ass religion has to be half a bubble out of plumb."

"I expect his mother's sharp enough to see through that. But, still, it can't hurt to have him pushing her along."

"At least she seems to be leaning our way. Worsham's fully on board. Now we just need to convince Thumper to let Myrna sell her part of the property. How's that coming?"

"My site agent says he's getting close to wrapping things up," Smith replied. "The tip from Nate Plummer was a good start and my agent's contacts have been busy tracking down the confirmation we need. Should have that finished up soon and once we have the irrefutable evidence, we can have a little chat with your cousin Thumper."

With a malevolent grin, Cuyler Corley said, "I can't wait to see the look on his face when we drop that bomb. How about the info on Shelton and the Costa Rica thing?"

"That's an easy one. He just needs to round up copies of the checks she's written. Of course, between you and me, that's all just a bluff, something to hold over the old lady if she needs a shove. I have some good friends who would prefer that not go public. But Rhetta wouldn't know that and just the thought of her precious granddaughter being implicated in something shady should do the trick."

"You've certainly got all the angles figured out," Cuyler said. "Even my old man could have learned a thing or two from you and Mr. P."

Bondurant looked toward the door through which Ryman had left. "Another thought just occurred to me," he mused. "One of those friends could make use of this Church of Foxhunting thing. Not in a way dear old Saint Hubert or his servant Ryman would appreciate, but that's of no concern to us. I've got to make a quick call."

****

The following morning Astrid was hustling along from her Arlington apartment to the PACA office when a large man appeared in front of her, blocking her path. As she tried to step around him, he moved to keep her from going forward.

"Hey," he said in a bright voice, "aren't you Astrid Stevenson, the head of People Against Cruelty to Animals?"

Always mindful of threats from those who opposed her work, she said, "Who wants to know?"

"My name's Korth. I've been a long time admirer of your work, especially your Costa Rica project. I have many friends there. There's also someone here in the States who's a mutual friend of ours."

"That's nice. I appreciate your support. But I need to get going. I have an early planning session with my staff and am already running late."

She tried to duck around him but he blocked her again.

"Our mutual friend said if I ever ran into you, he'd like me to give you a message, some information you might find useful."

His tone piqued her interest. "Who is this mutual friend?"

"His name is Smith."

"I know a lot of people named Smith."

"I'm sure you do, many with the last name Smith. But perhaps not so many with the first name Smith."

That got her full attention. "I'm listening."

Ten minutes later Astrid rushed into the PACA meeting room where her staff was waiting for her. "Clear the decks! Forget whatever was on the agenda! I just got some information that's going to shoot our fundraising through the roof!"

****

Ryman strolled into the showroom of McKendrick Farm & Home Equipment around mid-morning. Although not a hunting day, he wore his full autumn hunting kit—brown field boots, tan breeches, oxford shirt with a horse-and-hound themed tie, and tweed hacking jacket. He considered it his "clerical attire" and wore it every day as a mark of his position in the service of Saint Hubert.

After a year of such behavior, Bar Reinhardt was used to the display. But he still sniggered whenever Ryman made one of his rare appearances at the shop. "So what brings you into our humble little business today your reverend-ship? I don't suppose you've come to do any actual work."

"Work? In the service of our dear Saint Hubert, I'm working every day. And that work is about to be mightily blessed. I wanted to come by and share the good news."

"Unless it's that you've come to your senses and are ready to rejoin the world of sanity, I doubt the news is much good to us here."

"Oh, but it is! Saint Hubert has opened a path for his church to have a platform from which to preach the word, a platform that will reach many people and the word can be spread far and wide."

"Another one of your batshit crazy ideas no doubt."

"Doubt all you want, brother, but you'll see. I had a meeting yesterday with Cuyler Corley and Smith Bondurant. They've offered to set aside a special area at the resort they're planning that would serve as the base for the Ancient and Venerable Church of Ars Venatica. We can have regular services there, I can spread the word to all who come, and they've even mentioned letting me use the state-of-the-art high tech equipment they'll be installing to produce informational videos that will be seen around the world."

"And you believe all that crap?"

"It's not crap. It's for real. Now all I have to do is convince my mother to follow through on the offer they've made her."

"Good luck with that. Have you ever been able to convince your old lady of anything in your entire life?"

"I've never had Saint Hubert's help before. With his support, I believe she'll see what a great opportunity this is."

Ryman's enthusiasm ebbed as he realized what this would mean to Bar. "Oh, well, maybe not such a great opportunity for you. But I'm sure you'll find another place to live that's just as nice as what you've got now."

"Yeah, right. And I'm sure my birds will all just follow along wherever I go. But, hey, don't let that concern you. It all belongs to your old lady and if she decides to sell, well, the rest of us will just have to deal with it."

Miles Flanagan stepped out of the stockroom. He wore his tall black boots, canvas breeches, billowing white shirt, and gray cavalry jacket. "Do you really want your mother to sell out to those goddamn invaders and carpetbaggers?" he asked.

"Um, Cuyler Corley isn't exactly a carpetbagger," Ryman replied. "He's old Virginia, much more so than you are."

"Yeah, and he and his old man have spent their whole life ruining the countryside with their damn developments. And that other fella, what's his name, Bondurant? He's damn sure a carpetbagger. Shit, all the way from California. About as far away from Virginia as you can get. We gotta stop these people. Fucking invaders is what they are. And we in the 43rd Battalion know how to deal with invaders."

"First of all," Bar said, "watch your language in the shop. Second of all, how many times I gotta tell you to stop wearing your stupid re-enactor stuff to work? And number three, it ain't 1863 and you ain't reliving the Lost Cause." He looked at Ryman in his hunting attire and then back at Miles in his Partisan Ranger uniform. "Jesus, you're both batshit crazy." He walked away shaking his head and mumbling obscenities under his breath.

Ryman went to the office where Muriel Hudkins was processing invoices and Shelton was working on a spreadsheet of revenue projections.

"Good morning, Mister McKendrick," Muriel said. "It's so nice to see you."

"Nice to see you, too, Muriel. Everything going okay?"

"Just fine. And you?"

"Couldn't be better."

Shelton continued to stare at her computer screen.

"Miss Shelton," Muriel said, "your father's here."

"Huh?" She looked up with a vague gaze at Ryman. "Oh, hi Daddy. Sorry, I'm just really concentrating on this, didn't want to lose my train of thought."

"Sure. Sorry I interrupted. I gotta be going anyway." He gave Muriel a light wave and sheepishly backed out of the office.

Shelton's attention returned to her monitor.

"This invoice doesn't seem right," Muriel said. "I need to check on something in the stockroom."

When she was gone, Shelton picked up her phone and called Astrid.

"I can't talk right now," Astrid said. "Hugely busy. Have to call you back."

"We need to talk."

"Not a good time."

"How about dinner tonight?"

"No way. Gonna be working really late. We're gearing up for a new fundraising campaign. Huge opportunity and we need to get it done."

"When then? This is really important."

Astrid paused and looked at her schedule. "Okay, fine. The best I can do is squeeze in some time tomorrow afternoon, about three o'clock. Just for coffee and a quick chat. Can you do that?"

"I can."

"Okay. Usual place. See you then."

Chapter 28

Myrna heard the hunting horn off in the distance. She went to the front window of the cabin and waited to see if the hounds and hunters would pass by within view. Leeland Corley had positioned his cabin where woods framed the back and both sides while the front offered a panoramic view of rolling fields. The property was part of Montfair Hunt's prime territory and Myrna knew the Thursday morning action was likely to come that way.

Her patience was soon rewarded when she saw a reddish-brown figure dart into the scene running left to right. The fox stopped about a third of the way into the field, sat down and looked back toward where it had just come from. It was as if he was saying to the hounds, *Got you fooled back there with that trick at the creek, didn't I. But, okay, I'll wait a bit while you sort things out.* His ears pricked forward and Myrna heard the cry of the hounds strengthen as they found the line and came on in full chorus. The fox turned and resumed his lead, jogging at a leisurely pace, no hint of panic, confident that he could elude these inferior creatures at will.

Just as he went out of sight to the right of Myrna's field of vision, hounds emerged from the left. As a child she'd marveled at how Ivan Mooney knew every hound—as many as sixty or more in the kennel at any one time—by name, voice, and personality. The hounds now running before her were several generations beyond those of her youth. But Crispie O'Rourke had carried on Ivan's breeding program and these hounds looked very similar to those she'd known in her childhood. She almost expected to see Ivan—the wiry little man with the vein-marked bulbous nose who smelled of damp wool and fresh hay but always had a kind, gentle word and an elfish wink for an inquisitive little girl—coming into view behind his hounds.

It was, of course, Crispie O'Rourke—the lanky Irishman with a nose flattened by fights in barns and barrooms, a man Myrna barely knew—who burst into the scene. Where some huntsman in this situation would be cheering their hounds on with voice and horn, Crispie knew his hounds needed no such encouragement. He rode silently behind his pack, allowing them to do their job without interference. Myrna remembered hearing her father say many times that, "The huntsman who appears to be doing least is doing best."

"A lot of noise going on out there," a voice said from another room.

"The hunt's passing by," Myrna replied.

Smith Bondurant stepped out from the bedroom and joined her at the window in time to see Thumper leading his followers. They rode at a respectable distance behind Crispie, cantering gracefully across the field.

Myrna thought she saw Thumper turn his head briefly to look toward the cabin. She was glad Bondurant had parked his car behind the place. But did Thumper see him standing there at the window next to her?

"So that's what this foxhunting thing looks like," he said. "Seems kinda dangerous, don't you think?"

"It can be risky. But so are lots of other sports. I've had friends suffer some pretty serious injuries skiing. One person I knew even died."

He turned to face her. "Well, what's life without a little risk, eh?"

"My life will be more than a little risky if our deal doesn't go through."

"You know Cuyler and I are working hard on that."

"Are you? How much longer is it going to take? I can't keep going on like this."

"We're almost there. My agent is just wrapping up a couple of final details to make sure everything is solid and then we'll have a little chat with your brother."

"I can't believe you have something on him, something serious enough to force him to let me sell my part of Montfair." She turned back toward the window. "And mess up hunting for him and all the other hunt members."

"Well, we're not taking over the whole county. Just bringing some jobs and prosperity to a small part of it. They'll still have lots of land to do their silly foxhunting." He looked at his watch. "I've got to be going. You just stay tight here and I'll let you know as soon as we're ready to move."

As he drove away, Myrna's phone sounded with Glo's ringtone.

"Just wanted to see how you're doing," Glo said. "Holding up okay?"

"As well as can be expected, I guess. But this waiting is really starting to wear on me. Your boss keeps telling me to be patient, that he and Cuyler are working on some secret thing that will force Thumper to give in."

"When did he tell you that?"

"Just now, right before he left."

"He was at the cabin?"

"Yeah."

"Was Cuyler there with him?"

"No just him."

"Just him and you, alone?"

"Yes."

"Dammit! I was afraid this might happen. I should have never put you in touch with him."

"What are you talking about? He's my only hope. Maybe you don't fully understand the pressure I'm under. A very scary man keeps telling me I have to do whatever's necessary to make this deal happen. And if I don't, there are going to be much worse consequences than...well, worse than...you know..."

"Yes, I know. I know only too well. Better than you can imagine."

"What? You too?"

"No, not me, thank God. But let's just say there's a pattern here. I can't tell you what to do, I can only say be careful, that's all. I don't want you getting hurt."

"And I don't want to get hurt, which is what I'm facing if Thumper can't be convinced to let me sell. Do you have any idea what Smith and Cuyler are talking about?"

"I was never privy to inside family matters. But with the family so involved in politics for many generations, maybe there's something there, some dark secret from the past."

"Now that I think about it, Cuyler did make a comment that whatever it is may not be about Thumper's past, but someone else's, someone he cares about."

"So maybe they do have something. If so, let's hope they can use it soon, and it does what it needs to do. In the meantime, as your friend, just try to be careful. There are some people involved in this who don't care about anyone or anything other than what's good for them."

"You think I don't know that? To be honest, I suppose you could include me in that group. I'm willing to see my own brother forced to do something he'll totally not want to do, allow a bunch of outsiders to ruin his cherished lifestyle just to get me out of a bad situation. And one totally of my own making. So who's really using who here?"

Chapter 29

"You look tired," Muriel said.

Shelton sat at her desk, staring at her computer screen.

"Why don't you go home and get some rest," Muriel suggested. "You've been working day and night. The shop's doing fine. Bar and I can handle things for now." She chose not to say anything about Shelton's appearance. Between her efforts to keep the family business from going under and her unsettled rift with Astrid since the *Auntie Mame* incident, Shelton's sleep pattern had been erratic and her personal grooming slack. Her hair was a mangled mess and she looked and smelled like she'd spent the night in the clothes she was wearing.

"I can't," she said. "I have to drive into Arlington for an important meeting, something personal."

"Things not going well with your friend?"

"I don't know. But that's what I need to find out." She looked at her watch. "Damn, I have to get going. I may be back this evening, or maybe not till tomorrow morning. Depends on how things go this afternoon."

Two hours later an even more tired, disheveled, and self-questioning Shelton McKendrick sat at a tiny corner table in the Arlington Hyatt's Cityhouse restaurant, close to Astrid's PACA headquarters. On the drive in Shelton had fortified herself with a twenty-ounce dose of straight Starbuck's. No frilly drinks for her. She needed high-octane coffee, and lots of it.

She dangled one flat shoe from the toe of her foot and felt the twenty ounces of caffeinated beverage work its invigorating magic on her nervous system. Just as its effects began to press on her bladder, Astrid Stevenson strode in. Too late to hit the ladies' room now.

They embraced awkwardly, like unfamiliar cousins at a family reunion.

"Sorry I'm so rushed," Astrid said, taking a seat. "But some information has just come my way and we're not wasting any time moving on it. It's a gift from the fundraising gods."

"I'm sure that will help you further your good work for animal welfare."

"Yes, absolutely. And it's something you might find interesting too. But let's set the shop talk aside. You were pretty insistent about seeing me. This must be really important."

"It is to me. The question is, how important is it to you?"

"How important is what?"

Shelton flipped a finger back and forth between them. "Us, that's what. If you remember, the last time we saw each other we argued over a scene in a silly movie and you banished me to your couch for the night. I sneaked out the next morning and went home. Things have been…I guess we can say…a bit cool since."

"And you came here just to make up with me?" She reached out, placed a hand on Shelton's, and smiled warmly. "That's so sweet. And I forgive you for defending that horrible movie." She noticed Shelton's hand was shaking slightly.

Shelton drew her hand back as the waiter arrived. Astrid ordered regular coffee, Shelton asked for decaf.

"When did you switch to decaf?" Astrid asked as the waiter left. "I thought you loved your caffeine."

"I guess you can get too much of a good thing."

Astrid sat back and took in Shelton's appearance: the disarray of hair and clothing, eyes reddened from lack of sleep, the absence of even a hint of any cosmetic touches, hands shaking mildly, but a firm set to her square McKendrick jaw.

"Have we had too much of a good thing?" Astrid asked. "Did you come here to give me the brush off? If so, I must say it was very noble of you to do it face-to-face." Astrid folded her arms and gave Shelton a hard stare.

"No, of course that's not why I came. I came for the exact opposite reason. I wanted to know if it's you who plans to brush *me* off."

The waiter returned with their coffee and they both sat in uncomfortable silence as he placed the cups before them. "Regular for the lady, and decaf for...the other lady."

Shelton could not bear the sight of the sloshing brown liquid. The pressure on her bladder was approaching critical proportions.

"Is that what you think?" Astrid asked. "That I'm giving you the brush off?"

"The thought has crossed my mind."

Astrid took Shelton's hand again. It was shaking even more now. "No, I'm not brushing you off,"—a playful grin illuminated her face—"Sheltie Lou."

Shelton blushed and could not suppress a smile at the nickname Astrid had turned into a term of endearment. Her doubts eased, the "brush off" concerns waned, and she felt a renewed vigor to be with this vibrant, intoxicating woman.

"In fact," Astrid continued, "I need your help with this new project. It's in an area where you have special expertise."

Shelton assumed it had something to do with veterinary pharmaceuticals. "Um, well, sure, I'll be happy to help if I can. Why don't you tell me all about it over dinner tonight, and then we can..."

"It'll have to be a late dinner, I'm afraid. No telling when I'll get out of there. In fact, I need to get back pretty soon. Let me just give you a quick taste of what this is all about."

There was something else Shelton was longing to taste. But it looked like that would have to wait until later. "Can you give me just a minute to run to the ladies' room?"

"This won't take long. Remember the movie we were watching? *Auntie Mame*?"

"I really need to…"

"And you said you were into foxhunting as a child? And people you know still do it?"

Shelton's interest in her bladder was temporarily distracted. "Yeah, I remember."

"Well, of all things, a couple of days ago I received some information alerting me to a truly startling development. Some wacko out there where you grew up is trying to turn foxhunting into a *religion*. Can you *believe* that?"

Shelton was speechless. How did Astrid find out? And did she know the wacko was Shelton's father?

"Can you imagine the fundraising potential from something like this? We're working hard on the campaign now." Astrid became more animated than Shelton had ever seen her. Her eyes sparkled, her hands fluttered. A glow of pure energy shined around her. "This is even better than Santeria. I mean, their animal sacrifices are no less horrid. But they have this veil of cultural mysticism, which makes some people hesitant to interfere. Plus there was that annoying Supreme Court ruling in their favor. And besides, they pretty much limit their sacrifices to chickens. And only our most ardent supporters give a damn about chickens. But foxes! And rich white people thinking they can justify torturing and killing them, tearing them to pieces with a pack of wild dogs in the name of *religion*!"

"Well, they don't actually…"

"We're drawing up the press material now, putting together the graphics. This could make our entire year, put us way over the projections we'd made for…"

"I can't help you."

Shelton's blunt statement halted Astrid's enthusiasm.

"What do you mean? I thought you said you'd put all that behind you. And I thought you were as committed to helping animals as I am?"

"I'd like to think I am, or at least I was before I had to come back to Virginia to help save our family business. What I did every day as a pharma rep helped animals by helping the vets who care for them. I was out there on the road, in the vets' offices. I smelled the disinfectant, the urine, and the feces. I saw the animals, what they say with their eyes, the fear, the pain, the trust. I saw the owners, people who love their animals like their own children, who would do anything to help them, who will spend their last dime, even go into debt, for their beloved pet."

"Oh my God. That's beautiful. Yes, that was your mission. And maybe one day you can return to it, your true calling. We're both committed to the same thing, just in different ways."

"Maybe. We're certainly looking at it from different levels."

"What do you mean?"

"You're flying at thirty thousand feet, way above the situation on the ground. I was down in the trenches, doing the hard, gritty work."

"Are you saying what we do at PACA isn't hard work?"

"I'm just saying there might be a disconnect here."

"Oh, that we're not 'connected' to the animals?" Astrid sat back and crossed her arms again. Her sparkle faded. "I see. Just because we're, like you said, at thirty thousand feet, we're not as committed as you were."

"Oh, I'm sure you're committed. I'm just not sure to what."

"How could you say that? I've devoted my life to helping animals. It's what I do for long, grueling hours every day."

"Are you really committed to helping animals? Or are you mostly committed to raising money? I could almost see the dollar signs flashing in your eyes."

"Shelton, it takes money to carry out our mission. All the good intentions in the world don't matter if you can't act on them."

"And just what are your intentions?"

"What? What do you mean? You know what we stand for. We're about protecting animals, fighting cruelty…"

"Yes, yes, I know all that. But I've been doing some research into just how that mission is getting carried out. And, frankly, I don't see much real action. What I see is mostly fundraising and then spending the money on lobbying, salaries, a hefty pension fund, and then more fundraising."

"Where did you get that nonsense? Our enemies are always trying to spread those lies about…" A flash of insight blazed across her face. "Wait a minute. Foxhunting. The North American Fox Chasers Association. Their offices are out there, where you're from. That's always their line. 'PACA is just ripping people off, using animal rights as a way to raise money, but then not spending it on helping animals.' Please don't tell me you've bought into that BS."

"I'm not taking anything for granted, from either side. But I do know one thing. You're wrong about foxhunting, and I won't help you with this in any way." Shelton thought about what Astrid's efforts would mean to her family and friends in Crutchfield County. She imagined her father's image distorted into some crazed, cult-like figure, splattered on the Internet with a plea to send money to PACA so they could stop this hideous practice of terrorizing and killing foxes, breeding dogs to be nothing more than killing machines, putting innocent horses at risk of injury. And now, adding a whole new level of offense, claiming this was all done in the name of religion. Astrid was right about the fundraising potential. And her efforts had to be stopped.

"I see," Astrid said. "So you still have a soft spot for this…this barbarism. And you claim to have been out there on the road every day helping animals. Who's really the hypocrite here?"

"You think you know, but you don't. You just have your own prejudiced ideas. You've never been within a hundred miles of a foxhunt. You have no idea what really happens. You don't know these people or what their lives are really like. But you won't hesitate to destroy them so you can get people to send you money."

"Well," Astrid said calmly, an ironic smile wreathing her mouth, "it looks like we're right back to the *Auntie Mame* night. I think we're done here."

"I think so."

"Aren't you glad you came here just to see little old me?"

"As a matter of fact, yes, I am glad. Although not for the reason I thought I'd be."

"Well, it was fun while it lasted." Astrid stood up. "I need to get back to the office. I have a new campaign to develop."

Shelton stood and leaned across the small table, causing Astrid to recoil as her former lover's bulk intruded into her space. With her hair shooting out in all directions, a strong body odor hitting Astrid's tender nostrils, and the look of pure fury on her broad face, Shelton was a daunting image. "If you insist on going through with this, not only will I not help you, I'll fight you in every way I can. You have no idea what goes on out there, who these people are, what they do, or why they do it. But they're *my* people. And I love them. You do anything to hurt them, especially my father, and you'll regret you ever met me."

Astrid was ill equipped to handle physical confrontations. Her legs shook and her mouth went dry. How could this large, lovable woman turn into such a frightening figure? Her father? He was involved in this?

Perhaps this relationship had been doomed from the start. Thank goodness for *Auntie Mame*!

Shelton lingered for a moment, enjoying the fear and confusion in Astrid's eyes. Then she said calmly, "I have to use the ladies' room. Then I'm out of here. For good." She pointed at the two untouched cups of coffee. "You get the check."

She barreled out of the restaurant leaving Astrid standing by the table watching her go.

****

Shelton did not want to admit that she hid in the ladies' room, but she took her time. She waited as long as possible before she emerged from the stall and ventured out into the hotel lobby. Once she was sure Astrid was gone, she collapsed into a stuffed chair and let all the pent up tension drain from her tired body.

Her fingers went to the medallion around her neck, a movement ingrained from years of habit when deep in thought. It only took a second for her to realize what she'd overlooked in the heat of her encounter with Astrid. There was no way now for her to ask Astrid to return her original Saint Hubert medal. But there was another possibility. Not only had Shelton forgotten to ask about the medal, Astrid had failed to ask Shelton to return the key to her condo. Astrid would be tied up at her office for hours. Shelton remembered slipping the medals into the drawer of the end table beside the sofa where she'd slept that night. There was a good chance the other one would still be there.

With quick steps, short breath, and jangling nerves, Shelton covered the three blocks to Astrid's building and minutes later let herself into the condo unit. She pulled open the drawer and to her relief there was the precious medallion. She slipped the chain over her neck and laid the key on the end table. Turning to leave, she thought she heard something—a voice, Astrid's voice, coming from the bedroom. Then another voice, this one male.

Shelton's first impulse was to flee. She had what she'd come for. The relationship with Astrid was over. No need for another confrontation, and one likely to be even uglier if Astrid caught her sneaking into her home.

Then she heard the voices again, louder this time, with an urgent, rhythmic tone.

Shelton had to find out what was going on. She went to the bedroom door, gathered her courage, and flung the door open.

The first detail Shelton took in was the sight of a man's pale white butt cheeks. A pair of slender, feminine legs were wrapped around the back of his thighs.

At the sound of her entrance, the man rolled off Astrid and faced the intruder. "Holy shit! Who are you?"

Astrid sat up. "What are you doing here? I can have you arrested for breaking and entering."

Shelton's surprise morphed quickly into the realization that this was her hand to play. "Afraid not. I had a key, which you gave me. No crime there. But, hey, go ahead call the cops. I'm sure they'd understand what you're doing here with His Honor."

"You know who I am?" The man began to gather a sheet around him, as if covering his genitals would conceal his identity.

"Yes, I know who you are." Shelton reached into her jacket pocket and pulled out her phone. She pointed it at the bed and began taking pictures. "You're hearing the Thirteenth Amendment case that Astrid's pushing through the courts, trying to claim the 'involuntary servitude' thing applies to animals." She turned the phone toward Astrid. "Entering a motion before the bench, are you?"

"Bitch! You couldn't stand me dumping you, could you? Came slinking back to ask my forgiveness."

"Not hardly. If I'd wanted to do that, I'd have gone to

your office, where you're supposed to be, working on your new fundraising campaign. I came here to get something I left behind, and to leave your key as I sure won't have any further need of it. And look what I found."

She swung the phone back toward the judge and clicked another shot.

"Get that damn thing from her!" Astrid shouted at the man.

He obediently arose from the bed and moved toward Shelton. Middle-aged, paunchy around the belly, flabby in the arms and chest, Shelton did not feel particularly threatened by this naked, pathetic man.

He made a half-hearted effort to snatch the phone.

Shelton blocked the man's grab with her left hand.

His eyes widened at the strength of her grip.

She bent his hand back and he dropped to his knees.

Astrid started to get off the bed and try for the phone. But Shelton shot her a look that froze her in place. Astrid knew she was no match physically for the younger, stronger woman. "You won't get away this, barging in here like this. What I do in my own bedroom is none of your concern."

"It is now," Shelton said. "You'll do anything, use anyone, to get what you want. But you're not going to use my family and friends to line your own pockets. If you go after them with this new campaign, these photos of you and His Honor will be posted for the world to see. Do we understand each other?" She gave the judge's hand one more hard twist and then released it. He crumpled into a fleshy pile. "Court's adjourned."

Chapter 30

The image of Opening Day for formal hunt season is what most people see in the classic paintings that hang in hotel lobbies and on the walls of banks and dentist offices. Gentlemen riders don their scarlet coats, ladies ride in elegant sidesaddle finery, well-muscled horses gleam and prance, hounds swirl about, eager for the chase.

A semblance of this scene greeted Tobias Johnson as he drove up the Montfair driveway on Saturday morning, the last weekend of October. The reality was slightly less elegant but still impressive. There were several men, and two ladies, wearing scarlet. As a joint-master, Mildred Preston was entitled to wear red and Patti Vestor's position as professional staff entitled her to do so. But most of the gentlemen and all of the other ladies wore black coats. There were three ladies riding sidesaddle, their turnout partly identical to the images of yesteryear with flowing skirts and shadbelly jackets. But rather than the standard top hats and veils of old, both wore harnessed safety helmets and one had a protective vest over her torso.

The weather offered the chance for a decent day of hunting, although the conditions were less than perfect. A chilly wind rolled down from the mountains and the sky was iron gray. The sunless sky threatened at least a light sprinkle, maybe even a steady downpour.

Thumper, Janey, and Elizabeth rode from the Montfair barn out onto the main lawn where the hunters and spectators were gathered. Knobby mountains formed a sequence of gentle mounds off to one side, a scalloped line fading off into the misty horizon. Open fields lay before them, the verdant glow of summer now faded into a light greenish-yellow and flecked with patches of umber.

A stiff breeze rattled through the woods and scattered a tumult of leaves, billowing and swirling around the horses' legs. The wind passed and the leaves drifted down to the dank soil.

Thumper saw Tobias walking from his car toward the assembled crowd. A woman approached him and extended a hand.

"I see Shelton found your friend," Thumper said to Elizabeth. "He'll get a good tutorial on our wacky sport car-following with her."

Elizabeth studied the steel-gray clouds on the western horizon. "Let's hope we can get some sport in for him to see before the rain hits." She then looked around at the tents and tables where the post-hunt breakfast would be laid out.

Ryman appeared by her side. "Not to worry," he said brightly. "Saint Hubert has assured me it will be a glorious day, perfect for hunting, the rain will pass around us, and our celebration in his glorious name will not be marred."

"You're in an especially good mood this morning," Thumper said.

"And why not?" Ryman replied. "Saint Hubert is working in wonderful ways to assure his word will go forth for all to hear."

Janey listened intently and made mental notes of everything Ryman said.

"And how," Thumper asked, "do you see that happening when you don't seem to be able to get the word out to anything more than a corner of Crutchfield County?"

"Ah, a corner may be all that's needed. The trick is for the world to come to that corner."

"You're losing it more every day, old buddy."

"Not losing, old friend, gaining! Gaining and winning. His name be praised! Now let's welcome everyone and go have some fun."

With opening announcements made, Crispie moved off with hounds toward the south, behind the main house. A fox awaited just inside the woods edge where the land rose toward a sharp ridge. Hounds opened and the chase began. The fox jogged upward, made a sharp right turn, dashed back toward the Montfair front lawn, past the tents and tables, and picked up speed heading toward Fair Enough Farm.

The spectators and car-followers were still milling around and had to move out of the way as the riders came cantering across the lawn. Tobias focused on the form of Elizabeth as she raced past. She glanced over at him, raised her hunt whip in a quick salute, smiled, and then turned her focus back to the chase.

The fox led hounds toward the McKendrick house and then south again, back onto Montfair land, through Myrna's portion of the estate, and on to Worsham's. As Ryman had predicted, the storm clouds split and passed around the hunting action. The sky above turned to a powdery gray and the air remained comfortably cool for the heavily clad, hard riding chasers. The pursuit continued for two hours through much of Montfair's prime territory and everyone agreed it was one of the best Opening Meets in recent memory. A few were even willing to join in with Ryman when the fox finally went to ground in their praise of Saint Hubert's blessing.

Those following by truck and car also benefited from the fox's choice of path. Multiple times he emerged from the cover of woods into open fields and close to farm roads where the followers were afforded a panoramic view of Sir Charles in full flight, hounds in full cry, close but a safe distance behind. The field of riders, with Thumper in the lead and Elizabeth next in line, happily cruised along in the hounds' wake. Janey, still relatively new to foxhunting and absent any seniority, remained farther back.

Tobias, a skilled interviewer, found Shelton to be an excellent source of information as she provided a running narration throughout the action. On the drive back in, she reversed the roles and became the questioner.

"How did you and Elizabeth meet?" she asked.

"Through a UVA alumni group."

"I thought she still has one more year to go."

"She does. But as coordinator for the local chapter, I like to get out introductions to those who'll be graduating soon, give them a head start on being part of the group."

"How do you like being a reporter?"

"Well, it certainly is an interesting line of work, especially these days. Has its challenges, but I thrive on that. I like to get into the weeds on what I'm chasing, dig up the details, get the whole story, not just sound bites and sensational headlines. My main beat is Capitol Hill, but I have the freedom to work on other stories as well."

"Working on something like that now?"

"Got a few things I'm looking into."

"Such as?"

"Well, at the top of the list is an animal rights group that might be up to some shenanigans."

Shelton's stomach tightened. "Really? What group is that?"

"Something called People Against Cruelty to Animals. PACA for short. You might have heard of it. They get a lot of coverage for some of their more outlandish fundraising tactics."

"Yeah, I've heard of them. So what kind of shenanigans have they been up to?"

"Well, it's all still speculative at this point. I can't go public with anything until I have reliable evidence to back it up. But the suspicions have to do with their efforts to establish a branch operation in Costa Rica, some suggestions that this might actually be a front for something else. Although at this point it's still pretty shadowy about what that something else might be. Seems like a lot of money has been raised earmarked for that project and it's possible some of that's been done to evade taxes. The rest might just be from well-meaning folks who've been duped into thinking it's really for helping stray dogs in San José."

Shelton thought about the checks she'd written to PACA, for a hefty amount in total, and all of them with "Costa Rica" entered in the memo line. She tried to sound nonchalant as she asked, "So will this be, like, a TV investigative report when you're ready to go live?"

"That's the goal. Of course, we can only do so much on TV these days. The full details would be published online, might do a podcast on it too."

She turned into the Montfair main entrance.

"Well, we're back," Tobias said. "That was really quite an experience. Thank you so much for chauffeuring me and filling me in on all the details."

"Yeah, sure," Shelton replied absently, "any time."

She remained in the car as Tobias got out and walked toward the tables where an elaborate post-hunt breakfast awaited. Was she one of those duped by Astrid's Costa Rica project? Was it really a tax evasion scam? Or something worse? Could she be implicated in whatever it was because of her donations and her personal relationship with Astrid? For some well-meaning person to respond to a tear-jerking TV ad and send in a few dollars was one thing. But for a person sleeping with the head of PACA to make substantial contributions specifically noted for a potentially dubious cause…well, that might be a different matter.

As various scenarios ran through her mind, she saw herself forced to make a plea deal with government investigators. The video of Astrid in bed with the judge just might come in handy for something more than stopping her now ex-lover from using foxhunting as a fundraising ploy.

****

Thumper, Elizabeth, and Janey arrived at the breakfast to find Tobias chatting with the sidesaddle ladies. They were explaining how they found "riding aside" preferable to "riding astride" and defining the tradition and function of their attire.

Tobias took the arrival of the hosts to excuse himself.

"Doctor Billington," he said, "I wonder if I could have a few minutes of your time. Something I'd like to get your counsel on."

"Sure, fire away."

Glancing back toward Elizabeth, he added, "Well, more in private if we could."

Thumper was intrigued by the slightly conspiratorial tone. "Yeah, okay. Let's take a walk."

They nodded to Elizabeth and Janey, then walked off away from the crowd.

"Elizabeth's birthday is coming up soon," Tobias said.

"Yes, I know. I was there when it happened."

"Right. I was wondering…I mean…I thought you might have a suggestion if I wanted to…y'know…get her something."

Thumper found the young man's awkwardness endearing. The request also piqued his curiosity about the status of this budding relationship. "She's not easy to buy for, is she? I can relate to your situation. But to give you some help here, I need a bit more input. Are we talking a small, thoughtful friendship gift? Or something more serious, a personal, meaningful gesture?"

"Um, maybe somewhere in between?"

Thumper chuckled and placed a hand on Tobias's shoulder. "A pivotal point for you two?"

"Possibly."

"Okay, here's what I'd suggest. She'll love anything from the Horse Country store in Warrenton. If you want to lean more toward the casual end, just do a gift certificate. It'll show you recognize what she likes, more personal than, say, an Amazon gift card, but far from a suggestion of intimacy. However, if you want to go more that way, they have some really nice jewelry to pick from, some of it antique, most of it very distinctive. Pretty wide price range."

"Sounds perfect."

"If you decide to go with a piece of jewelry, ask for the owner, Marion Maggiolo. She knows Elizabeth and would be able to suggest something suitable. Of course, if you opt for the gift certificate, you can just do that online."

Thumper could see the wheels turning in Tobias's head. Which way would he go? Thumper would be on the lookout to see if a new piece of jewelry showed up on his daughter.

Their stroll had taken them to the crest of a gentle hill that looked down onto the main lawn where nearly a hundred people were gathered—eating, drinking, talking, laughing. Both men stood in silent contemplation watching the crowd below.

Thumper's parents would have recognized that scene. The attire of some non-riding attendees varied from how folks dressed in the previous generation's time, as did the size and shape of most of the vehicles parked along the lawn's edge. But there was not a shred of difference in how the hunters looked. All scarlet and black coats had been replaced with earth-tone tweed hacking jackets worn over vests and white stock ties, above breeches and mud-splattered boots. With helmets now hung in trailers, the headgear consisted of billed caps (most bearing the Montfair Hunt name and logo), straw hats, or tweed newsboys. Thus the nearly universal presence of harnessed safety helmets would not have interfered with the sight of hunt caps, bowlers, and top hats that were standard headgear in Thad and CeeCee's time.

The surrounding landscape would not only be recognizable to Thumper's father but to his grandfather and others before him as well: the sweeping expanse of the lawn down to Montfair Lane, the stately oaks lining the half-mile long driveway, the pastures and outbuildings, and just to the east, a portion of the McKendricks' house and barn could be glimpsed through the trees.

That view, enjoyed by generations of Billingtons and shared with their friends and neighbors, would be devastated by the appearance of a massive resort facility if the Pymsdale project went forward. It would mean a sudden and vast upheaval to the way of life for virtually everyone, not just the privileged few, in that part of Crutchfield County.

Tobias was first to break the silence. "Thank you, Doctor Billington. You've been very helpful."

"Please, drop the 'Doctor' stuff. 'Thumper' is fine."

Tobias nodded. He turned and noticed a small, enclosed area just behind them. A wrought iron fence, about four feet high, enclosed what appeared to be a small cemetery. Tobias saw perhaps a dozen tombstones, most of them thin and plain. Some leaned at a slight angle, others were sharply tilted, close to toppling over. Two or three graves were marked simply by flat stones on the ground. Where inscriptions were still visible, they were faint at best. The carvings had not been deep when first made and had since been worn down from long exposure to the elements. A large oak tree along the back of the enclosure provided some shade but little shelter.

The plot was neatly trimmed and the iron fence showed a recent coat of black paint. A gate hung along the front fence line, the latch secured by a padlock.

"The final resting place of your ancestors?" Tobias asked.

"Ah…no," Thumper replied. "Not any Billingtons buried there." He turned and started to walk back toward the gathering below. "C'mon. The ladies will be wondering what's taking us so long."

"Who then?" Tobias asked, catching up with Thumper.

"Oh, mostly people who lived and worked here at the farm."

"Family had a lot of 'workers,' did they?"

"It was a big, productive farm at one time. A very labor-intensive operation, back before motorized machinery. So, yes, the family had its share of help."

"'Help'?"

Thumper stopped. "Okay. A lame euphemism. Not a piece of family history we're especially proud of. Can't change the past though. We can only press on for a better future."

"Amen."

Tobias looked back once more at the grave plot as Thumper continued to amble toward the party.

Rejoining Elizabeth, Tobias said, "You don't see many old private cemeteries these days. It must really give you a strong connection to the land to have people who lived and worked here buried right on the property."

"I guess for some," she replied. "But it was always just a creepy old place to me."

"I thought it looked very nice. The size and condition of the grave markers suggest the people buried there weren't very prominent folks. But I will say it's nicely maintained."

She pointed toward a second story window at the corner of the house. "That's my room. Kind of weird to grow up with a cemetery right outside your bedroom window. My grandfather gave it a lot of attention, and my father has Voytek keep up. But I pretty much avoid it."

"Your father didn't seem to want to give it much attention when we were up there just now. We were having a nice chat, but when I asked about the cemetery, he just walked away."

"He has a lot on his mind, a difficult family situation we're dealing with. I'm sure he didn't mean to be rude or anything."

"Oh, he wasn't rude. Just…well, I suppose he wanted to get back to the party."

"I'm sure that's all it was."

Thumper was chatting with Bing Sensabaugh when he glanced back up toward the cemetery. He missed the rest of what Bing was saying as a segment of his recurring nightmare—the image of a crushing wave of asphalt washing over the ancient graves—flashed through his mind.

Chapter 31

"Seems like I've become right popular these days," Rhetta said to Myrna as they sat at the kitchen table at Fair Enough Farm. "First you, then I got Ryman coming by later and Thumper after him. 'Course, your cousin Cuyler and his new buddy, that Bondurant fellow, are pushing me to sell the place."

"I don't want to push you. You have to do what you think is best. But just so you know, the only way I can make the deal happen on my side is if you also agree to sell."

Rhetta smiled and gave Myrna an affectionate pat on the hand. "I remember how you used to gab with your mother and me about the movies. We'd all sit around this same table and go on and on about which actors and actresses were doing what, which movies we liked and which we didn't. Your mother and me agreed on most things, but you had your own opinions, being the younger generation. We liked the sweet romantic things, with lots of music. You were more into the edgy stuff."

She took a sip of coffee and continued. "I gotta admit I was jealous when you quit school and took off for Hollywood. I just knew you were gonna make it big." She shook her head. "But I guess things didn't work out. You got a lot more talent than most of those gals who became stars. Just bad luck I reckon. I expect most of them got where they are by sleeping with the right people, and I knew you'd never stoop to that, being a Billington and all."

"Maybe I wasn't really as talented as you thought I was. And let's be honest, I wasn't going to make it on my looks alone."

"Bah! You got your own beauty. Don't let nobody tell you different."

"What I have got is a load of trouble if this deal doesn't happen."

"And I'm sorry you're in a tough situation. But let's be honest, no matter what I decide to do, do you really think your brother's not going to do everything possible to keep you from selling that part of Montfair? And, like you said, unless we both do the deal, and Frank Worsham too, the whole thing's off anyway. So I reckon we're all just whistlin' Dixie."

"We know Frank's hot for the deal," Myrna said. "He was already planning to sell his farm even before this Pymsdale project came up. And, well, Cuyler tells me he might have some way of persuading Thumper to agree to let me sell. He won't say what it is. Sounds kind of cloak-and-dagger like. So I have to ask, if there is a way to make that happen, will you be willing to sell too? I've got to know there's some hope this will work out. If it doesn't, I'll be in some really bad trouble."

Rhetta studied the desperation on Myrna's face. Was this for real? Or was she a better actress than most people thought? "Y'know, I always wished I'd had a daughter. I kinda envied CeeCee having two girls, and naming them after two of our favorite actresses. Things didn't go very well with my two boys. One died young, for no good damn reason, and the other's gone nuts. There was no point asking Fergus to go with the names of any of my favorite actors. Had to be old Scottish-sounding family names. I kinda look at Shelton as a daughter now. Her real mother abandoned her years ago. So I guess my main concern is what selling the farm would mean to her."

"And...?"

"Well, she's not interested in keeping the place going as a working farm. And I guess there won't be any more little McKendricks coming along, given her...y'know...lifestyle and all."

Myrna thought about pointing out options such as adoption and in vitro fertilization but realized that would just provide more reason for Rhetta to not sell and caught herself in time. Instead she said, "So she might be better off not having to deal with what to do with this place if, well, y'know if something happened to you."

"If? Hell, child, you mean when. I plan to be around a while longer, but ain't none of us gonna be here forever. Tell you what, I'll give it some more thought on my end, you see what kind of cloak-and-dagger crap Cuyler's got up his sleeve, and we'll see how things go from there. You okay with that?"

Myrna realized that was the best she was going to get at that point. "Yeah, I'm okay with that, for now."

****

Rhetta kept her session with Ryman to the front porch. She could only tolerate his Saint Hubert ravings for a few minutes at a time.

"I just wanted you to know," he began, "that Saint Hubert wants you to make the deal with Pymsdale."

"Well, ain't that nice of him. He's branched out from sending you messages about foxhunting to advising you on land deals. Got yourself a multi-talented saint there, don't ya?"

"But this land deal *is* about foxhunting. Cuyler and Smith have said there will be a section of the resort dedicated to it, its history and practice, and they want me to be in charge of that. It'll be a wonderful platform for spreading Saint Hubert's message, one that will reach far beyond just the actual foxhunting community. Everyone who visits the resort will get to hear Saint Hubert's message. And that means people from all over, not just this country but from around the world."

"Are you really dumb enough to believe they're going to let you do that? They're just using you to help persuade me to do the deal."

"No, it's true! I had a meeting with them last week at Cuyler's office. They showed me the plans and everything. Every Pymsdale resort has a theme tied to the local history. And the theme here will be about Virginia's horse history, not just foxhunting but racing, with a big spread about Secretariat, polo, the part that horses played in the Revolution and the Civil War, Teddy Roosevelt's famous ride from Washington to Warrenton and back all in one day, the old remount station in Front Royal that supplied the army with horses right up till the end of World War Two. Someone needs to oversee all that and they said if I was willing to take the job, I could include a section about Saint Hubert. I mean, he is the patron saint of hunters, so there's some connection there, right?"

"Yeah, I suppose so. Are they offering to pay you for all this? Or does your Saint Hubert buddy want you to do it for free in exchange for spreading his word?"

"It's a paid position, and a pretty nice figure, too. Sheltie Lou, Bar, and Muriel have the shop under control. So I can devote all my time to the resort project and not have to rely on the shop for any income."

"Huh. Well, it would be nice for you to finally have a real job. Even if it does mean you won't be giving up your stupid-ass Saint Hubert crap. Now you do realize that if I agree to sell the farm, that means your buddy Bar and all his damn birds will have to find some other place to live."

"Yes, I know. We talked about that the other day after I met with Cuyler and Smith. I was kinda surprised, but he seemed sorta okay with it. I guess with Daddy dying last year, Sheltie Lou coming back to help out, and Bar taking over more duties at the shop—hell, he's even gotta wear a shirt and clean overalls now—maybe he's accepting the fact that sometimes things just have to change. No matter how much you'd like them to stay the same."

"I reckon that's true. I'm giving this whole thing a good thinking over. Cain't say just which way I'm leaning, but I'll let you know once I make up my mind. Whichever way I go, it's gonna make some folks right happy, others not so much." She looked down at Abel who'd been sitting beside her throughout the conversation. "C'mon, dog."

She turned and went back in the house with Abel behind her, leaving her son standing alone on the porch.

****

Thumper pulled up a few hours later. He noticed the old horse in the side paddock. "Minnie Dee, hey buddy. I hope we didn't cause you any problems when we came by the other day. Looked like you were ready to go along with us."

The horse did not lift his head, just kept munching on the fresh pile of hay set out for him.

Thumper continued on into the house and took a seat in the kitchen where Rhetta had a cup of coffee waiting for him.

"We can't let this happen," he said. "I won't let it happen. You know I'll never give my permission for Myrna to sell her share of the property. If Frank Worsham wants to sell his place to Cuyler for a retirement home, that's a separate matter. And we might be able to work around that. But this Pymsdale resort? No way, not a chance."

"It ain't for me to know all the details about how your folks set things up with the family property, but I reckon they made you the boss of it."

"Not exactly. The will states that if one of us wants to sell, the other two have to agree. I've talked to Claudette and she's leaving it up to me."

"Kinda puts you in a tough spot, don't it?"

"Not really. I can understand her being less adamant about it than I am. I think she's always felt guilty that she wasn't a better sister to Myrna, should have tried to be more supportive and helpful instead of just brushing her off as a starry-eyed, airheaded kid."

"And you don't have any brotherly guilt?"

"Yeah, sure. I suppose I was also dismissive. Never really took an interest in her acting career. Such as it was. But not so guilty that I'd allow generations of our family heritage to be destroyed because she's let herself get in a tough situation."

"Any idea just how tough it is?"

"No, not really. But I can't imagine it's a life-or-death kind of thing."

"Maybe you need to find out."

"Look, my parents made me the steward of Montfair. I may only be a one-third owner, but they entrusted me to watch over the estate and do whatever I could to preserve it. You know how they felt about it. No one was closer to my mother than you were. I don't think she'd want to see everything around here turned upside down by some massive resort facility, do you?"

"I can't speak for what your mother would want. I expect she might be inclined to put some thought into her daughter's welfare in a time of need. Maybe put that above what happens to a piece of ground."

"Montfair is more than just a piece of ground. And Fair Enough means a lot to the McKendrick clan too. Could you really see yourself letting this place go? Not pass it on to Ryman, or Shelton? And whoever comes after them?"

Rhetta rose from the table, went to the counter, and refilled her coffee mug. She could see Minstrel's Delight through the side windows. Still looking at the horse, she said, "Did I ever tell you about what losing the family farm did to my daddy?"

"No," Thumper said. "I don't believe you ever did."

"It wasn't much, but it was *our* place and my daddy was right proud of it. He scratched out enough to make a living, but most of us kids—there were eleven of us—had to start working young to help make ends meet. For me it was breaking and training horses for folks like your father and his friends." Her grim memory lightened briefly to a wistful smile. "That's how I met your momma." The sadness returned. "Anyway, there were some bad years. Too much rain, or no rain at all. Some blights destroyed the crops. Like most small farmers, the place was mortgaged to the hilt. Well, long story short, the bank foreclosed and we lost the farm. No one else wanted it as a working farm, so some speculator bought it, figuring it would be ripe for splitting up and putting houses on it in a few years. Meanwhile, the place just sat there. The ground went fallow, the house rotted down to a shell, the barn fell into a pile of kindling.

"Meanwhile, all Daddy could think about was getting that damn place back. It was a matter of pride to him, thought he'd failed as a man. He took any job he could find, usually two or three at a time, saved every damn penny he got his hands on. He was gonna buy that goddamn farm back if it killed him. This went on for about ten years or so. Then one day that speculator started building houses on it. Daddy went by every day and watched them bulldoze what was left of the house and haul it all away. He watched them grade out the land, put in the sewer lines, pour the foundations, lay out and pave the streets, and then build a bunch of little brick houses. 'Ramblers' they're called. Didn't look like they rambled much to me. Not much bigger than a tractor shed. But people bought them up.

"That was when Daddy finally realized he was never going to get the farm back. Wasn't any farm left to get back. Once it was all paved over and built on, that was it. Kinda sent him off the deep end, I reckon. He started spending the money he'd saved up all those years on hard liquor. Didn't work much after that. Pretty much stayed drunk 'round the clock. Took him about two years to drink himself to death. Probably would of happened a lot sooner with most men but, y'know, us Keanes come from right sturdy stock. Takes awhile to kill us even when we're trying."

Her misty blue eyes came slowly back to Thumper. "And now I've got a piece of land. And some big-talking developers want to give me a whole lot of money for it, more than it's actually worth from what Cecelia tells me. Maybe I should take the money while I can, get one up on the developers to even things out a bit for what happened to my daddy."

Thumper sat in silence for several seconds. The steamroller dream flashed through his mind and the illusionary odor of creosote tingled his nose. He then said, "And your pig-headed neighbor stands in the way. If I won't let Myrna sell her land, the deal's off for you."

"Yep, boils down to that."

She turned back to the window and pointed a bony finger toward Minstrel's Delight. "That damn old horse already outlived Ivan. And Fergus too. Now just a matter of which one of us goes next." An impish grin lightened her face. "I'm betting on me winning that one."

He rose to leave. "I have no doubt you will."

As he started backing his Jag out of the driveway, his eye caught a gray lump in the paddock. He pulled back in, got out of the car, and walked toward the enclosure.

"Minnie Dee?" he called out.

No response.

He clapped his hands three times.

Nothing.

He looked carefully to see if there was any movement, even a hint of breathing.

Not a trace.

He rested his head on the top fence board. "Well," he said aloud, raising back up, "at least you got to see the hunt one last time. And I expect you and Ivan are back together, chasing foxes around through the fields of Elysium."

He remembered how invigorated the horse had looked a few weeks earlier—a final burst of energy before succumbing to the inevitable passage into eternity.

Turning from the paddock, he went back to the house. Standing in the front foyer, he called out, "Rhetta? Where are you?"

"I'm right here. No need to holler," she said as she came down the hallway from the kitchen. "You have a change of heart about letting Myrna sell?" she teased. But when she saw the expression on Thumper's face, she recognized the characteristic look of a Billington bearing bad news. "What is it?" she asked coolly.

No sugarcoating was required. "Minnie Dee's dead."

Her expression did not change at first. But then one corner of her mouth turned up into a faint smile. "Told you I'd outlive that old horse."

Chapter 32

A white van rumbled along the driveway to Worshams' house. Frank waited on the front lawn, Merle at his side. The van stopped, Cuyler Corley stepped out from the driver's seat and opened the sliding door to the passenger area. An elderly man, wearing a rumpled brown suit, sat in a wheelchair. Cuyler operated the controls that lowered the chair from the van onto the ground. Once securely in place, Cuyler let out a sharp whistle and two black Labrador retrievers leapt from the vehicle.

The dogs bounded over to Merle and the threesome took off for a fun romp around the farm.

"Been a long time since they've had a chance to run free like this," Cuyler said to Frank. "Daddy was still duck hunting right up till he had the stroke, spending a lot of time at his place down on the river. Never went anywhere without Lukey and Danny. Been tough on them the past year."

"They're welcome here anytime," Frank replied. "How's your father doing?"

"He has good days and bad. The physical situation is pretty much stable. Mentally and emotionally it's kind of up and down. Some days he doesn't know where he is or who's who. Doesn't even recognize me. But he always knows who Lukey and Danny are. They pretty much never leave his side." He looked at the three dogs cavorting across the fields. "Except for a chance to do something like this. And then some days he's more lucid. His speech is slurred, but you can understand most of what he's saying, when he feels like talking."

Cuyler turned to Leeland. "Daddy, this is the place I was telling you about. You remember Frank, don't you? You and Momma used to ride through here with the hunt. If you look off that way, you can see Montfair." He pointed toward a spot where a portion of roof could be seen through the tattered remains of fall foliage. "They're hunting around here this morning, we might even be able to see or at least hear them if they come this way."

Leeland showed no visible response to his son's words. He gazed blankly at the rolling countryside before him.

Cuyler continued. "Frank here has agreed to sell his place to us. We're going to build a lovely retirement home right on this spot. It'll be a wonderful place for you and others. Lots of fresh air, beautiful views, best of care in every way. And if things work out for the McKendricks' place and part of Montfair, the rest of Frank's property will be part of a fabulous resort the Pymsdale folks are planning to build."

The sound of Crispie's horn in the distance caught Cuyler's ear. He turned toward the direction it came from and saw a few hounds emerging from the woods below. They were still searching for a line to follow, spread out and working hard with sterns aloft.

Leeland's head snapped up at the sound. His vague gaze changed to a focused stare.

"Better call the dogs in," Frank said.

"Right," Cuyler replied. "Lukey! Danny! Come boys!"

The two labs obeyed, along with Merle, and the three dogs sat obediently between the men as they all watched the hounds working below.

One hound let out a loud "Awooo!" and the others went to him, circling around the spot and searching for the scent. Another hound confirmed the find, then another and with that the pack was off on the line heading up the hill toward Worsham's house.

Leeland Corley began to make a clucking sound. His hands moved from the sides of the wheelchair to his lap. He raised his hands slightly and closed his fingers as if holding reins. He rocked back and forth in a gentle, rhythmic cantering motion.

A flash of reddish fur appeared at the crest of the hill.

"Tally ho!" Leeland called out, in a loud, clear voice that took Cuyler and Frank by surprise. "There he is! On to him! On to him!"

He eyes widened and the pace of his motion, though bound in the chair, quickened.

"That's right, Daddy," Cuyler said. "The hunt's coming right by us. Just like when you and Momma were following hounds. Isn't this great!"

The fox saw the men and dogs ahead and made a sharp turn to his left. He knew where Frank's cattle pastures were and it would be a handy place to foul his scent and throw the hounds off.

Hounds soon reached the spot where the fox had turned. The sudden move put them at a loss briefly as the lead hounds overran the line. But the wiser members of the pack knew the trick, quickly regained the line, and got their mates back on the right path.

Crispie rode behind his hounds, letting them do the job they were bred and trained to do. The field of riders, with Thumper in the lead, came a short distance behind.

Thumper saw the men in Worsham's front yard, doffed his hunt cap and saluted them as he rode by. The followers, all wearing harnessed safety helmets, raised a hand to acknowledge the landowner who allowed them to hunt on his property.

Leeland raised his right hand and returned the gesture. "On to him! On to him!" he shouted again.

Cuyler was dumbfounded at his father's behavior. "You all right, Daddy?"

"I'm fine boy! Just fine!" He continued to watch as the riders cantered along, heading toward a coop between two pastures. Cuyler could hear him softly counting strides as each rider approached the jump. "One, two, *three*! Nicely done. One, two, *oops*, took it long. One, two, three, nope, chipped in. One, two, three, ah that was a good one."

"This is the most alert he's been since the stroke hit," Cuyler remarked to Frank. Turning back to Leeland as the last rider went out of sight, he said, "Enjoy that did you, Daddy? Remind you of old times?"

Leeland looked up at his son, his eyes still clear and sharp. "What was that you said about building something here? Some kinda retirement home? And a resort those Pymsdale people want to build?"

"That's right. A lovely retirement home right here. And down there,"—he pointed toward Montfair and Fair Enough Farm—"a beautiful, elegant resort. First class, a real international jewel, people will come from all over."

"Like hell they will!" Leeland snapped.

"Of course they will, Daddy. Pymsdale properties are very popular. This one will be packed from day one."

"It won't be packed if it doesn't get built. And you're not going to build it."

"Well, sure, the deal's not finalized yet. Frank here has signed a letter of intent. We're still wrapping up some details on the McKendrick place and the part of Montfair that we need to make it work. But we'll get that hashed out and this will be Corley Development's jewel in our crown."

In his anger, the old man tried to rise from his wheelchair. The failed effort only served to fuel his rage. "Part of Montfair! You're going to build this thing on Montfair?"

"Well, just a part of it," Cuyler said sheepishly. "It won't touch the main part. Not the house or anything."

"Boy, you touch one square inch of Thad and CeeCee's place, and I swear to God I'll cut you off from everything!"

"Daddy, it's not Thad and CeeCee's place anymore. They're both gone now. You remember, there was that plane crash and…"

"I know they're dead, damn it! What? You think just because I can't walk I've lost my mind? But it will always be their place to me. And I'll be damned if I'm going to let you mess it up."

"Daddy, you need to calm down," Cuyler pleaded. "The doctor said you're not supposed to get excited or worked up. You could have another stroke."

Leeland took a breath and his irritation ebbed. "Look, son," he said gently. "We've made enough money to last several lifetimes. You've done well taking over the business. I'm proud of you for that. But maybe it's time to give it a rest. Leave this land alone, at least for now. Let an old man hold onto his memories a while longer." He looked again to where the last rider had gone out of sight into the woods below Worsham's house. The light in his eyes faded to a hazy glimmer. "Get me back in the van," he muttered.

****

Merle trotted behind Frank Worsham as the inseparable twosome entered the McKendricks' shop. Miles Flanagan was waiting behind the service counter with the repaired chainsaw Frank had come to retrieve. Frank was now accustomed to seeing Miles in his Partisan Ranger uniform. The only elements missing were his plumed hat, saber, and two black powder pistols. Bar had given up trying to stop him wearing the shirt, breeches, and boots. But he drew the line at the hat and weapons. Miles could be an annoyance and his behavior sometimes bordered on delusional. But he was a whiz at repairing handheld gear such as chainsaws and string trimmers, which allowed Conway Purvis, Bar's young protégé, to focus on tractors and other large equipment. Miles' work habits had also improved since Ansel Hart took him in and made him a member of the 43rd Battalion of Virginia Cavalry.

Frank was just wrapping up at the service counter when Bar and Ryman stepped out from the office.

"Didn't expect to see you here," Frank said to Ryman.

"Just a quick visit to go over a couple of business details with Bar and Sheltie Lou," Ryman replied. "Speaking of visits, looks like you had some visitors at your place this morning, watching the hunt as we came by."

"Yeah. Kind of a weird thing."

"How's that?"

"Cuyler brought his old man out to show him where he was going to build the retirement home. And he also told him about the Pymsdale plans, how that would be built on your family's farm, part of my place, and part of Montfair. Leeland didn't seem very lucid, not much response to anything Cuyler said. Then he saw the fox and he perked up. Shouted 'Tally ho!' and called to the hounds to get after him. And when the riders passed by, I swear it looked like he thought he was on a horse riding with y'all. He got pretty lucid after that, and ripped Cuyler a new one about building anything, mentioned something about Thumper's parents, called Montfair 'Thad and CeeCee's place.'

"Cuyler apologized before they left, said he'd come back later without his father and we could have a chat. But I kinda got this feeling the deal might be on shaky ground."

"Good for old Leeland," Miles said. "About time someone stood up to those damn carpetbaggers."

Bar shook his head. "For Christ's sake. How many times you gotta be told the Corleys ain't carpetbaggers?"

"Maybe not them," Miles replied in his usual defiant manner, "but they're in bed with those damn Californians. At least I hear Thumper ain't going along with this crap. And as long as he stands in their way, it ain't gonna happen. So they might as well just take their goddamn plans and shove 'em."

Bar cleared his throat and looked at Miles as he nodded toward Worsham.

"Oh, well," Miles said, a hint of apology in his voice, "I reckon building that retirement home at Frank's place ain't such a bad thing. At least that's something for Virginians built by Virginians. Just not the whole damn resort those Pymsdale assholes want to build."

Merle whimpered and looked up at Ryman.

"What is it?" Ryman asked.

"Oh, shit," Bar said, "here he goes again, thinking he can talk to the animals."

Frank was less skeptical of the ability Ryman believed came from Saint Hubert after he diagnosed a tumor on Merle's hip a year earlier. He insisted Frank get the dog to the vet immediately, the vet confirmed the diagnosis, and said Ryman probably saved the dog's life.

The men all stood silently as Merle and Ryman appeared to be sharing unspoken thoughts.

Ryman turned to Worsham and said, "He doesn't want to leave his home."

The words hit Frank Worsham in the gut. "How could he know what's going on?"

"Dogs are more perceptive than people give them credit for. They think in images rather than words, but they're more aware of things than most folks realize. Merle knows what you and Cuyler have been talking about. He told me Leeland's dogs were there and they had a great time running around in the open fields. They told him they really hate being cooped up in the house since Leeland can't move any more."

Aware of Bar's disbelief, Frank said to him, "I didn't say anything about the other dogs being there."

Bar scoffed. "Hell, Frank, you know Leeland never goes anywhere without those dogs. Even if he's in a wheelchair, those dogs are with him. No great feat of psychic power there."

211

Ryman continued to look down into Merle's pleading brown eyes. He wanted to comfort the dog, tell him it would be okay. But Ryman's agenda ran counter to what Merle wanted. The position as historical curator for the resort, the opportunity to spread Saint Hubert's blessed word, meant more than one dog having to move to a different home. Or did it?

"Don't you worry," Ryman said. "Your home is wherever Frank is. No matter what or where, you'll always be with him."

Merle barked once.

Bar and Frank took that as acceptance of Ryman's reassurance. But Ryman knew the dog was not convinced. Yes, he loved Frank. But he also loved his home: the fields to run in, the creeks and ponds to wade and swim in, his four dog beds in his favorite places in the old farmhouse. His days revolved around the daily routines he accompanied Frank on: tending to the cattle, mending fences, cutting hay, hauling feed. What would life be like without all that to fill his days? And, worse still, what if Frank ended up like Leeland, and Merle had to live like Lukey and Danny, still with their pack leader but never being able to run free like they were used to?

Ryman knew he'd done nothing to assuage the dog's fears.

Miles also sensed Merle's anxiety. He reached down and stroked the dog's head. "Good boy. Nice to know at least the dog's on our side."

****

Corley's Cadillac Escalade was parked in front of Worsham's house when he returned to his farm. Cuyler stepped out of the car as Frank got out of his truck. Merle hopped out and stopped when he saw who was there. In typical Golden Retriever manner, Merle was always happy to see any visitor. But instead of bounding over to Cuyler with wagging tail and joyful smile, he curled up his lip, showed one gleaming white fang, sneezed, then turned and trotted up onto the porch where he plopped down.

"I just wanted to apologize for my father's behavior," Cuyler said. "You know his mind's not all there. He thinks Montfair still belongs to Thumper's parents, looked like he thought he was riding with the hunt instead of being stuck in a wheelchair. The deal's still on as far as I'm concerned."

"I don't know. Maybe your old man had a point."

"You can't be serious. I'm making you one hell of an offer. You were the one who said you were thinking about selling. I've acted in good faith, and I thought you were a man of your word."

"Ah, c'mon, Cuyler. You know there's no way in hell Thumper's ever going to let you have part of Montfair for your resort project. Rhetta might agree to sell, but without that piece of Montfair, plus my place, you've got no Pymsdale deal. And the only reason you're making such a sweet offer for my land is you need a big chunk of that too. The retirement home idea is probably just a ruse to make me think my land will be used for a noble purpose."

"That's not true, Frank. And it's not fair either. You saw the plans. It'll be a first rate facility. And it won't be a problem for the hunt. No more so than your house and outbuildings are now. Hell, you even ask them to stay out of some of your pastures during calving season, and that won't happen any more once you and all the cows are gone. I thought you were through with farming. Too hard to make a living at it anymore you said."

"It's not just about me."

"What? The missus doesn't want to move?"

"Nah, Betty's okay with it."

"Something or someone else then?"

"Yeah, kinda that." Frank looked toward the porch. Merle lifted his head and his expectant gaze and furrowed brow seemed to say, *Go ahead, tell him. Please, tell him.* "It's Merle."

"What? The dog? Are you nuts?"

"Yeah, I probably am. But I've given it some thought, and I can't do this to Merle."

"Now you really are joking. You'd pass up this deal because of a goddamn dog?"

"He's not a goddamn dog. He's my best friend. And he depends on me. This is his home, he loves it here, and I can't ask him to give it up."

"Listen, Frank, I don't know what's going on here, but this is bullshit. You signed a letter of intent."

"Yeah, well, sometimes intentions change."

Cuyler looked at the dog, who seemed to be returning a victorious smile. "You know, Frank, dogs don't live forever."

"Are you threatening my dog's life?" Frank took a step toward Corley.

The smaller man moved back and raised his hands. "No, that's not what I meant. I just meant, well, this deal won't be on the table forever, and dogs, well, y'know, they have a lifespan…"

Worsham squared his shoulders and hovered over Corley. "I don't like what you're insinuating. Yeah, dogs have a lifespan. And Merle's has a long way to go still. So nothing better happen to him. Or it just might have an impact on *your* lifespan."

Corley backed toward his car. "Now you're the one making threats, Frank. You need to calm down and think this through. Take some time and come to your senses. I'll be in touch."

"Don't bother."

Corley jumped into his car and drove away with dust and leaves flying in his wake.

Frank looked at Merle and the dog's grinning face seemed to say, *Atta boy!*

****

Bar arrived home that evening to find Drago reclining in a lawn chair in front of the trailer, a six-pack of Budweiser, with one can removed, on the bare ground beside him. As Bar got out of his truck, Drago raised the can in salute.

"Cheers, old pal. Figured I'd pay you a visit and give you a heads up before all the shit hits the fan around here. I suppose I owe you at least that, considering what a help you've been." He patted the other chair next to him. "C'mon, have a beer with me for old times' sake."

Bar plopped down into the chair and grabbed a beer.

"You don't look too happy to see me," Drago said.

"I'll be happy to see your ass leaving."

"Yeah, well, too bad you'll also be leaving. Thanks to certain friends I have in influential positions, I've just finished rounding up some very interesting information about your neighbors. Seems you and I aren't the only ones around here with, shall we say, a rather shady past. I mean, really, who'd have thought there'd be a couple of former Russian operatives hiding out here in little old Crutchfield County, masquerading as a farm manager and housekeeper. That ruse about being Polish circus workers stranded here when the 'parent company' collapsed, I don't know if Billington's old man fell for it or knew all along what was up. Either way, he snuck them around the official channels so no one could find out what they'd really been up to. Pretty handy to have a powerful congressman in your corner who gets to play by his own rules."

He took a long pull on the can of beer and continued.

"And won't his exalted legacy be smeared if that comes out. And your buddy Thumper will have to stand and watch as his trusted servants get frog-marched out of the big house…and carted off to that other Big House, the one with razor-wire fences and tiny windows. Hot damn! Won't that be a sight?"

Bar wanted to smash the sneering smile from Drago's face. But that would do nothing to save the Nutchenkos and, in retaliation, Drago would drop his promise to keep quiet about the darker aspects of Bar's past. The only other option was to permanently silence Drago. Bar was still thinking through how to accomplish that. A failsafe plan had not yet emerged, and he knew time was running out.

"And," Drago said, "let's not forget your precious little 'Sheltie Lou' and her involvement with that bogus Costa Rica project her lady friend has set up."

"She's got nothing to do with that. Whatever's going on there, it doesn't involve her in any way."

"Oh, really? She doesn't know this is all a tax scam, and possibly some other nasty stuff going on down there? Whatever it is, it ain't about animal welfare. And yet she's written all these hefty checks earmarked for 'PACA Costa Rica.' And her being such a smart business person, so good with numbers and everything, who just happens to be sleeping with the woman running the scam."

"Look, do whatever you want with the Nutchenkos. That's no skin off my ass. But that should be enough to get the job done. You don't need to go after Sheltie Lou too."

"That all depends on the old lady. Seems she's leaning toward doing the deal, and as long as that happens, the info about her granddaughter is off the table. And the same goes for Billington. He let's his sister make the deal, and the Polacks get to stay. For now, though, you'll keep all this to yourself. Any leaks to the wrong people and, well, old friend, there are still some folks we used to hang out with who would be very interested to know where you ended up. Left us all so suddenly, we didn't even have a chance to say good-bye. Or to settle up some scores. But as long as you keep your mouth shut, my lips are sealed too."

Drago looked off into the woods encircling the tiny trailer. He could see Bar's flock of pet vultures gathered on the ground feasting on a deer carcass Bar had set out for them that morning. "But, sorry to say, when the deal does go through, your ass is gonna be outta here. You and your filthy, disgusting damn birds." He waved his hand in a wide arc. "All this will be covered in asphalt, your lovely little paradise paved over."

He yanked another beer from the pack, got up from the lawn chair, and walked to the edge of the woods. He popped the can open, drained it in one swig, belched loudly, and then hurled the empty can at the vultures. They hissed at the attack and scattered into the trees.

Bar gripped both arms of the lawn chair. He resisted the urge to leap on Korth, pound him into a pile of bloody pulp, and feed his remains to his vultures. As he remembered, Drago was cunning and malicious, a man who enjoyed inflicting pain and inspiring fear in those weaker than him. But, despite Korth's size and menacing appearance, Bar was the faster and stronger one in their partnership. While both had slowed down over the years, Bar had no doubt he could still outmuscle Drago in hand-to-hand combat.

There was, though, another alternative. It was risky, but definitely worth considering.

****

Glo's phone rang and Caller ID showed the number she least wanted to hear from.

"Time to tell our friend that everything's ready," Drago said.

Chapter 33

Saturday's hunt met at Fair Enough Farm. In addition to the riders, several spectators had turned out as well.

"As you all know," Thumper announced, "Minstrel's Delight passed away a few days ago. Many of you will remember him as he was Ivan Mooney's number one hunter for many seasons. He carried our huntsman well, no matter the terrain, the obstacles, or the weather. We owe as much to him for the wonderful sporting days we enjoyed as we owe to the huntsman and the hounds. He'd been living out a peaceful retirement here thanks to Rhetta, and she selected a lovely spot, just up the hill behind the main pasture, for his final resting place. We'll be stopping there to pay our respects before we go hunting today."

Rhetta fired up her John Deere Gator and led the way across the field to the gravesite.

Crispie moved off with hounds at a controlled walk, flanked by Patti, Ryman, and Nardell keeping the pack in order.

The riders came next, followed by those on foot.

The November air was pleasantly chill, perfectly suited to formal hunting attire for the riders and mid-weight jackets for the spectators. The autumn foliage bowed to the coming winter but clung to a vestige of its multi-hued palette.

Once everyone was gathered by the gravesite, Thumper offered a few remarks about the splendor of horses in general and the noble spirit of Minstrel's Delight in particular.

Rhetta then stepped forward and everyone awaited her benediction on this solemn occasion.

Her blue eyes, cloudy with memories, drifted up from the pile of loosely packed soil, first toward the crest of the tree-covered mountains, and then out over the eastern vista stretching away across the Piedmont toward the distant horizon.

"I recall how my daddy thought there wasn't anything so important in all the world as one damn piece of land," she said, more to her herself than to those around her. "Losing that land made him turn kinda crazy. Wanting it back kept him going. Realizing he was never going to get it back, once they'd paved it over, killed him."

The others cast sideways glances, having expected nothing more than a few kind reminiscences about the deceased horse. Thumper made a subtle hand signal and flashed a look at the crowd that said, *Give her a break.*

"I guess I've never really thought of this land as mine," she continued, her gaze still directed out toward the eastern panorama. "It's been McKendrick land for about a century and a half now. I've only been a McKendrick for about sixty years. But I reckon that's still a long damn time. And now it's up to me to decide if it stays McKendrick land or not. Fergus is gone. Our son Teedy's gone. Sheltie Lou's got no use for it." She looked at Ryman, shook her head, and said, "And Ryman, well, he seems to have other plans. So I was thinking there wasn't any good reason for me to stay here. Now I'm not so sure. Once this place gets paved over, like my daddy's farm did, you can't get it back."

She paused for a moment and a hint of sadness softened the weathered creases of her face. "It just never seemed right to me that Teedy died so far away from here. Bad enough I still don't really know what for. But at least when Fergus went, he dropped dead in the family shop. And now even Minnie Dee gets to rest here on McKendrick land. That is, he can rest here till those Pymsdale people start tearing everything up and paving it over."

She brought her focus back to those assembled around the grave. Turning first to Thumper, she said, "I reckon you're right about not letting Myrna sell her part of Montfair. That money they've offered to me looked awful good, maybe take it and go live the high life for awhile, leave the rest to Sheltie Lou. But the more I think about it, the thought of dropping dead on the carpet of some damn con-DOH-minium doesn't sound quite so appealing anymore.

"I don't imagine we can hold off the developers forever. But at least we can keep this resort from getting built, keep this land like it is for the rest of my days, maybe for many more of yours too."

She then addressed Elizabeth directly. "It's not very likely that this will still be open land by the time you reach my age, maybe not even by the time you reach your daddy's age. But you just remember what it was like." She tapped a finger against the side of her head. "Fix it in your mind when there weren't houses every twenty yards and gas stations and Seven-Eleven stores on every corner and traffic covering the roads all the time. Remember when you could still climb on a horse and ride through open country galloping behind a pack of hounds on a cool winter's morning.

"I suppose nothing lasts forever. Minnie Dee didn't. I won't. None of y'all will. Not even the land itself." She kicked at a clump of clay around the edge of the grave. "Come a time when this will just be *dirt*, just dirt growing grass for show. Not for grazing or making hay. Not for growing crops or keeping livestock. Not for riding and hunting on. Not for any useful purpose at all. Only *land* is useful. When it ain't useful no more, it's just dirt. Then I reckon it might as well get paved over and built on. But y'all remember when it was still land. And y'all remember the difference."

She looked back out toward the east once more, as if scanning the horizon for signs of the coming invasion. Her eyes then dropped down to the pile of freshly dug red Virginia earth. Her expression revealed a sudden remembrance of why everyone was there and a realization that she had yet to say anything about the departed one they had come to eulogize. "Minnie Dee was a good old horse. Reckon I'll miss him."

She turned from the grave and stepped into her Gator. The others silently watched as she rumbled back to her house.

****

Rhetta wasted no time calling Cuyler to tell him the bad news. Steeled for the confrontation, she felt a flush of relief when she heard his voicemail greeting. She left a terse message telling him she'd decided not to sell.

She then drove to the Corley cabin. Cuyler would be disappointed, but he'd make another deal somewhere else. And even if he didn't, he'd be okay. Rhetta still doubted there was any way Thumper could be convinced to let Myrna sell her part of Montfair, but without the McKendrick property, the deal was dead regardless of what Thumper might be persuaded to do. Still, though, she felt Myrna deserved the courtesy of being told about her decision in person.

The message was delivered short and to the point, typical for Rhetta. She didn't wait around to counter Myrna's pleading or console her with motherly understanding. That wasn't her style. Courtesy done, she was in her truck and pulling away before Myrna could stop her.

Glo Devereaux could barely understand what Myrna was saying through the sobs over the phone. "Myrna, take a breath, try to calm down, and tell me what's happened."

"I'm done, it's over! My life…nothing…they'll come for me and I can't stop them. This was my only hope."

"We'll figure something out. There has to be some other way. Just don't do anything rash. Will you promise me that?"

"How can there be some other way? They'll want the money or else…or else…oh, God! I can't even think about it."

"Look, just stay where you are. I'll get there as soon as I can and we'll figure something out. Can I trust you to just sit tight? Don't leave the cabin, don't talk to anyone else. I'm on my way."

Myrna's reply was barely audible but it sounded close enough to "yes" for Glo to end the call and hit another number.

A young woman answered, surprised that her boss was calling her personal number so early on a Saturday morning.

"I'm sorry to bother you on the weekend," Glo said, "but I'm afraid a family emergency has come up and I have to leave right away. I'd like you to cover for me while I'm gone. Mr. Bondurant will also be away for at least a few more days, so you'll mostly just be fielding phone calls and keeping things in order while we're both gone."

"Oh, yes, I'll be happy to cover for you. I hope it's nothing terribly serious."

"I won't really know till I get there. The cell signal isn't very reliable where I'll be, and given the sensitivity of the family situation, there might be times when I can't answer my phone even if the call does get through. So if you need to reach me, just leave a message and I'll get back to you as soon as I have the chance."

The young woman was about to ask Glo where she was going and how long she thought she'd be gone, but the call ended before she could say anything more.

Glo was quickly on to her next task, booking the first available flight to Virginia.

****

Rhetta's phone rang just as she stepped through the mudroom door and into her kitchen. Caller ID showed it was Cuyler. She hesitated for a moment, but decided he, too, deserved the courtesy of a direct response.

"Got your message," he said. "You really need to reconsider your decision. You know you'll never get another offer like ours."

"Look, Cuyler, you and I both know this was all pointless anyway. There's no way Thumper's going to let Myrna sell her part of Montfair. Whatever you and that Bondurant fellow think you've got up your sleeve, you're kidding yourself if you believe it's going to make him change his mind."

"You might be surprised. If he does agree to let Myrna sell us her acreage, would that change your mind?"

"Probably not."

"You said 'probably,' not 'definitely.' So maybe there's a bit of wiggle room. How about Smith and I stop by and we discuss this, just the three of us, nice and friendly."

"I don't see where there's anything to discuss, but if it would make you and your pal Smith feel better to come out and flap your gums some more, I reckon I can give you that."

"Great. Smith's down in North Carolina checking out some other possible sites. Nothing comes anywhere close to what we want to do in Paradise Gap, but we'd be poor planners to not have some tentative backup plans."

"Well, I hope those other folks don't give you as much grief as we're giving you."

"And I hope we don't have to deal with them at all. Smith will be back here Monday, around midday. We can clear whatever else is scheduled for that afternoon and pay a visit to Fair Enough Farm. Say around five o'clock?"

"I'll have the coffee pot on. Unless you boys would prefer something stronger."

"Coffee will be fine."

Cuyler called Smith next. "The old gal's changing her mind. She's agreed to meet with us Monday afternoon, but it sounds to me like we're going to need some heavy persuasive power. Your site agent is all set?"

"He passed the word along to me last night through our contact point. Everything's wrapped up, conclusive evidence on both counts. He has the documentation, and best he holds on to that till we need to play our hand. Wouldn't want it to get out to the wrong people and go public, it would be of no use to us as a bargaining tool then. And as long as only he has it, there's no chance of that happening. I'll get word to him about when and where to meet us, have him at the ready if we need to use the info. And once we're done convincing the old lady, we can go next door and pay a visit to your cousin."

Bondurant called Glo next. She spent a few seconds staring at his name on the phone screen. Knowing what she was about to do, she didn't want to talk to him for fear her tone might give something away. She let it go to voicemail.

As it was still early Saturday morning on the West Coast, Bondurant wasn't surprised to hear Glo's voicemail greeting. "As soon as you get this, I need you to call my site agent. Tell him to be in place at Site Two Monday afternoon, no later than five o'clock, with the information in hand. He's to wait out of sight behind the house and look for the signal when he's to join us."

After listening to the message, Glo considered her options. If she didn't convey the instructions, the consequences for her could be severe. But knowing where Bondurant and Korth would be on Monday afternoon might be useful. They were clearly laying a trap. Perhaps she could arrange a trap of her own making.

She called Korth, gave him the message, and clicked off before he had a chance to respond.

Chapter 34

Bar was enjoying a leisurely Sunday morning in his trailer, what he feared might be a dwindling number of such mornings, when a black sedan pulled up and two men got out. Both wore dark suits, white dress shirts, and red ties. Clean-shaven and with neatly trimmed hair, Bar assumed they were from an organization commonly known by its initials. He guessed the first letter was an "F." Or it could be a "C." Either way, this was not a pleasant social call.

"Mr. Reinhardt?" one of the men asked as Bar stepped outside.

"You were expecting someone else?" Bar shot back.

"No need to be coy, Mr. Reinhardt. We're just here to ask you a few questions."

Yeah, right, Bar thought. What could this be about? Had his past finally caught up with him? Had that SOB Korth gone back on his promise to leave Bar out of whatever was happening if he cooperated and helped him get a handle on the local scene?

"Do you know someone named Dragomir Korth?" the man asked.

Was this a trap? Had Drago himself sent these guys to find out if Bar would turn on him?

"Korth? Yeah, I knew him once. Long time ago."

"Have you seen him lately?"

"You mean around here?"

"Yes, Mr. Reinhardt, around here. As in, right around here." He waved his arm in a circle toward Bar's front yard.

"What would Dragomir Korth be doing around here?"

"You're not answering the question, Mr. Reinhardt. Have you, or have you not, had contact with Mr. Korth recently, as in the past few days, and around here, as in..." He pointed straight down. "...*here?*"

"Who wants to know?"

The man let out an exasperated breath. "Mr. Reinhardt, my partner and I are with the FBI. You're no doubt familiar with that organization."

"Heard of it. You got some ID?"

"Yes, of course we do."

Both men flashed what, under quick inspection, appeared to be legitimate credentials.

"Satisfied?" the lead man asked.

Bar shrugged.

"Fine. Now, it would be very helpful to the pursuit of public safety if you would please answer our questions. We have reason to believe that Korth is in this area. There are multiple warrants out for him, some of them international in nature. We know you and he were associates many years ago on the West Coast. None of that is our concern. However, he's been very active in several illegal operations since and we're part of a task force to bring him and others to justice. Our efforts have traced him to this area, which is not part of his usual operating territory. Given the relationship the two of you had, we thought he might have contacted you."

"And just how did you gentlemen know where I was?"

"That's not germane, Mr. Reinhardt. The relevant issue here is whether or not you might be able to help us locate Mr. Korth."

Bar considered his options. Were these guys really FBI? Did that matter? Whoever they were, if they were able to snag Drago before he could use the evidence he'd claimed to have about the Nutchenkos and PACA, that would be a good thing. Make this damn Pymsdale resort thing go away, and his little oasis in the woods, his paradise, would not be paved over. If this was a setup by Korth himself, well, the consequences could get ugly. But he'd deal with that if he had to.

"Yeah," Bar said, "I've seen him. He popped up a couple of months ago, just appeared out of nowhere. Said he was working on a couple of angles for clients, wanted me to help fill him in on the lay of the land, who's who, what's what, that sort of thing."

"And did you cooperate?"

"Yeah, kinda. I didn't tell him anything that isn't already common knowledge around here. But I guess it was stuff you wouldn't know if you weren't familiar with our little community."

"Do you know where he is? How to contact him?"

"Seriously? C'mon, you guys know better than that. What? You think he gave me his business card with this phone number and address? He pops up when you don't expect it, and then disappears."

"Yes, we know. He's very good at that sort of thing. Had some excellent teachers. And now has some very powerful handlers. Did he mention who the clients are he's working for?"

How much detail did Bar want to give these guys? Besides, he was pretty sure they already knew most of it. And he'd now implicated himself by admitting he'd had contact with Korth. Might as well tell the rest, some of it anyway. "It's got something to do with the land deal for the resort the Pymsdale company wants to build here." He didn't think it was necessary to go into any further details about the Nutchenkos and PACA. If they already knew that too, they didn't need his input. And if they didn't, best to not tip them off.

The two men looked at each other and nodded.

The lead agent withdrew a card from his pocket and handed it to Bar. "If you do see him again, we'd like you to contact us. Can we count on you to do that, Mr. Reinhardt?"

"Yeah, sure. But there's no telling if he'll ever show up again."

"We understand. Thank you for your time, you've been very helpful." He noticed several large black birds stirring in the trees around the yard. "You have a flock of buzzards for neighbors?"

"They're vultures, not buzzards."

"They feed on carrion, don't they? Only eat dead things?"

"Yep. They can pick a carcass clean in no time at all."

"A lot of carcasses around here, are there?"

"I make sure they always have something to munch on. Some folks think it's a dirty job. But it's my way of keeping the neighborhood clean and tidy."

"It seems, Mr. Reinhardt, you and I have more in common than you might have thought."

Bar watched them pull away. If they did catch up with Drago, he'd be lucky if they really were FBI agents, people who had to play by the rules, even if those rules were sometimes stretched a bit. The alternative was much darker. Bar had never been more than a bit player around the edges of some shady deals. But he knew that the people behind those deals did not play by any conventional rules. That realization was what propelled him to slip away without notice, use some of the skills he'd picked up from his brief time in that other world to conceal his identity, and find the perfect cover and hiding place just outside the little known village of Paradise Gap.

And now that life was threatened with destruction one way or another. And the lives of many of his friends and neighbors would also be dramatically altered if Drago Korth and those he worked for succeeded with their plans.

He wasn't sure if he or anyone else could stop him, and he knew what might happen if his efforts went awry. But he was now certain it was a risk he had to take.

****

It was mid-day when Glo arrived at the Corley cabin. With no seats on a non-stop flight available, she'd had to go through two connections with layovers. An early morning arrival at Dulles Airport was followed by the lengthy drive in a rental car out to Paradise Gap.

Myrna rushed out of the cabin and threw her arms around her the second she was out of the car. "Oh my God! I can't believe you're really here. You have no idea what I've been going through." She released Glo from her embrace and stepped back. "Jesus! You look terrible."

"You have no idea what *I've* been through!" She smiled and the two old friends laughed. "But it was worth it to get here for you. Coffee! I need coffee."

Once inside, they got down to the serious business that had prompted Glo to travel three thousand miles on short notice.

"You know how much it means to me that you came all this way," Myrna said. "But, to be honest, I don't see how there's any way you can get me out of this mess."

"And to be honest back at you, you sounded so panicky that I was afraid you might…well, you know…do something…stupid."

Myrna looked out the cabin window. "I considered it. It felt like…like if someone's about to be sent to prison and knowing how horrible that will be, they decide to just end it all instead. Being stuck here, all alone, hours and hours to just think." She looked down and shook her head. "It was pretty bleak." Then a sardonic grin crinkled her face. "Maybe what saved me was that I ran out of wine and was too scared to go out and buy more. Being sober probably stopped me from doing the deed."

"Whatever kept you going, I'm just glad you've stuck it out." Glo steeled herself for what she was about to reveal. "Look, I have a confession to make. My reasons for coming here weren't just to be supportive to you, although that's a big part of it. I'm embarrassed and ashamed, and I need to get a few things out in the open, something I have to do face-to-face. It might mean some very nasty consequences for me, pretty much put us both in the same situation, and with similar people."

"What are you talking about? You can't possibly be involved in any of this."

"I am, more than you'd think." She closed her eyes, took a breath, and said, "Okay, here goes. Smith Bondurant has a long history of sexual assaults. And I've been complicit in covering them up for him. It started as a minor thing. A young employee at one of the resorts filed a complaint a few years ago. He insisted it was an innocent misunderstanding, that he'd done nothing wrong, never would, and she was just trying to profit off his position. He seemed so sincere. I'd been working as his personal assistant for a couple of years and I'd never seen any hint of that sort of behavior. He said he could either fight it publicly, put himself through all that scrutiny, and be judged guilty in the court of public opinion regardless of the outcome, or he could just work out something privately and put it behind him.

"I asked if he meant have a lawyer offer a settlement in exchange for a non-disclosure agreement. He said 'Something like that, but better to not make it a matter of public record.' He knew someone who could get it done discreetly. But he'd have to channel the funds to him privately. And that's where he needed my help. As his personal assistant, I could transfer money from his private account to other accounts without raising any questions. And as that was beyond my official duties as a Pymsdale employee, he'd be happy to compensate me for the additional service. It all seemed so innocent and logical. Although it did seem like the amount he wanted transferred wasn't very much, and what he was paying me for a simple transaction seemed like a lot."

Glo looked around the room. "Are you sure there isn't still some wine here somewhere?"

"Believe me, if there was, I'd have found it by now. Maybe we can make a run to the store. But I've got a feeling this isn't the end of your story."

"I wish it was. I did what he asked, felt I was helping a good man protect his reputation."

"It happened again, though, didn't it?"

"About a year later. That's when I started to question whether or not I should go along with this. He swore it was another set-up, that someone in his position was vulnerable to this sort of thing. A powerful man, spends much of his time on the road, staying at exclusive resorts where there are a lot of young women on the staff, some of them looking for the chance to exploit an innocent situation to their advantage.

"When I said I felt badly for his situation but was uncomfortable serving as the go-between, he didn't get upset, didn't threaten my job, or anything like that. He just said he understood and he'd figure some other way to work it out. It was the next day I met his 'friend.' "

Myrna was starting to sense where this was going. "Let me guess. A large, scary man showed up out of nowhere and convinced you to change your mind."

"I was coming back from lunch, minding my own business, walking along West Olive, when there he was, standing right in front of me. He seemed friendly and mildly apologetic at first. Said we had a mutual acquaintance. When I questioned who that could be, he said a gentleman who was having some difficulties with a trumped up sexual assault charge, a situation I might be able to help him out with. I said I'd already helped him once before and wasn't comfortable doing it again. That's when his mood changed. I could just feel the waves of threat coming off him even before he said anything."

"I know that feeling. It often wakes me up at night just thinking about it."

"He told me I was now on record as being involved in the first situation. 'Complicit' was the word he used. He said it was my choice not to help with the current 'problem,' but I should understand there could be some unpleasant consequences if I didn't. He then smiled, that hideous grin, and said that, on the upside, I stood to earn some generous compensation for my efforts."

"How many have there been so far?"

"Six at this point. We've become a well-oiled machine. Smith has his way with vulnerable young women, they then realize he's used them and they threaten to go public. Drago shows up, scares the crap out of them, smoothes things over with a modest offer for them to keep quiet, and a stern warning of what could happen if they don't. I facilitate the pay-off so it doesn't come directly from Smith, no one else knows about Drago's role in this, I get some extra spending cash on the side, and the problem goes away.

"I've been doing a brilliant job of rationalizing my role in this. Mostly it's because I fell for Smith's game the first time and got myself implicated in his cover-up. So I had to choose between exposing myself to all the accusations of aiding a sexual abuser or being part of the effort to keep it all hush-hush. Then there was the threat of what Drago might do if I tried to get out. The money Smith was paying me wasn't much of an issue. I was doing okay without it. But—and this is maybe the worst of all my rationalizing—I tried to tell myself that these young women were somewhat responsible themselves for what happened, that they probably led him on, went to his hotel room willingly, always late at night, poor judgment on their part and, you know, 'men will be men.' "

"Yes, I know about all of that. And it isn't just 'young' women who can fall for it. Especially when you're desperate and he's the one person who might be able to help you out of a hopeless situation."

"I should have warned you. But, well, please don't take this wrong, I just thought...you know, the other women were all, like, in their twenties, more gullible, not yet wise to the ways of the world, easier targets for Smith to take advantage of. I figured you were smart enough to not fall for his crap."

Mryna reached out and put her hand on Glo's. "It's okay. It was different with me. My fate really was in his hands. Still is, I guess. I've had to do whatever necessary to make this deal happen. And that big, scary guy has kept popping up, even here, to remind me of that."

"Another thing I have to be honest about," Glo said. "I knew Drago was the scary man you mentioned when we met for lunch."

Myrna was surprised at this revelation. "How did you know that? Like he's the only scary guy working that part of LA?"

"He'd been watching us and called me afterward, asked how I knew you and why I'd written you a check. I told him it was a loan so you could get to Virginia where you owned a valuable piece of property. He asked if that was on the level and I said it was. I tried to ask what his interest was in this but he cut me off. I'd assumed he wasn't only working for Mr. Bondurant, that he was probably what I guess they call 'freelance muscle.' So it made sense he was also working as an enforcer for the loan shark you're into."

Myrna's mood darkened. "And I'm still into him. Cuyler keeps telling me that he and Smith are working on something that will convince Thumper to change his mind. But, come on, you know Thumper as well I do. What could anyone possibly have on him that would be so bad it would make him give in about selling my part of the family property?"

"It's not about him directly."

"What? You know about this?"

"My role as what they call the 'buffer' between Drago

and Smith has expanded beyond just covering up the sexual assaults. I've also been required to channel information back and forth so there's no record of direct contact between them. I don't get all the details, but enough to figure out that Drago's been using his underworld contacts to track down some information about the Nutchenkos. It seems preposterous, but it's something about them being spies, that working for a Polish circus troupe was just a cover. And when they wanted to defect, your father pulled some strings with contacts at the State Department to hide them out at Montfair where they became his personal helpers on the farm."

"Oh, my God! We always thought that was just a family joke, something to make them seem exotic and sort of mysterious. No one took it seriously. Although my father did make it absolutely clear that we were never to mention that to anyone, not even as an amusing family story. And if someone asked, we were to say we knew nothing about that."

"If it's true, and if Drago has the proof he claims to have, then one word to the wrong ear, and their cover could be blown, they could be deported or maybe even imprisoned."

Myrna needed a few moments to process this. "But...you mean...do you really think Thumper would go so far as to let me sell part of Montfair just to save the Nutchenkos? Okay, so, sure, that puts him in a tough situation. But I have to think he'd place the preservation of the family property over the Nutchenkos' welfare."

"It wouldn't just go badly for them. First of all, it would harm your father's legacy if it became public that he'd used his office and influence to get special treatment for two illegals who had been spying on our country and who he then made his personal servants. The press could easily make that out as abuse of power, maybe even implying slave labor. You know how much Thumper's reputation depends on your father's legacy, especially now with all the attention his book is getting.

"But it's worse than that. If Thumper knew about this, he could be considered complicit in harboring fugitives from justice. So it's not just about his reputation for always being truthful, that he was bluntly honest about your father in his biography, but he could also face some legal problems of his own. And pretty serious ones."

Myrna remained silent as she took all this in.

She then said, "I can't believe Smith would stoop this low. And Cuyler along with him, my own cousin."

"Um, well, let's not forget it was you who started this in the first place. I don't want to lay a guilt trip on you, but this all began because you wanted to sell your part of the family property."

"Okay, yes, you're right. It's all my fault. But I had no idea it would come to this, that it would get so ugly. Smith told me they were going to offer Thumper a nice position with the resort, even name the conference center for our father. When he turned that down, Smith said he and Cuyler had another angle they were working on, but I assumed it was just a better offer to butter him up before hitting him with the news that my share of the property was part of the deal, make it easier for him to give me permission to sell. Then Rhetta blabbed to Cecelia, Cecelia told Elizabeth, and I've been imprisoned here, completely cut off from Thumper and out of the process, just waiting to find out if Smith and Cuyler really have figured out a way to get Thumper to agree or if I'll have to go back to LA still broke and face the consequences."

Myrna's dark thoughts about the likely outcome sparked another realization. "Crap! What about Rhetta? That's what really sent me over the edge when I called you yesterday. Now she's decided not to sell her place. So it doesn't matter what anyone has on the Nutchenkos and Thumper's involvement in that. They couldn't possibly have anything on Rhetta to get her to change her mind."

"Well, like with Thumper, not exactly on Rhetta herself."

"Don't tell me Ryman is also a spy."

Glo chuckled at Myrna's attempt at a note of dark humor. "No, no one's a spy. And it's not Ryman, it's Shelton."

"Shelton? What could she have done?"

"It was all innocent, and she still doesn't know, but it seems that PACA, the animal rights group, has something funny going on in Costa Rica. It's really just the organization's leader, some woman named Astrid Stevenson, who's behind it all. She's channeling money to a private account as a tax dodge for herself and others."

"I can't imagine Sheltie Lou being involved in something like that."

"She's not. Not directly anyway. But she's been making some substantial contributions to PACA, all earmarked for the Costa Rica project, and all while she's been having an affair with this Stevenson woman. Doesn't make it look very good even if she's really just been making these donations in good faith. If this hits the news, she'll at least be implicated and the McKendrick name will suffer. Probably won't do the family business any good. The lawyer fees alone to defend herself could bankrupt her."

Myrna stood up and walked to the front window. "When I was growing up, I never really appreciated what we had here. Not just all this open country, the beautiful scenery, but the sense of family and a sort of community cohesion. It didn't matter if you had money or not, if you had horses and rode with the hunt or were a hard working farmer and your sports were things like deer hunting or fishing. Yeah, there was the occasional oddball, or some newcomers who moved to the country with the wrong impression of what it was really like. But they either adopted our ways or moved on, for the most part. Sure, it wasn't all perfect because human beings aren't perfect. But, looking back, I should have stayed. Hollywood! Yeah, right. Look how that worked out."

She turned from the window to face Glo. "We have to stop them. I don't care what happens to me. For once in my life I have to face reality and take responsibility for my own choices. I don't know how we'll do it. And it's going to be tough on you too. But I get the impression you're ready to call it quits."

"I am. I'm not sure what to do either, but I do know what the next move has to be."

"What's that?"

"I need to go have a chat with your brother."

Chapter 35

Thumper was in the middle of scrubbing out a water trough at the barn when he heard a vehicle rumbling along the Montfair driveway. He looked up to see it was Bar's truck, the unmistakable, mint-condition, '72 F-100 pickup, a two-tone job in aqua blue and bright white that was Bar's pride and joy.

Janey was in the tack room hanging up a bridle she had just finished cleaning. She also saw the approaching truck and called out to Thumper, "I'll go see what he wants."

Bar noticed Thumper bent over the trough, shirtsleeves rolled up, working a heavy bristled brush against the inside walls. He stepped out of his truck as Janey emerged from the barn, wiping her hands on a small towel. Unruly strands of hair curled out from the edges of the sweat-stained cap she wore and bits of hay clung to her shirt and jeans.

"So much for the elegant life of the country squire and his lady," Bar said.

"It's Sunday, Natasha and Voytek's day off. They're still at church. Since the Ledesmas left, Thumper and I have been pitching in to pick up some of the slack."

"Still can't find someone to replace Javier and Bettiana?" He referred to the Argentine couple who had been part of the resident staff, living in the apartment above the barn. Highly skilled professionals, they had moved on to a larger training facility a few months earlier.

"Some applicants but no one that's met Thumper's high standards. So, to what do we owe the pleasure of your visit?"

"I wish it was about pleasure, but I'm afraid that ain't the case. Got some pretty serious shit I need to discuss with the Squire, if we can pull him away from his chores for a few minutes."

"I'll go get him." She quick-stepped through the barn and out to the side paddock where Thumper was refilling the trough. "Bar needs to talk to you. He says it's something serious."

Thumper turned off the hose, grabbed a towel, and followed Janey out to where Bar stood waiting. Bar always had a slightly menacing aura, even more so when he wasn't wearing a patch over his destroyed left eye, which directed the focus to the azure sheen of his remaining eye. But the grim look on his disfigured face caused Thumper to pause in his tracks.

Before Bar could say anything, Thumper's phone rang. He recognized Glo's ringtone. They kept in touch, but usually only regarding issues concerning their two children. He raised a finger to Bar and answered the call.

"Sorry to bother you on a Sunday," Glo said, "but there's something we need to talk about."

"Is Augie okay?"

"Oh, yeah, he's fine. Not about him. But something serious you need to hear about."

Thumper looked at Bar. "That seems to be the order of the day."

"I'd like to come over, if that's all right."

"Come over from where?"

"I'm at the Corleys' cabin, with Myrna. I could be at Montfair in a few minutes."

"What are you doing in Virginia? When did you arrive?"

"I tell you when I get there."

"Bar's here now, said he also has something serious to tell me. So, fine, sure, come on over. Join the 'something serious' party. But you may have to wait your turn." He clicked off the call and waved a hand to Bar. "Okay, the floor is yours."

Bar explained what he knew about the Nutchenkos and PACA, how Drago had told him Corley and Bondurant planned to use that information to persuade Thumper and Rhetta to go along with the Pymsdale project.

He was just wrapping up the details when Glo arrived. She explained her reason for the sudden trip to Virginia, that she was worried Myrna might do something desperate. She then started to recount the information she had, but Thumper interrupted her and gave a quick synopsis of what Bar had already told him and Janey.

"Does that line up with what you were going to tell us?"

"Yes, exactly the same." Turning to Bar, Glo asked, "But how did you know about this?"

"I might ask you the same question," Bar replied.

"As Mister Bondurant's personal assistant, I'm privy to inside information that no one else knows about."

"And in your role as Mister Bondurant's assistant, does that ever involve dealing with a certain person he refers to as his 'site agent'?" Bar added air quotes around "site agent" with his beefy, oil-stained fingers.

"How…how could you know about his 'site agent'?"

"Let's just say we knew each other many years ago," Bar replied. "And many miles away from here. Never thought I'd see him again. But damned if that son-of-a-bitch didn't just show up one day, like out of nowhere. More like out of a bad dream. I think he wanted to fill me in on what was going to happen just to piss me off, that I was going to have to move when they started building the resort and there was nothing I could do to stop it. And if I didn't keep my mouth shut, he knew some people who might like to know where I'd been all these years."

"So aren't you putting yourself at risk telling all this?" Thumper asked. "And here Glo turns up with the same info."

"Well, shit," Bar said with a sardonic smile, "if I'd known Miss Glo was coming I'd have kept my big damn mouth shut. But too late now. So I reckon I'm in the game as much as y'all are."

Janey was confused with this exchange between Bar and Glo. "What to you mean by 'site agent'? And with the finger quotes? Who is this person?"

Bar motioned to Glo to give the response.

"He's what I guess some might call a 'fixer.' He takes care of things for people in prominent positions. He's able to track down information that would be hard for others to find. He has connections in some shady places, and he can be very persuasive in person."

"And your job involves working with someone like this?" Janey asked.

"Sadly, yes, it has in recent years. But I'm happy to say that's about to end."

Janey wanted to know more about Thumper's ex-wife's involvement with this mysterious 'fixer," but before she could ask another question, everyone's attention turned to see the Nutchenkos pulling in, returning from services at the local Catholic church.

Surprised to see Bar and Glo there, Voytek slowed down. When he saw the expressions on the faces of Thumper and Janey, he stopped the car.

"You are not looking well," he said. "Something is wrong?"

"You'd best join us," Thumper replied. "Yes, something is wrong."

Voytek and Natasha got out of the car and stood with the others.

Thumper took the lead and repeated what Bar and Glo knew about the information Drago had about them.

Natasha began to shake and tears welled in her eyes. "I must sit." She staggered over to a bench along the front of the barn and plopped down.

Voytek remained stoic. "We have not spoken of this for a long time, many years. We thought it was all forgotten by now." He shrugged. "I am guessing not everyone has forgotten."

"Spies!" Natasha spat out the word and her exclamation took the others by surprise. "We were not spies! We did not want to be part of any of that. We just wanted to get out of Poland. Things were so bad, no freedom, no opportunities. We heard about America and we wanted to be here. But we had no way to do that. You couldn't just leave, they wouldn't let you. So we thought maybe working with circus would be a way to escape. We were just poor farm kids, but Voytek was good with animals and machinery and I was good cook. So we got jobs and thought when circus visited America, we could slip away, and no one would notice."

She looked at Voytek, and he nodded, knowing what she would say next.

"But then we found out circus wasn't what we thought," she said. "Yes, it did things like regular circus does. But there were other people, supposed to be just workers like us. But they were something else. And they made us do things we did not want to do. They said if we did not cooperate, things would go badly for our family still in Poland. So when they told us to take a package somewhere and give it to someone, we did what we were told. We never looked in package. We did no spying. We had no idea how to do such things. These other people just used us and we had no choice."

She looked around at what had been her home for many years, the main house, the cottage in the back, the barn, pastures, crop fields, outbuildings. "And then circus closed. It was no longer needed. Everything changed. And we were left on our own. God was merciful. He arranged for it to happen when we were, of all places, right here in America. And then He sent Mister Thad to help us. We were not even speaking English, only just a little. But he said we could come here, at least until our status could be sorted out. We are hearing nothing more about that, so we thought all was well. We never asked, best to not bring it up."

Glo turned to Thumper. "Did you know about this?"

"Sort of. It was before you and I were married, before Augie and Elizabeth were born. I was working on Capitol Hill, living in DC. There were some rumors. But my father dismissed them, told me he'd handled everything correctly. But years later, when he was getting ready to retire, he told me the truth. He really did pull some strings, used his influence to skirt around some technicalities so Natasha and Voytek could come and work here. He planned to make everything legal at some point, but the longer he put it off, the more difficult it became. And facing reelection every two years, if the opposition ever got wind of this, it might have cost him his seat in the House. But he swore me to secrecy and made me promise I wouldn't mention it when I wrote his biography."

"So you really are complicit in this," Glo said. "Jesus, what a mess."

Natasha stood up, squared her shoulders, and did her best to maintain her composure. "Yes, very much a mess. And all our fault." She turned to Voytek. " Come, we must pack our things. We will face consequences. We will not bring harm to these people who have been so good to us."

"You're not going anywhere," Thumper said. "Montfair is as much your home as it is mine. You've earned your place here and I'm not going to let assholes like Cuyler Corley and Smith Bondurant run you off or kowtow me into giving them what they want."

"But," Natasha replied, "Mister Corley is family, your cousin. And Miss Myrna, she is even closer, your sister. You cannot put Voytek and me above your family."

"They haven't behaved like family, trying to pull something like this. You and Voytek have shown something more important over all the years you've been here, honesty and loyalty."

Natasha was about to respond but Glo cut her off. "I think there may be a way to work this out, to get Smith to back off, take his resort project idea somewhere else."

Everyone looked at her, awaiting her revelation. Did she want to admit her role in aiding Bondurant's sexual misconduct in front of everyone? "Let's just say I have a bargaining chip I'm willing to use if necessary. And there's a time and place where it can be played. Cuyler and Smith are planning to meet with Rhetta tomorrow afternoon. Maybe some of us should be there when they arrive. Surprise guests you might say."

"Are you going to tell us what this bargaining chip is?" Thumper asked.

"Not just yet. But I know the meeting is set for five o'clock and they're planning to use that other information they have about Shelton and her contributions to PACA to persuade Rhetta to change her mind and agree to sell. And if they need some extra incentive, the 'site agent' has been told to stand by and join in if he gets the signal."

"The 'site agent' waiting for a signal," Bar mused. "Do you know how that's going to work?"

"I don't know what the signal is, but he was told to wait behind the house."

"Good cover back there, with an open view of the kitchen windows. Yes," he muttered to himself, "that could work." Turning back to the others, he said, "You all worry about what's going on in the house, I'll take care of what's happening outside."

His eerie grin and twinkle of light from his crystal blue eye sent a chill up the spines of everyone standing around him. They were glad he was on their side.

****

"Okay, great, we'll get there a little before five o'clock. Probably best we park behind the barn so they're not on alert if they see another car there. Then we can all be waiting in the kitchen when they arrive. See you then." Thumper clicked off his phone. "Rhetta's on board," he said to Janey and Glo.

Bar had returned to his trailer, the Nutchenkos to their cottage. Thumper, his former wife, and current live in partner were now seated around the kitchen table.

"I hear you write books about weird religions," Glo said to Janey.

"Yes, I've written a couple of them. And several articles."

"My daughter tells me you were also a college professor."

"I was. But now I'm taking time to focus on my writing."

Glo noted Janey's attire—dust-covered barn boots, well-worn riding breeches, and a flannel shirt with bits of hay stuck to it. "Writing…and riding it would seem."

"That too."

Glo leaned back and smiled warmly. "Elizabeth said she's very happy you and her father have become a couple. He's a good guy. There were just some irreconcilable differences between us. He's East Coast, I'm West Coast. He likes horses, I'm sane."

All three chuckled at that remark, glad for a more relaxed moment from the day's unexpected drama.

The levity didn't last long.

Turning to Thumper, Glo said, "We need to talk about Myrna."

"Do we? Really?"

"She's your sister, and she's at her wit's end. We're all in agreement that letting her sell her share of the estate, especially for something like a Pymsdale resort, isn't going to happen. But you have to understand the danger she's in because of that."

"Danger of her own making. And it was her choice to cut Claudette and me off after our parents died. She didn't like the way they'd left things, making it clear they didn't trust her to act wisely with a direct inheritance. And that proved to be good judgment on their part since it didn't take her long to blow through the money they did let her have. But Claudette and I had nothing to do with how they'd set up their wills, and yet Myrna seemed to blame us for it."

"Does any of that really matter now? The amount she owes this guy seems like a fortune to her. I admit, she's in pretty deep, more than I could help her with. I'm guessing, though, that it wouldn't put much of a dent in your portfolio. I hear the book about your father is doing very well. Must be some nice royalties flowing in from that. And, of course, he was Myrna's father, too."

"Yes, the book's doing okay. So, what? I should use some of what I'm earning from that to bail Myrna out again, and then get busy on my next book so I can do the same when she gets herself into another harebrained predicament?"

"I think you'll find she's changed. I'd say this one's been a real wake-up call, shocked her into reality. You should at least go talk to her. She could use a big brother's support now, if just an arm to lean on."

He looked at Janey.

"It's up to you," she said. "My family has all stayed close back in Minnesota. I guess I was sort of like Myrna, the only one to leave with a dream of a different life. It's worked out okay for me. Hasn't made me rich and famous, but it's taken me to some very interesting places around the world, some of them pretty dangerous. I'd like to think if something had ever gone wrong, my brothers would have dropped everything and come to my aid, whatever that took." She paused briefly, then said, "I think you should at least go talk to her."

Thumper nodded. "I don't suppose either, or both, of you would like to come with me."

Glo shook her head. "Nope, time for you to brother-up." She then had another thought. "But you might want to take along a bottle of wine. Maybe two."

Chapter 36

Thanks to a heads-up call from Glo, Myrna was not surprised when she saw Thumper's Jag bouncing along the farm road leading to the cabin. She opened the front door at his knock and found him standing with one hand behind his back.

"Glo said you might need this." He pulled his arm around to reveal a bottle of cabernet sauvignon, Myrna's favorite.

"Oh, God, yes!"

She grabbed the bottle and trotted to the kitchen. Thumper followed. He extracted the cork while she found the last two clean glasses.

Looking around the small kitchen, cluttered with dirty dishes, glasses, pots and pans, bits of debris dangling over the edge of a stuffed trash can, he smiled and said, "I see your housekeeping skills haven't improved much."

"Well, unlike some folks, I don't have a full time, live-in housekeeper to tidy up after me." She immediately regretted saying that. "I'm sorry. I shouldn't play the 'poor me' card. My situation is purely of my own making. And I'm really glad you came to see me. Here." She handed him a glass of wine. "Let's go sit where you don't have to look at all this mess."

Seated in the living room, she said, "I guess Glo has already told you what's going on."

"Yes, she has. There is no sitcom, is there?"

"No, I lied about that."

"And about your real reason for being here."

"That too."

"You know I can't agree to you selling your part of our family property, certainly not for something like this Pymsdale resort project."

"Yes, I know. And now that I know what Smith Bondurant is really like, and the depths both he and Cuyler are willing to stoop to if it'll get you and Rhetta to change your minds, I wouldn't sell to them even if you let me."

"So what are you going to do?"

She sipped some wine and sat silently for a long moment. She then said, "I guess I have no choice but to go back to LA and face the consequences for my own mistakes and poor judgment."

"Maybe not."

"What other choice do I have?"

"Glo told me how much you owe this guy. It's only a fraction of what your share of the property would be worth if it did sell."

"Yeah, I know that. I was hoping to start over with a nest egg, keep my shop going but have some cushion, some nice, safe investments for security. I guess none of that matters now. Once I get back to L.A…" She shuddered, then took another sip of wine. "But we have some things to deal with here first, like standing up to those two assholes. The asshole in LA will just have to wait a couple more days."

"Look, I know Claudette and I haven't always been as supportive as we should have been. You had a dream and, looking back, I think we admired you for trying to follow it. I sort of had my own form of rebellion when I refused to enter politics and become the next Billington to hold public office." He attempted a poor imitation of a raspy-voiced Don Corleone. "Senator Billington, Governor Billington."

"But you're not a pezzonovante." Myrna's imitation was even worse than Thumper's, and they both laughed.

"Glo made a pretty good case on your behalf. I had some time to think about things driving over here."

Summoning Brando's voice once more, he said, "I'm prepared to make you an offer you can't refuse."

Myrna perked up. "I'm listening."

"I can loan you what you need to pay off your debt. But there's a catch."

"Go on."

"I need barn help. The couple that had been working for me moved on and I haven't found anyone to replace them. You've been away from the horse life for a long damn time, and there's a lot of physical work involved. But I expect shoveling shit, feeding horses, sweeping aisles, cleaning tack, and stuff like that would still be more appealing than what you'd be in for if you went back to LA still broke and unable to pay this guy off. You remember the old apartment above the barn? Nothing fancy, but serviceable and livable. The deal is you move back here, take that apartment, and work off the loan that way." He smiled mischievously. "And I'll only charge you half the exorbitant interest the asshole in LA is charging you."

Myrna sat silently. Her impulse was to leap off the couch and throw her arms around her brother. But she wanted to maintain at least some shred of dignity. She took another sip of wine, set the glass down, and said, "When do I start?"

"So it's a deal then?"

"Oh, my God, yes!" She pounced on Thumper and hugged him tightly. "Thank you, thank you, thank you! You've saved my life. Really, I mean it."

"And you're endangering mine with that choke hold." He pried her loose and she sat beside him. "Jesus, you're stronger than I thought. The barn work shouldn't be all that hard for you after all."

"So now we can tell Smith and Cuyler to take their resort and shove it." Myrna's enthusiasm dimmed. "But what about the information they have on the Nutchenkos and Shelton's connection to the Costa Rica thing?"

"We've got some cards of our own to play, thanks to Glo and Bar. We'll all be paying a visit to Rhetta's tomorrow, a little surprise for Smith and Cuyler. Should be an interesting afternoon."

Chapter 37

"Starting to slide into the slack season," Bar said as he surveyed the empty showroom. "Happens every November about this time."

"Plus it's Monday," Shelton added. "Never that busy of a day for us anyway."

"So maybe I'll knock off a little early. Got some stuff at home I can work on. That'll be a better use of my time than standing around here with nothing to do."

"Can I knock off early too?" Miles called out from behind the parts counter.

"Not you, shithead. You got deliveries to make. We got parts orders to go out, and some repair jobs that can be dropped off."

"If you're going home early, could you do me a favor?" Shelton asked.

"Sure, whatcha need?"

"Before I left for work this morning, Grandma mentioned that she agreed to meet with Smith Bondurant and Cuyler Corley this afternoon, at five o'clock. They're going to try to talk her into changing her mind about selling the farm. I know she's a tough lady, but those two are pretty slick. I'd feel better if you'd check in on her, make sure she's got some backup if she needs it."

"I'll give her some backup!" Miles said. "I'd love to get my hands on those goddamn carpetbaggers."

"Jesus," Bar said, shaking his head. "You just don't quit, do you? Bad enough I let you get away with wearing your stupid ass reenactor costume to work. But I'm fed up with listening to your damn psycho ravings. Get your sorry ass in gear, get those deliveries loaded up, and make yourself useful for a change." Bar turned back to Shelton. "You know Thumper's not going to let his sister sell her part of Montfair, don't you? So it don't really matter what your grandmother decides. The deal's finished."

"I told her the same thing, but she said Cuyler mentioned something about that still being on the table."

"Well, if it will make you feel better, I'll stop by then."

"I can stop by, too!" Miles offered.

"You still here?" Bar asked. "Hit the damn road. Now!"

Miles muttered a colorful curse under his breath. Returning to the stockroom, he carried the parts and equipment to be delivered out the backdoor and loaded them into his truck. To make room for a few smaller items in the cab, he tossed some of his cavalry gear—artillery jacket, plumed hat, saber, ammunition belt, and his two-gun pistol rig— into the back seat.

Still mumbling about "damn carpetbaggers," he stomped on the gas and drove off.

****

Bar did not stop to see Rhetta when he returned home. He drove past the house to his trailer deep in the woods. He didn't stop there either but continued farther down an old, overgrown logging trail where his truck would not be seen. Once out of the truck, he put on a set of camouflage coveralls, pulled a camo balaclava over his head, and hung a set of high-powered binoculars around his neck. As a one-eyed man, the device functioned more correctly as a monocular. But after decades of one-eyed life, his depth perception had adjusted sufficiently to monocular vision that he could judge distance well enough. He then checked the pockets of his coveralls for his standard gear: a coiled up length of thin rope, large handkerchief, cell phone, and folding Buck knife. One other item rested in his shirt pocket: the card left by the "agent" who had visited him the day before.

His sniper skills were rusty after so many years of disuse. But he retained enough of the basics from his Marine days that he was able to conceal himself adequately. He walked through the woods to his chosen spot—a tree-stand Frank Worsham used when deer hunting on Fair Enough Farm property. The elevated platform provided ample cover with plywood walls on three sides and a sweeping view of the area behind the McKendricks' house. He knew Drago Korth's tactics from their time working stakeouts together. When Korth settled into his position to watch for Bondurant's signal, Bar would be ready.

****

Thumper, Janey, Glo, and Myrna arrived at Rhetta's at 4:30. Thumper parked his Jag behind the barn where it wouldn't be seen when Bondurant and Corley pulled in.

The foursome joined Rhetta in the kitchen and they all sat nervously discussing their plans to confront Smith Bondurant and squash the Pymsdale project.

****

As Bar scanned the woods with his binoculars, he noticed his vultures had found a deer carcass about halfway between the tree-stand and the house. He hadn't placed it there, but deer, like all animals, die of one cause or another, most wild ones out of sight of humans, and the carrion feeders go to work. This one may have just been old or sick. Vultures are equipped with gastric juices so low in pH—lower than car battery acid—that virtually no amount of bacteria can harm them. They are, as Bar was fond of pointing out, nature's perfect clean-up machine. He watched them for a minute, happy to see them enjoying a good meal, and then returned to his surveillance.

Aiming his binoculars toward the house, he saw Thumper, Janey, Glo, Myrna, and Rhetta seated around the kitchen table. Rhetta stood up and pointed toward the hallway. The others nodded in agreement to whatever it was she was saying, then got up and left the kitchen.

Ah, Bar thought, *hiding in another room, waiting to make a surprise appearance at the right moment. Good idea.*

His plan began to bear fruit around 4:45 when he heard a twig snap in the woods behind him and off to his right. As he expected, Drago wasn't concerned about being detected as he moved to his position. He knew Bar never left the shop any earlier than 6:00 on a weekday. But Bar assumed that Drago, not one to take foolish chances, would have first checked out the trailer to confirm Bar wasn't there, nor would he have seen the well-hidden truck.

Bar watched as Drago, also equipped with binoculars, crept toward Rhetta's home. He settled on a spot between the tree-stand and the house, a position that afforded him an adequate view of the kitchen window through his binoculars while remaining far enough away to not be easily seen.

Raising his binoculars, he saw the old woman sitting alone at the kitchen table, thin legs crossed, one foot swinging in rhythm with a spoon she was tapping on the table. *The old gal looks nervous,* he thought. *She'll be a helluva lot more nervous once Bondurant drops the news on her about what we've got.* He touched a hand to his chest where, inside his jacket, was the envelope that contained all the incriminating evidence on both the Nutchenkos and PACA, including the contributions Shelton had made earmarked for the Costa Rica project.

Bondurant and Corley arrived promptly at 5:00. Rhetta didn't bother going to the door, she just hollered, "Y'all come in! I'm in the kitchen."

Two sets of binoculars focused on the scene. Bar and

Drago watched as the two men pled their case before the old woman, who now sat rigidly upright, arms folded tight across her chest, and her head shaking emphatically to everything they said. Frustrated by her refusals, they sat back, looked at each other, and nodded.

Knowing what this meant, Rhetta saw that the time was right to spring their trap. She called out something, and seconds later the four surprise guests appeared in the kitchen.

Bondurant and Corley bolted up. Fingers were pointed, accusations made, and denials countered. Corley raised his hands in defense, pointed at Bondurant, and shook his head. He knew nothing about Bondurant's misdeeds and was appalled at such alleged conduct.

Bondurant, red-faced and furious, pointed at Glo and made threatening gestures.

Glo stood, head high, and firmly defied her boss, despite the likely consequences of her actions.

Watching all this unfold, even though he couldn't hear a word that was said, Bar was delighted to see the cornered expressions and postures of Bondurant and Corley. It looked like the plan was working fine so far.

Drago, however, was dumbfounded. What were all these others doing there? It was supposed to be just the two men and the old lady. As persuasive as they could be, Drago figured the old gal wouldn't cave and the signal for him to join the discussion would come at some point. But these others weren't supposed to be there. Especially Glo. Thumper, Janey, and Myrna were puzzling enough. But Glo should have been in California. And she knew about the information they had. However she'd gotten involved in this and shown up in Virginia, it could not be good for their plan.

He needed to get closer, try to hear what was being said, and be ready to spring into action when Bondurant gave him the signal.

Bar watched as Drago arose from his concealed spot

and started creeping toward the house. His path took him toward the deer carcass where the vultures were feasting. Accustomed to the presence of a large man who provided them with food, the birds ignored Drago's approach and continued to peck at the remains of the dead animal. Frustrated by the glitch in the plans and annoyed that the vultures didn't get out of his way, he starting waving his arms and kicking at them.

Bar dropped down from his perch with a quick and light descent, a surprisingly agile action for man his size. He moved rapidly toward Drago, who continued tormenting Bar's pets. Between his focus on what was happening in the house and the hissing of a flock of large, angry birds, Drago did not hear Bar's approach.

When Bar reached the hind end of the carcass, he reached down, grabbed a leg, and pulled it up along with a large section of haunch. Bar took one more step toward Drago, who heard the sound behind him at the last second and turned just in time to see a deer haunch flying toward his head. Bar swung the leg with all his considerable might and the hunk of decaying meat and solid bone collided with Drago's temple, sending him reeling to the ground where he landed in a shattering pile of rib bones and entrails.

With Korth in a semi-conscious state, Bar went to work quickly. He pulled out his rope and had his nemesis firmly bound and tied to a tree before he could recover enough to resist. He then reached for the "agent's" card and entered the number in his phone.

"Bar Reinhardt here. You asked me to call if I had anything to report as to the whereabouts of one Dragomir Korth. Well, I'm looking at him right now, all nicely trussed up, a package for you if you'd like to come get it. Kinda messy, but that couldn't be helped. Same place you were at yesterday, but behind the main house. Shouldn't be hard to find. That quickly? Jesus, you guys don't fuck around, do you?"

He then turned to Drago, who had regained consciousness. "Your pals from the FBI will be here shortly. I'm sure they'll be happy to see you."

"You son-of-a-bitch. You don't know who you're dealing with. Those assholes aren't FBI. They're with a clandestine organization, with international power. People you don't want to fuck with."

"Apparently they're people you've fucked with. So that's your problem, not mine. My only gripe is how you treated my poor, innocent birds, just trying to enjoy a nourishing meal. I can overlook most of the shit you're trying to pull, but not that. Oh, but there is one other thing before your new best friends arrive." He started patting down Drago. "Where is it? I know you've got it on you. Ah, there it is." He reached inside Drago's jacket and withdrew the envelope. "You and your buddies won't be needing this. I think we'll have a nice little bonfire back in the woods tonight." He stuffed the envelope inside his coveralls.

"There's more going on here than you realize," Korth said. "I'm not only working for Bondurant, but there's another client who's owed a hunk of money from that Myrna woman. If I don't complete the mission to get her to pay up, he'll just send someone else. And he may not be as patient and understanding as I've been. So if only for her sake, and your friend Thumper, maybe you should rethink this whole…"

"How about you just shut the fuck up?" Bar stuffed the handkerchief in Drago's mouth and tied it tightly behind his head. "You can tell all your sad stories to the guys who'll be here soon. About time you face the consequences for all the shit you've done over the years. I'm glad I got out when I did, should have bailed sooner. But I'll sleep better at night now knowing you're off the streets."

Drago struggled at the ropes and tried to speak. But Bar's bonds held secure and only muffled muttering could be heard.

Bar was admiring his handiwork and enjoying his victory when a movement off to the far side of the house caught his eye. He saw Miles Flanagan, decked out in full Ranger attire, moving toward the side kitchen door

"What the hell?" He shook his head. "Sorry to leave you here all alone, but it looks like I've got another asshole to deal with. Best of luck to ya."

Leaving Drago straining and muttering, Bar moved closer to the house. Sliding along the wall, he was able to peak through a corner of a window without being seen and could now hear the conversation inside.

"If you go public with this," Bondurant said to Glo, "I'm taking you down with me. And the rest of you, too."

He turned to Thumper. "Your Russian servants."

"They're Polish," Thumper replied coolly.

"Whatever." Then to Rhetta, "Your granddaughter."

"What you say you got on her is bullshit. Won't none of it stick. So do your damndest. Men like you need to be taken to the woodshed."

Cuyler waved his hands and called for calm. "Look, we've got an impasse here. Simple solution. We'll take our resort project and go somewhere else. We won't use the evidence against the Nutchenkos or Shelton, and Glo doesn't go public about Smith's...um...indiscretions. And he won't do that any more. Will you, Smith?"

"Nice try, Cuyler," Bondurant said dismissively. "Frankly, I think Glo's bluffing. Aren't you, Gloriana? I mean, do you really want to be revealed as the person who facilitated the payoffs? And you'll have to convince those women to also go public or whatever you say won't matter. And we both know that our mutual friend gave them ample reason to keep their mouths shut, no matter what. You wouldn't want to be responsible for anything that might happen to some of them, now would you?"

He saw the hesitation in Glo's eyes. She knew how convincing Drago Korth could be.

"Ah, there," Smith said. "So maybe Cuyler's right. We'll take our project elsewhere. Glo will leave Pymsdale with a..." He cracked a smile at the play on words that occurred to him. "...*glowing* reference, a healthy severance, and she can easily find other employment. We'll keep a lid on the information we have regarding other parties. As long as nothing goes public concerning me, everything about your friends and family will stay quiet too." Turning to Myrna, he said, "As for you, sorry the deal won't work out. But, hey, that's not my problem. It was fun while it lasted. Maybe I'll have my new personal assistant send you a gift basket when we get back to LA"

He turned toward the window and said, "Now, just to close the deal, there's someone waiting outside who might have a few words to add. I just need to give him the signal." He started to raise his hand when another voice filled the room.

"Stop right there!"

Everyone froze as a small man wearing a Confederate Partisan Ranger uniform stormed into the kitchen. He held a large pistol—.44 caliber black powder Navy Colt Revolver—in his hand, aimed directly at Smith Bondurant.

"You're not signaling anyone, you goddamn carpetbagger. Bad enough you think you can come here and change everything, no respect for our customs and way of life. But now I find out you've been mistreating womenfolk. We don't put up with that sort of thing around here. No siree, we don't."

That crazy little shit, Bar thought. *Now he's really lost it.*

He ducked under the window and made his way around to the side door Miles had used. Moving as swiftly but as quietly as he could, he crept into the house toward the kitchen.

"I was planning to just threaten you," Miles continued, "put the fear of Jefferson Davis into your sorry Yankee ass and send you back where you came from. But now that I hear what you been doing to women, and how you're planning to ruin the lives of some fine folks around here, I reckon I can't let you go. Gotta set things right once and for all." He pulled back the hammer on the pistol and took careful aim at Bondurant.

Before he could pull the trigger, he turned at the sound of loud footsteps behind him. Bar body slammed the much smaller man, caught Miles' hand, and raised the gun upward. It went off with a dispatch that left everyone's ears ringing as a pistol ball tore into the ceiling. Shards of drywall showered down and black powder smoke filled the room.

Bar yanked the pistol away from Miles and pushed him against the kitchen counter, holding him in place with his other hand firmly gripping Mile's white linen shirt right at the neck.

"Sorry to interrupt your party," Bar said. "This crazy little shit's become quite an annoyance lately. I'll see to it he doesn't bother y'all any more."

Everyone in the room was visibly shaken and speechless, but none were as ashen as Smith Bondurant. Standing next to him, Thumper could tell that Smith's custom-tailored suit was going to need some special cleaning, if it could be saved at all.

Before anyone could respond, their attention turned to the sound of a vehicle pulling up behind the house.

"Oh, don't worry about that," Bar said. "Just some folks coming to pick up a package I left for them in the woods back yonder."

Miles struggled to get loose from Bar's grasp. Bar tightened his grip and pushed him harder against the counter. "You just stay put, you crazy little fucker. If you're lucky, you just might get out of this without a lengthy prison sentence. But you're gonna need some professional help."

Turning to Smith, he said, "That 'package' being picked up contains a friend of yours. I'm afraid he won't be responding to your signal, now or likely any time in the future. Seems some other folks have a few scores to settle with him. Oh, and the information you and Corley think you have about certain people? Sorry to say that won't be seeing the light of day either. So you can just take the little shit's advice and pack your sorry ass back to wherever you came from, leave all these fine folks alone. You, too, Corley. A sorry fucking excuse for family you are."

With everything happening so quickly and unexpectedly, no one noticed that Miles was wearing his two-gun rig. Bar still held the pistol Miles had drawn from the right holster, but the other one remained in place on the left side. Miles slowly slid his hand across his body, then grabbed the second pistol, and cocked it in one smooth motion as he pointed it toward Bondurant before Bar could react.

As Miles squeezed the trigger, Thumper waved his hands, shouted "No! Don't!" and stepped in front of Bondurant just as another ear-piercing explosion erupted in the cramped kitchen. A yellow flash flared from the pistol and a haze of heavy, acrid blue-black smoke swirled through the room.

Chapter 38

Thanksgiving morning arrived clear and crisp. The mounted members of the hunt were assembled on the front lawn of Montfair, where the annual Blessing of the Hounds had been held since the days of Thumper's great-grandfather. The riders were all turned out in their finest hunting kit, each piece of tack oiled to a lustrous sheen, metal fittings brightly polished.

Volunteer servers—non-riding social members and friends of the Hunt—circulated among the riders with trays of libations and finger food. Most popular of all the offerings were Natasha's Scotch eggs.

Reverend Davenport, adorned in his formal clerical robes, stood at the front of the spectator crowd. Close behind him were Rhetta McKendrick, Myrna Billington, and Glo Devereaux. Farther back in the crowd were Bar Reinhardt and Shelton McKendrick.

Everyone—riders and spectators—held a small printed program detailing the order of service.

All eyes turned as two riders appeared in the distance, moving off from the Montfair barn and heading down the driveway toward the lawn. Both wore black hunt coats. As they came closer into view, it could be seen that it was Elizabeth and Janey.

When they reached the others, Elizabeth rode up to where Mildred Preston and Ryman McKendrick were waiting for the signal to begin the ceremony. Crispie O'Rourke, Patti Vestor, and Nardell Raithby held the hounds off to the side.

"My apologies," Elizabeth said. "Can you believe it? He forgot to fill his flask."

"Goodness," Mildred replied. "This has to be the first time that's ever happened."

Another rider appeared, this one wearing a scarlet coat and moving quickly on a dark bay. When he reached the apex of the lawn, he doffed his cap and nodded to the others.

"Sorry," Thumper said, "last minute equipment detail."

"And a most important one," Mildred remarked. "Are we ready then?"

"Yes, please proceed."

She signaled to Reverend Davenport, who called the ceremony to order. When the chatter had stopped and all eyes were on him, he said, "This is always a special occasion, a time when we can reflect on our good fortune to be where we are and to do what we do. That the custom here is to hold the Blessing of the Hounds on Thanksgiving Day makes that awareness all the more relevant." He paused and his customarily somber demeanor revealed a playful smile. Turning toward the masters, with particular focus on Thumper, he added, "The fact that the holiday bears the endorsement of a certain Mister Lincoln notwithstanding." Then back to the crowd. "So if you will all refer to your programs, let us begin."

As Davenport recited the blessing, Thumper's thoughts drifted elsewhere. He'd heard these words every year since childhood and could recite them flawlessly from memory. His gaze drifted off toward the nearby westward mountains, each crest punctuated by a ragged line of trees. Only a shred of autumn color remained on this late November morning. The few stubborn leaves clinging to the starkly barren trees—a fading confetti of dingy gold and speckled red—filled him with reassurance that another season would roll through its cycle here in Crutchfield County. These last leaves would fall, snow would follow, and spring's verdant growth would again spill down and blanket the fields and pastures.

The steamroller dream had not tormented his sleep the past few nights. For now, at least, Paradise Gap, Montfair, Fair Enough, Worsham's, and other properties would not fall prey to the suffocating black death of asphalt pavement.

Thumper's attention returned to Davenport as he caught the closing words of the blessing. "...to all who shall take part in the hunt, grant protection of body and soul; make us all ever mindful of, and responsive to, the needs of others that the spirit of true sportsmanship may prevail in all that we do.'"

And the people all said, "Amen!"

****

The chase led them from Montfair to Fair Enough, where hounds and riders passed close by the grave of Minstrel's Delight. It was as if the fox was paying homage to a departed player in their sporting theatrics.

From there they cantered to Frank Worsham's. He and his wife Betty, along with Merle of course, stood in the front yard, waved as they rode by, and watched as each rider jumped the coop from one pasture to the next.

The fox obligingly went to ground in the hillside den at the back of the McKendricks' property.

****

Thanksgiving Day hunts are purposefully kept short and the usual tailgate socializing is skipped so everyone can get home for family gatherings. There would be some additional guests at Montfair this year. Along with Thumper, Elizabeth, Natasha, Voytek, and now Janey (attending for her second year), plus Ryman and Nardell, Myrna was now part of the resident crew and Glo had postponed her return to California till after the holiday.

Rhetta was not one for large group gatherings, holidays or otherwise, so she and Shelton were enjoying a small, quiet dinner at home. It was a good opportunity for Shelton to tell her grandmother all the details of how her relationship with Astrid Stevenson had ended. Rhetta asked, gently, if that meant Shelton wouldn't be making any more contributions to Astrid's fundraising efforts. Shelton said it certainly meant that. Not another dime from her, ever. Without revealing why, Rhetta just said she was glad to hear that.

Glo had spent much of Tuesday and Wednesday grappling with her dilemma about Bondurant. Leaving Pymsdale was a given. But should she remain silent, knowing he might take advantage of more young women? Or should she expose herself to legal jeopardy by going public, admit her role in the cover-ups, but put a stop to his predatory behavior? And what if, in retaliation, he blabbed about the Nutchenkos and Shelton's PACA contributions? By Wednesday evening she sought Thumper's advice. Myrna joined them and together they devised a plan to ensnare Bondurant in his own game.

Myrna would return to LA, contact Smith, tell him she was there for a brief visit to close her shop and wrap up some details before moving back to Virginia permanently. She wanted no hard feelings and would like to meet for a drink. She's sorry things didn't work out, but she has to admit she'll always have some fond memories of spending time with him. Her acting skills would be put to good use and Glo was sure he'd leap at the chance for one more tryst with her. She'd play the coquette over drinks in the hotel bar and then invite him up to her room.

Once there, he'd find himself facing a very large, scary man with one eye and ear missing. Bar would remind Bondurant that he owed Bar his life, but that life could just as easily be taken away. If Bar had outwitted and outmuscled Drago Korth, a slug like Smith Bondurant wouldn't have a chance. And if a crazy little man like Miles Flanagan literally scared the shit out of him, he sure as hell wouldn't want to deal with any of Bar's old West Coast buddies. So he'd best be on good behavior from that point forward. Certain people would be watching. Oh, and if anything ever comes up about a couple from Poland or a young woman who gave some money to what she believed was a worthy cause, he'll want to find another planet to live on.

Thumper called Bar and proposed the plan to him. Glo would use some of the money she'd gotten from her role in the payoffs to fund the trip. She would then donate the rest of the money to a women's shelter in LA, but could hold out a portion to compensate Bar for his help.

Bar needed no compensation. Just let him know when he needed to be there. He was happy to help.

With details concluded, Thumper filled three double Old Fashioned glasses with a healthy pour of Wasmund's Copper Fox single malt Virginia whiskey and the three conspirators toasted their brilliant plan.

****

Natasha was in her happiest element on Thanksgiving Day, in the kitchen preparing mounds of food. Her years cooking for a circus troupe made portion control a difficult concept for her. Thanksgiving was one occasion where she could cook and bake with abandon. There would be ample leftovers, but nothing would go to waste.

She was humming her favorite Polish folksong when Bar appeared at the mudroom door. "Ah, you are here! Come, I have pie for you."

Bar entered and she handed him a freshly baked pecan pie. "Thanks. Muriel and all her family sure love your goodies."

"Is nice you are having Thanksgiving with them. You should not be staying alone in little trailer." She paused, wiped her hands on a kitchen towel, and faced Bar squarely. "Voytek and I can never thank you enough for what you have done. We were thinking it was all over for us, that we would be sent away, maybe even to prison. You are hero to us. And I am also thanking you for saving Mister Thumper's life. He is not talking about it, but Miss Myrna told us what you did."

"Hell, if I saved anyone's life, it was that asshole Smith Bondurant's. And I did that more to keep Miles from making things any worse for his dumb-ass self than they already are. He coulda shot Bondurant to hell for all I care. And if the little shit had thought to load his other pistol with live balls instead of the blank rounds they use for their reenacting stunts, it would have gone a lot worse for Mister Thumper. I guess Miles figured six shots was all he was gonna need. Lucky for all of us."

"Well," Natasha replied, "lucky you were there. And lucky for Miles that you did not turn him in to police. Are you sure that was right thing to do?"

"Look, I know you and Miles have had some issues. And no one knows better than me what a royal pain in the ass he can be. But I think realizing he might have killed Thumper scared the crap out of him, kind of jerked him back into some semblance of reality. He's agreed to get help, counseling and meds kinda stuff, and Ansel will keep an eye on him. No one actually got hurt. And I told Rhetta I'll patch up the hole in her ceiling."

"You are very kind man. Maybe too kind."

"Well, we'll see what happens."

"Yes, we will see."

Myrna returned to the kitchen from her duty setting the dining room table. Bar noticed she still looked worn and tired, but her mood had improved considerably. She seemed less jumpy, no longer startling at every shadow.

"Are you sure you can't join us for dinner here?" she asked Bar. "Or at least come back for dessert?"

He hefted the large pie. "I don't think I'll have any room for dessert after this. Which ain't like me. But thanks for the invite."

Myrna's tone turned somber. "I've been avoiding it, but I have to ask. How did you know about Korth? And who were those people who came for him?"

"Let's just say that old Drago and I knew each other a long time ago, another place, another life. The details best left alone." He turned to Natasha. "A lot of details from the past best left alone."

****

After dinner Thumper and Ryman went for their traditional walk, a practice they'd been observing on holidays since they were teenagers.

"I guess I'm glad they're not going to build the resort," Ryman said. "But it could have been such a blessing to Saint Hubert's work, a way to spread the word to so many more people."

Thumper stopped walking, turned to his old friend, placed a hand on his shoulder and said, "Ry, you know they were just stringing you along, right? If they did manage to get all the property they wanted and build that damn thing, there's no way they were going to let you preach your Church of Foxhunting stuff there. They were just trying to get you on their side to help persuade your mother to sell. If the deal had been done, they'd have dropped you like a hot horseshoe fresh out of the forge."

"Maybe. But they seemed pretty sincere."

"Did you get anything in writing?"

"Well, no, but they said…"

"Ry, what guys like Smith Bondurant and, I'm sorry to admit, my own cousin Cuyler say doesn't count for squat. You and I were raised to be men of our word, gentleman's honor and all that. Did you ever know Fergus to go back on his word, even if something he'd promised turned out to be a loss for him? Or my old man either?"

"No, of course not. Everyone knew they could trust my father's word, no matter what."

"Well, other people are cut from different cloth. I think, in the long run, Saint Hubert was watching out for you. I expect he's got some other plans in store, something probably better than that old resort place would have been anyway."

"You really think so?"

"Pretty sure."

Ryman nodded and they continued their walk in the late afternoon air.

****

In past years Thumper had hired extra help to handle all the clean up work as a favor to Natasha. But this year, Myrna, Janey, Glo, and Nardell volunteered to handle that duty. They hustled the Nutchenckos out the door, over mild protests, and ordered them to their cottage for a relaxing evening and a good night's sleep.

Although Elizabeth was eager to be off to meet her friends in DC, most notably Tobias Johnson, the others roped her into sticking around to pitch in. Her only task was to help clear the table, and then she was free to leave.

"She seems pretty sweet on that fellow," Myrna remarked.

"I've yet to meet him," Glo said. "But Thumper speaks well of him. And that carries a lot of weight when it comes to our daughter."

"I don't think there's been a weekend when she was home from school that she hasn't spent at least some time with him," Janey noted.

"She hasn't shared much with me," Glo said. "I mean, after all, I'm just her mother. Always the last to know, right? Do you think it's serious?"

"I've tried to get a sense of that from her," Janey replied. "She insists she's in no hurry to get involved in a serious relationship. So many plans ahead for her, graduating next year, already has some law school applications brewing."

"Doesn't hurt to have the Billington legacy behind you." Myrna's comment carried a hint of bitterness.

"Well, she's a very bright young lady in her own right," Janey said. Turning to Glo, she added, "I'm sure she won't make any foolish choices. After all, Thumper's already looking forward to being there when she gets sworn in as an Associate Justice of the United States Supreme Court."

They all chuckled at that, and continued on with their clean up chores.

****

Their work was just wrapping up when Thumper and Ryman returned.

Thumper looked out the kitchen window and said to Myrna, "Hey, kiddo, looks like there's a wee bit of light left. And I still need to walk off some more that that fabulous dinner. What say you and I go for a little stroll?"

Their wanderings took them across the front lawn, up the gentle hill along the western side, where the ancient oak tree stood guard over the old cemetery.

"I can't thank you enough for what you're doing for me," Myrna said. "I promise I'll work hard to pay you back."

"Don't worry. I plan to work your ass off."

Myrna flexed her bone-thin arms. "Bring it on! I'm ready."

"Yeah, right."

They continued along in silence for several minutes until they reached the gate to the cemetery.

"Elizabeth couldn't wait to get out the door so she could go meet Tobias," Myrna said. "On the upside, I think it was the fastest the dinner table has ever been cleared. Did you notice that lovely pin she was wearing? She said it was a birthday gift from him."

Thumper grunted absently in response.

"He seems like a very nice young man," Myrna added.

"Uh huh."

They both leaned on the gate and looked out over the collection of small grave markers. Several of the inscriptions were difficult to read even in bright sunlight. But as the late November rays were fading, almost gone, the headstones appeared to be little more than indistinct tablets set at jumbled angles.

Myrna's attention focused on one marker in particular. She knew what the name and dates were without having to read them in the dark.

"Does Elizabeth know?" she asked.

Thumper remained silent for a long moment. "I don't think so. She always thought this place was scary. She avoided being near it as much as possible."

"Well, she's a grown woman now. Maybe it's time she knew."

"Yes, I suppose it is."

To be continued...

If You Liked This Book...

For more information on the works of J. Harris Anderson, visit www.BlueCardinalPress.com where you can:

- Read excerpts from current and upcoming books.
- Read the blog "Postings From Paradise".
- Sign up for the newsletter.
- Receive advance information about new releases.
- Contact the author.

Reviews are always appreciated!

Also by J. Harris Anderson

The Prophet of Paradise
A Paradise Gap Novel

Foxhunting, Faith, and Pheromones

Life around Paradise Gap, in Virginia's Crutchfield County, has been cadenced to the comfortable traditions of foxhunting for many generations. And then Ryman McKendrick receives a vision.

Inspired by a message from Saint Hubert—or so he believes—Ryman launches The Ancient and Venerable Church of Ars Venatica, aka The Church of Foxhunting. Even the skeptics can't ignore Ryman's uncanny new powers. The Venatican ranks swell, hunters sing—literally—the praises of the sporting life, and a current of titillation flows among the participants, from teenagers to octogenarians. The two meanings of "venery" (pursuits both sporting and erotic) blend happily into a single drive for many of Ryman's ardent followers. But support is far from universal. Is one of Ryman's detractors committed enough to go to the ultimate extreme?

The Prophet of Paradise takes you inside a rarified world of foxhunting, religion, and sex—a powerful cocktail of passion that can lead to pleasure or pain.

The Prophet of Paradise
Chapter 1

Crutchfield County, Virginia
Friday morning, September 2
The Visions Begin

THE HEAVY HEAT of late summer lingered in the Piedmont. Horsemen scheduled their exercise rides early before the air turned to steam and the sparrow-sized horseflies massed for full assault. Thumper Billington rode out from his home, Montfair, shortly after sunrise. Cantering down a shady tunnel through the pine woods, he saw Ryman McKendrick walking across the open field ahead.

McKendrick's appearance showed he'd taken a tumble. He walked stiffly, with a limp in his left leg. His hardhat sat askew on his head. Grass stains smudged the back of his white polo shirt. A smear of gritty soil slashed across one cheek of his blue jeans.

"Ry," Billington called out, "you okay?"

Ryman stopped and turned to face the approaching rider. Billington knew well the unfocused look of a concussion. He'd seen it dozens of times on the faces of others, a few times in his own mirror.

"Damnedest thing," Ryman said. "Biggest deer I've ever seen. A buck. Must have been at least a twelve-pointer, maybe fourteen. And this thing—something in the middle of its rack. Couldn't tell what."

Thumper dismounted and gave Ryman a critical assessment. "Deer spook, huh? Anything broken?" He lifted a hand, three digits raised. "How many fingers am I holding up?"

"Sumbitch flew out of the woods. I mean he really flew.

Like airborne. Right in front of my horse. What was that thing? Shiny. Like it was hanging between his antlers."

"Ryman, listen to me. What day is it?"

"I musta gone over the horse's head. I was riding Colby, that youngster just off the track. Probably never seen a deer that close before." Ryman looked around. "Musta hightailed it home. Or he could be halfway back to Charles Town by now."

"Okay, Ry, you got yourself a royal concussion. We can skip the President of the United States question." Thumper pulled out his cell phone. "I think we'd better arrange for a trip in the red light limo."

"And there was this mouth." Ryman's eyes suddenly regained their focus and he grabbed Thumper's arm before he could push the 911 button. "It was, like, floating above me. I was on the ground, on my back. And I could see the mouth, with the lips moving, trying to tell me something. But I couldn't hear any sound. And it wasn't human. I…I remember thin lips, black maybe, and square teeth." He released his friend's arm and the unfocused gaze returned. "Where's my goddamn horse?"

"I'm sure he went back to the barn. I'll get you home. Then we'll get you checked out."

Ryman's hand shot forward again and blocked Thumper's second attempt to push the button. "You were holding up three fingers, it's Friday, and the President of the United States is your typical asshole who says one thing, does another. Half the country thinks he's God and the other half thinks he's a commie."

"Damn, that was a quick recovery."

"I probably do have a concussion. Hell, just another day at the office, right? But I really did see this, Thumper. Huge goddamn deer, enormous rack. And something else. It all happened so fast. I was galloping along the edge of the woods over by Caleb's Forty and this sumbitch just came outta nowhere, right in front of me. Next thing I knew I was on the ground, horse was gone. When I sat up, the deer was standing across the field, looking at me. The sun was shining off some strange thing, like it was…sort of…suspended above its head. I stood up to get a better look and the damn deer just…disappeared."

"I don't know, Ry. A nasty head bump can come back to bite you later."

"Shit, Thumper, I've had a lot worse than this. So have you. I'm awake and standing upright, ain't I? Besides, I don't have time for all that medical crap. I gotta get to town, run some errands, then get to the shop."

Billington put his cell phone away. "All right. But I'm escorting your ass back home."

During the long walk to the McKendricks' place, Fair Enough Farm, Thumper kept Ryman's bruised brain engaged with light banter, discussing the success of the summer exercise program for their horses and hounds. Joint-masters of the Montfair Hunt, the most important concern to both men was that the informal season of the foxhunting calendar was scheduled to begin the following morning.

The conversation drifted in and out of lucid exchange. At times Ryman spoke with clarity of a specific hound, a promising new entry, and his expectations of how well the hound would hunt. Then he mumbled the same remarks about the deer that spooked his horse, the height of its leap, the size of its rack, his glimpse of some strange object between its antlers, and the image of moving lips floating above him as he lay on the ground. He then looked around, wondered where his horse was, and the loop—hound, deer, leap, rack, mysterious object, moving lips, where's my horse?—repeated.

They found the young Thoroughbred outside the Fair Enough barn. It hadn't taken him long to learn where his new home was and the pull of the herd guided him back. The only damage was a broken set of reins.

After untacking and turning the horse out to pasture, Ryman limped toward his F250.

"You sure you're okay to drive?" Thumper asked. "Looks like it's not just your head that got smacked."

"Ah, hell, I'm fine. Back's a little sore. Hard damn ground to be landing on. Nothing broken though. Got some ibuprofen in the truck, gotta hit the ABC store for some scotch to wash it down with. That'll fix me up."

"Maybe the errands can wait. Have Nardell keep an eye on you. If you were having hallucinations, you probably have a more serious concussion than you realize."

"They weren't hallucinations. Anyway, Nardell's got appointments this morning and I got things I gotta do. I'll see you at kennels tomorrow morning, bright and early."

Thumper watched as Ryman drove down the dusty road leaving Fair Enough Farm. He could only hope in some vague way that his friend would not pass out behind the wheel. Neither of them were praying men. Chasing foxes was their faith, scotch whiskey their savior's blood, ham biscuits their wafers. Their "Hallelujah!" was "Tally-ho!" and "Amen" was "Gone to Ground."

The Foxhunter's Guide to Life & Love
An Inspirational Novel

Humorous, lighthearted, and earnestly practical advice to improve your love life, and your love *of* life.

J. Harris Anderson, through the voice of his popular character Thumper Billington, presents a compelling premise: Life is about The Chase. And foxhunters know how to *Embrace the Chase.*

Whatever you're chasing—an enriched relationship, overcoming challenges, learning a new skill—this book reveals the principles of the Foxhunter Model that anyone can use to get more out of life.

J. HARRIS ANDERSON

The Foxhunter's Guide to Life & Love
Chapter 1

Thumper Billington and Janey Musgrove stood on the front porch in the predawn darkness. The Virginia countryside rested in a peaceful quiet on this Friday, the day after Thanksgiving, as if every creature was sleeping off the holiday's indulgence.

"You know I have to go, right?" she asked.

"Yes, I know," he said in a half-whisper.

That morning should have been the essence of domestic coziness, Thumper and Janey waking well after sunrise, perhaps repeating the pleasures of the night before, their first night together.

"I can't pass this up. It's the chance of a lifetime."

He nodded. "I understand. Go. Get the story."

"Look, last night…I didn't mean for it to end this way."

"Is it ending?"

"Well, no. I don't mean that. I just mean…y'know, me taking off like this."

"You have to go. But if you want to come back…"

"Yes, of course."

"Okay, then. Off with you!" He made an exaggerated gesture of shooing her down the steps to her car.

She'll be back, he told himself.

And when she does come back, what's next?

He shuffled to his study, sat down at his desk, and checked his email. There was one from his agent.

"Sales of your father's bio going well, a good start on Christmas orders. Three new reviews, all glowing. Will send copies. Any thoughts yet on what's next?"

What's next?

His most recent work was a well-received biography of his late father, who served eighteen terms in the House.

So…what's next?

He kept an old photo of his parents at the edge of his desk. It was taken on Thanksgiving Day, the first year of their marriage. They were in formal foxhunting attire, assembled for the Blessing of the Hounds—he in top hat and scarlet coat, she in elegant sidesaddle finery with a flowing black skirt and veiled top hat, both of them mounted on well-muscled, gleamingly groomed Thoroughbred horses. Thad and CeeCee Billington were the image of privileged youth and unlimited promise.

"How did you do it?" he asked the photo. "All those years together, some rocky spots along the way, but always a team. What have I been doing wrong?"

He had only known Janey Musgrove for three months. She was an ill-timed presence in his world. Although it was an uneasy acquaintance at first, his coolness soon softened, first to acceptance, then to friendship, and then to something more. But how much more?

They had turned a page the night before. What did the next chapter hold? He knew he wanted this new relationship to continue. Was it love? Did he even know what love was? His track record in that field was not great. And he wasn't getting any younger.

Still addressing his parents' photo he asked, "How can I make this one work?"

The photo did not answer but a thought began to form.

There had been one constant in his life, one commitment that had never wavered, no matter the adversities, difficulties, discomforts, and challenges. It gave him the most gratification. He had gained much from watching the behavior of others, their successes and failures. Of all his accomplishments, this one passion had taught him the most about patience and persistence.

How could those lessons, amassed over a lifetime of involvement in an arcane, misunderstood pastime, help assure that Janey Musgrove would return to him? And if she ever had to drive away again, that she would always come back?

As he rumbled these thoughts around, a broader picture appeared. If he could apply those lessons to his own love life, perhaps others could benefit from his experience.

And it wasn't just about his love life. This pastime was a major source for his love *of* life.

He looked again at the photo of his parents. "That was it. You knew the secret, and you passed it along to me. I'd just never realized it until now."

Thumper Billington spent the next three days cloistered in his study. He only broke the flow for a few hours on Saturday when, as senior master of the Montfair Hunt, he was required to lead the field for that day's sport.

By Sunday evening a structure had formed, an outline was finished, he'd written his introduction, and had decided on a title. The rest would take shape as events unfolded.

Leaning back in his chair, he nodded in satisfaction, happy for the chance to let his writing take a different path. For once he could keep the serious academic, the respected historian, on the shelf and let his true persona—Thumper the Smart-Ass—run loose on the page.

On Monday morning he emailed the introduction and outline to his agent with a simple message: *"Here's what's next."*

About the Author

J. Harris Anderson attended the University of Virginia and George Mason University, where he earned BS and MBA degrees. A member of Mensa, his career as a marketing specialist took him through the banking, hospitality, and construction industries. He has served as a consultant to several organizations and as Senior Writer for a firm specializing in training programs and corporate communications.

As a committee member for the Masters of Foxhounds Association's Centennial Celebration, Anderson assisted with editing the commemorative book *A Centennial View*. He also created the accompanying DVD, *A Centennial Run*, an archival collection of information, histories, photos, and videos from every recognized foxhunting club in North America—165 of them.

He is currently the managing editor of *In & Around Horse Country*, a national publication covering foxhunting, steeplechasing, polo, and other horse sports.

An avid foxhunter, he has served as a field leader, whipper-in, and racecourse outrider. He lives on a Virginia horse farm and rides regularly with the local hunt club.

PAVING PARADISE